BRAINSTORM

Margaret Belle

Margaret Belle
Visit my website at www.MargaretBelleBooks.com

Printed in the United States of America
ISBN 978-1976810831

To my crazy, wonderful family.

PROLOGUE

Rochester, NY - 2003

"So, Audrey," said Dr. Collins, "we've come to the end of our last session. I have to say, you've done a lot of soul searching and self-discovery over the past two years."

"No offense," I laughed, "but it feels longer."

"In *any* case," she said, feigning hurt feelings, "you're about to head out into the world with your new marketing degree – are you nervous?"

"Maybe a little," I admitted. The faint aroma of Frankincense drifted to me; incense that Dr. Collins, my therapist, burned to relieve stress and anxiety. I liked it. I would take the memory of it with me as a reminder of the time I'd spent here, safe and comfortable in "my" chair, with Dr. Collins' gentle strength propping up my own shortcomings, preparing me to deal with the days that fell between one session and the next.

During my sophomore year, suffering from insomnia and extreme fatigue, I'd gone to a general practitioner, who in turn sent me to Dr. Sandra Collins, a psychologist, who'd determined that I suffered from Generalized Anxiety Disorder, or GAD. Once I heard the diagnosis, it made total sense. Back then I'd agonized incessantly over my grades and worried about everything, from whether I should brush my teeth up and down or sideways, to whether a plane flying overhead would plummet to Earth if I stared at it too long. I'd spun out horrifying scenarios of the imagined consequences of my thoughts and actions, as well as those of others, until I was so overwhelmed I would completely shut down. I called it my spin cycle.

"You have coping skills now," she continued, "and relaxation techniques to take with you." She pulled a business card from a pile on her desk and placed it in my hand. "You're always welcome to call me, but here's the card of Dr. Karol Steele, a colleague of mine in the Syracuse area; I suggest you contact her to continue with your therapy. And remember, Audrey, you've earned the right to be happy."

"I'll be fine," I said, hoping that was true. "I appreciate everything you've done for me." *If only I'd been honest with you even once*, I thought.

She walked me to the door like a mother putting her Kindergartener on the bus for the first day of school; all she needed was a camera. "One last thing, Audrey," she said. "You know that your anxiety can re-emerge in the face of highly stressful situations, so take things in stride when you're able and use those calming techniques when you need to." I gave her a hug and left her office for the last time.

Out on the sidewalk, as I waited for a cab in the June heat, a man darted around the corner and plowed straight into me. His eyes – dark brown and intense – locked onto mine before he shoved me hard against the building and took off. Soon after, two police cars careened around the same corner and sped by with their lights flashing, sirens wailing, tires squealing.

With my heart hammering in my chest, I lowered myself to the sidewalk. Sweating and feeling faint, I attempted the slow breathing technique that Dr. Collins had practiced with me, holding each inhale to the count of six, exhaling slowly between intakes of air, but I had difficulty following through.

My vision swarmed with gnat-like specks, but something crumpled on the ground near me caught my attention and I reached for it. It was a black ski mask. Unable to loosen my grip on the damp piece of wool, I leaned against the building and waited for darkness to swallow me.

MARGARET BELLE

CHAPTER 1

Syracuse, NY - 2013

My name is Audrey Dory, and I'm in the advertising business. I persuade people to buy product A over product B, choose brand C over brand D, and of course, my job isn't finished until they purchase whatever it is from the company I want them to, instead of from one of the fifty other companies that carry it. I manipulate minds until my targets no longer want the product or service they thought they did, but instead crave the one I want them to.

Whether I use facts, comedy, or play on emotions to do the job, the success of my business depends on my ability to separate people from their money.

Ten years ago, fresh out of college, I began selling air time at a local radio station and quickly realized that I had a knack for writing commercials that were creative and perfectly timed to thirty or sixty seconds. It became clear that the people in the advertising agencies I serviced were no more creative than I was, so I set out to learn everything about the business from selling, to billing, to scheduling, to collections; the following year I left my job and opened my own agency, Silent Partner.

The experience has been a satisfactory one for the most part, although I have occasionally found myself with a client who didn't pay - who went out of business and left me hanging, or died and left me on the hook. I became meticulous about doing credit checks on new clients before signing them up, yet somehow I still manage to be left holding the bag now and then.

I flipped through my Rolodex for Fergal Finnegan's phone number – "Ferdy" to those of us who know him well. Ferdy is the owner of an accounting firm and has been a client of mine for three years.

He'd left a message that he wanted to start work on a campaign regarding a piece of tax preparation software, for which he'd been granted a new patent. I knew from experience that he would drive me up a wall before the campaign was put to bed, but I'd put up with it, because although Ferdy was a pain the ass, he didn't owe me a dime. Plus, I had high hopes that his business acumen would translate into big bucks for him, and in turn, for me.

As I dialed the phone, my assistant, Harley Bud, attired in one of her tie-dyed, hippie-dippie, maxi dresses, and clogs, clomped in. Her long dark hair was pulled back and tied at the nape of her neck by something with beads that I couldn't identify. She placed a decorative bag on my desk. "Happy birthday, Curly," she said, referring to my mostly unruly auburn hair.

About two years ago, when my assistant left without notice, Ferdy had saved my butt by recommending Harley, and surprisingly, she had taken the job. Surprisingly, because she is a well-trained techie with knowledge and proficiency she will never get to use in my employ, and has mastered software she is not likely to ever find in the confines of my office.

Harley'd had the opportunity to work for a big firm in another state, but stayed here because her grandmother, who was all the family she had, was failing and needed her help. I was able to offer her a flexible work schedule so she could take her grandmother to see her army of doctors and a good benefits package, but next to nothing in salary. She walked past me and dropped her tote on top of her desk, which was all of six feet from mine.

Ferdy's secretary picked up. "Cat," I said, "it's Audrey. Is Ferdy around?" Harley rolled her eyes at the sound of his name.

"He didn't come in this morning."

"I'd ask if he was taking a mental health day," I said, "but I know that's not him – he'd crawl in if he had to."

"No kidding," she said, "it isn't like him to just decide not to come in." I picked up on the worry in her voice and paid more attention.

"Did you try his phone?" I asked.

"I've been calling his house and his cell. I think something's wrong."

"He left me a message," I said, "but I don't know if it was from this morning or yesterday after we closed. The time and date thing on my machine needs to be reset."

"Did he say where he was?"

"No," I said, "he just wanted to set up a meeting about his new software."

"Do you think I should call someone?"

"Like who?"

"I was thinking the police," she said.

"I don't know – that might be jumping the gun, but if you're worried, why don't we meet at his house? If I leave now I can be there in twenty minutes."

"All right," she said. "But I hope it's not like on TV, when someone doesn't show up at work and then a co-worker goes to check and finds the person dead."

"I'm sure it's nothing like that. I'll see you there." I grabbed my purse and checked to be sure my cell phone was in it. "Harley..."

"I know. I heard," she said. "Go."

* * *

Ferdy lived alone in a tony section of the city, and soon I was standing at his front door with Cat right behind me. I rang and knocked, but there was no answer.

"Now what?" asked Cat.

"Let's see if his garage has a window." We followed a rose-bordered, brick sidewalk around to the side of his garage, where we found not one, but two spotless windows. Ferdy's car was there. "Okay," I said, "now we call." I pulled out my cell phone, punched 9-1-1 into the keypad, and reported what little we knew.

A police car arrived within minutes and the responding officer, who introduced himself as Officer Morey, tried the door and found it unlocked. "Why didn't we try that?" I asked Cat.

"Wait here," the officer said.

From what I could see from the porch, Ferdy's front room was in disarray. A lamp, sofa pillows, and the pages of a newspaper were strewn on the floor; what appeared to be a cup of coffee was overturned on an end table. Right then, I knew that Ferdy Finnegan, a self-described neat freak, would never have left his home in this condition, and that something really bad had occurred.

Cat was beside herself. "What could have happened?" she asked. "Where the hell is Ferdy?"

I put my arm around her as we waited on the porch. Officer Morey walked toward us, and as he did, his radio crackled. I thought I heard the dispatcher say a private aircraft had crashed into Onondaga Lake.

"What did that just say?" I asked, as I pointed to his radio. Tony Bravada, the air traffic reporter for this market, was also a client of mine, and I was hoping against hope that it wasn't he who had just plunged into the drink. A check of my watch told me that Tony should be in the air, nearing the end of his morning shift. Crap.

"Small plane went into the lake," said the officer. "Unofficial report says it's the air traffic guy."

Cat pulled me away from the house and toward her car. "We can listen to the radio."

We sat in absolute shock as we listened to a witness describe how Tony's plane, The Soul of Syracuse, had plunged into the lake; no word on Tony; not even whether he'd survived. What the hell was going on? So far today, I had one client go missing and another crash his plane.

"There's nothing we can do here," said Cat. "Do you want to drive over to the lake?"

MARGARET BELLE

CHAPTER 2

When we arrived on the south side of Onondaga Lake, Air One, the county police helicopter, was circling above the wreckage of Tony's plane. Emergency vehicles were lined up on the roadside and an ambulance waited near the shore; police directed traffic in an attempt to keep rubberneckers moving along. There were more flashing lights than I'd ever seen in one place. My stomach lurched, as I watched divers in black wetsuits working in the water.

I tried not to cry. Tony was a good guy; a local celebrity, who was well liked and well respected, and now maybe he was dead. The press arrived. Cameras rolled. Microphones were thrust in the faces of police officers; everyone wanted to know what had happened to Tony. Including me.

Cat grabbed my arm and pointed to the divers. We watched as Tony was floated to shore strapped to a board, not moving as far as I could tell. Finally, the ambulance took off with him in it, and we followed the speeding vehicle to the E.R. at St. Joseph's Hospital, where we reported to the women behind the reception desk.

"Are you relatives?" she asked.

Cat pushed me forward. "No," I said, "I work with Tony."

"Does he have any relatives that you know of? Someone we could call?"

"He has siblings, but I don't know how many or where they live," I said. "I can tell you that he's 58, and I've never heard him talk about any medical problems."

"Are you thinking about waiting here?" she asked. "Because there's nothing you can do right now and we can't give you any information. You might as well go home."

"At least he's still alive," I said, as we walked back out to the car.

Cat drove me back to Ferdy's to pick up my Jeep. Police cruisers and vans filled the driveway, and men and women in law enforcement uniforms traveled in and out of the front door. Cat and I hugged, agreed to keep each other in the loop, and then went back to our respective offices.

The light on my answering machine was flashing, and I listened to panicked messages from the general managers of the radio and television stations who had Tony under contract to deliver traffic reports every weekday morning and afternoon. How was he? Was he even alive? Did I have someone to deliver air traffic reports in his absence?

"Hey, Harley," I said, "Do a search to see if you can come up with any of Tony's relatives while I return some of these calls."

Even though I resented the fact that the station managers seemed to care more about their traffic reports than about Tony, I couldn't afford to piss any of them off by not getting back to them. We'd had tough negotiations getting Tony's current stations on board when he'd first hit the air eight years ago, as the voice of Syracuse traffic. Now his whole livelihood was at stake, and I, as his agency of record, had to try to keep his network together until I found out how long he would be out, or if he would be able to go back to work at all.

I returned call after call, and with as little sarcasm as I could muster, promised to try and find a private pilot who had his or her own plane, and who could fly it while watching the sky above and the streets and highways below, report traffic problems, provide alternate routes to drivers, read advertising copy, and do it all while keeping track of which station he was on the air with at any given moment. Sure. Dime a dozen.

As far as Tony's condition, I had no answers. Not being related to him, I'd have to get my information from radio or TV reports like everyone else – unless I could find one of his siblings who could pass information along to me.

"Here's a sister," said Harley, as she handed me a slip of paper, "she lives three to four hours away, in Newburgh."

Rose Bravada answered the phone, and although she was very upset at the news, assured me that she would notify her other siblings and then drive right to the hospital. I asked her to let me know whatever she could about Tony and gave her the number to my cell. When I finished the call I turned to Harley. "What about Ferdy's next of kin?"

Within minutes she had a number for a brother, Sean, who lived in Pennsylvania. I called him and explained what little I knew about Ferdy. He said he would be on the next flight to Syracuse. I gave him my cell number and told him to call when he arrived and I'd pick him up at the airport. Then I called Officer Morey and told him that Ferdy's brother and Tony's sister would be in town shortly. If he needed to speak with either one, he would find Rose at Tony's bedside and Sean, since Ferdy's home was a crime scene, at the Crowne Hotel. Then I called the Crowne and made a reservation for him.

It was five o'clock, and although I had deadlines looming and needed to get Harley started on a website re-design, I was exhausted and hungry. "Want to grab something to eat?" I asked.

"Right behind you," she said, "just let me finish this one update and I'll lock up and meet you at Krabby Kirk's."

Krabby Kirk's Saloon was an establishment in the village of Camillus, a small suburb west of Syracuse. The best thing about the saloon is that I live above it. I most often do "take up" instead of "take out," since it's simply a matter of picking up my food at the bar and walking up the back stairs to my apartment.

I know what you're thinking. Advertising executives are supposed to be well-heeled and prosperous, live in large sprawling homes with panoramic views and drive BMWs. And that may be the way owners of large agencies roll. But when you own a two-person shop and your clients are people who run small businesses and cannot afford to pay large commissions and outrageous hourly rates, you keep your overhead low. And anyway, I like my little apartment. It has a great living room window that looks out over Main Street, where once a year, the Memorial Day parade marches by. Even though it's always the same, never any surprises, I cherish the tradition and look forward to it every year. I do love a parade.

I ordered a beer and wondered where Harley was; a call to her cell went to voice mail. Fifteen more minutes went by and another call went to her voice mail. I paid for my beer and began the trip back into the city to see where the heck she was, worrying the whole way that she'd had a flat tire, a fender bender, had run out of gas, or been mugged and left stranded or hurt in a bad part of the city where anything could happen; I stepped on the gas as my spin cycle whispered to me.

Her car was in the driveway, which should have relieved me, but did not, and I pulled in next to it. The office door was ajar and I pushed it open. "Harley?" Filing cabinet drawers stood open and papers were all over the floor; a soft cry brought me in. Harley was lying on the floor in the far corner of the office. "What happened?" I asked, as I helped her up and walked her over to her chair.

"This guy appeared out of nowhere when I was locking up," she cried. "He had a gun and forced me to come back inside."

"Did you recognize him?"

She shook her head. "He had one of those knit hats with eye holes pulled over his face." She hugged herself and sat rigidly on the edge of the seat.

"You mean a ski mask?" I took a deep breath, remembering the one that had been dropped at my feet a decade ago.

"Yes – one of those," she said, as she rubbed her arm.

I got her a glass of water. "Did he hurt you?"

"He grabbed me and I hit my back and my head when he pushed me down," she winced.

"I'm so sorry," I said, as I reached for the phone on her desk. Wondering what anyone could possibly want from this office, I dialed 9-1-1, and within a few minutes two patrol cars and an ambulance were in the driveway. Officer Morey was first through the door.

"We meet again."

"This is my office," I said. He waited with me as the EMTs checked Harley.

"And the young lady works for you?"

"She does."

"How long?"

"About two years."

"First two of your clients and now your assistant," he said. "Someone unhappy with you?"

"With *me*? No," I said, a little put out, "of course not." The EMTs loaded Harley into the ambulance. "I'd like to ride with her."

"I need you to stay here and check the place," he said, as he glanced around at the mess. "Obviously this person was looking for something. Can you tell if anything's missing?"

I attempted to take stock, but it was impossible to concentrate. The equipment was all here and we didn't keep anything of value on the premises. There was no art collection to steal or even award statues that could be sold for scrap. We had won many of those over the years, but we always gave the statues to our clients. It was our way of reminding them that Silent Partner was a small firm, but a good one.

I opened my top desk drawer and withdrew the $500 I had in there. "This was in my desk," I said, holding up the money, "and the drawer wasn't locked, so they weren't looking for cash." I folded the bills and put them in my pocket. "It's going to take me a while to sort through this stuff, get it back into the right folders, and then look through it all to see if anything is missing."

I led Officer Morey through the rooms of the 100-year-old house that I had turned into the agency's office. There was a storeroom for supplies, a small conference room, a bathroom, a little kitchenette, and the front office where Harley and I worked. The second story was closed off to conserve heat or AC, depending on the season, but we climbed the stairs and entered the first bedroom, which contained two cots; each piled with blankets, sheets, and pillows, all packed in plastic bags. "Why the beds if you don't use this floor?"

"For winter," I said, "in case the weather turns ugly and we don't want to tackle the roads."

I followed him as he walked through the rest of the upstairs. "I wouldn't have put carpet up here," he said, "I would have refinished all of the floors."

"Well, I wasn't going to live here," I said, "I just wanted to update it little by little. I got a deal when I had this part done, as I pointed to the room with the cots; do one room and get a second room free, if I used the same carpet. So I did this one bedroom and instead of a second bedroom, I had them do the stairs."

"Huh," he said, as we headed back down.

I really had no interest in following him down to the basement, but he insisted that I look around with him. The lighting was dim because I'd put in low-watt bulbs to save energy. "What's all this?" he asked, referring to a number of boxes and crates that were haphazardly stacked against one wall.

"I don't really know. Stuff from a former tenant, maybe, or the owner's. I don't come down here."

We trudged back up the stairs where the air smelled better. Officer Morey moved toward the door. "This place is now a crime scene, so you'll have to stay away for a day or so. An evidence technician is coming to dust for prints. When your assistant is able, we'll talk to her about a description of the guy."

"She said he had on a ski mask, so I don't think she'll be much help." He nodded and made notes in his little book. "If you don't mind," I said, "I'd like to head to the hospital. Where did they take her?"

"St. Joe's; I'm headed there now myself." He dug in his breast pocket. "Here's my card. Call me if you find anything's missing." I took the card, grabbed Harley's tote and my purse, and walked out, leaving my office to the mercy of the Syracuse PD. "And," he called after me, "you should have an alarm system installed. Like yesterday."

"I'll do that," I said, scolding myself for not having done it already, and made a mental note to call a security company first thing in the morning. As I drove out of the driveway, the evidence technician arrived in his truck. "This day just sucks," I informed myself.

When I arrived at the hospital, Harley had been sedated and was sleeping soundly, so I decided to check on Tony, but the nurse at the desk shook her head. "He's just out of surgery and won't be allowed non-family visitors until his doctors say so."

With nowhere to go and nothing to do, I headed home, wanting nothing more than some comfort food and my bed. I sat at the bar and ordered a cup of tomato soup and a grilled cheese.

"You okay, Aud?" asked Dick, my landlord and owner of Krabby Kirk's.

"Sucky day."

"Want to talk about it?"

"Talking about it would only mean reliving it," I sighed. "I'll just take my order and go upstairs."

I kept the food warm in the oven while I did my best to wash the day away in the shower and changed into my PJs. I needed even more calming than the steamy shower could provide, so I lit a stick of Frankincense and spent a few minutes practicing slow breathing before I carried my dinner to the couch.

Hoping for an update on Tony, I turned on the TV and was immediately assaulted by a pharmaceutical commercial; I reached for the remote before the inevitable disclaimers (vomiting, blurry eyesight, constipation, boils, hair loss, stroke, and death) made me lose my appetite. I changed to a cable channel with 24/7 news and found amateur video from two different angles, showing Tony's plane falling into the lake; both were horrific to watch. The aircraft had come in low, with its wings waggling from side to side, before it nose-dived into the water. I put my dinner aside.

The news anchor began a second story. Rochester police were reopening the case of a decade-old unsolved armed robbery, during which a customer was shot and killed. On what they claimed to be an anonymous tip, they named one Danny Stearns as a person of interest. "In New York State," said the reporter, "there is no statute of limitations if someone dies during the robbery. Three million dollars was taken at gunpoint from the National Bank of..."

My cell phone rang and I clicked off the TV. The face of another client, Carrie Ashton, smiled at me from the screen. Now what?

CHAPTER 3

"Hi Carrie," I said, trying not to let the exhaustion I felt creep into my voice.

"So sorry to call you after hours, Audrey, but our website has been hacked or something. It's crashed – frozen – I don't know what happened, but we can't get into it. Our password doesn't work. We need Harley up here first thing tomorrow to look at it."

Rather than go into the whole story, I told her Harley was out sick, but promised to do my best to locate a techie for her. It was the best I could do at the moment. If I'd been perfectly honest, I would have told her to call a local high school and get a guidance counselor to recommend a student. A lot of kids today can do as much as formerly trained IT pros, albeit self-taught.

"Good," she said, "because you know we sell 90% of our products on-line. We're losing money every minute the site is down."

So here was client #3 who was having a problem – certainly not as big a problem as Tony, or Ferdy, but still an event had occurred that was significant enough to bring her business to a halt, at least temporarily. No business, meant no advertising. No advertising, meant no income for me.

After a restless night's sleep, I met Ferdy's brother, Sean, at the airport and drove him to the Crowne Hotel. The stress was visible on his face – Ferdy was his only living relative. There was no other family member to share in the torment he was experiencing; no one to talk to about it. I knew how that felt.

I gave him my cell phone number and told him to call me when he needed to go to the police station, or anywhere else, for the next few days. He hadn't been in Syracuse for several years, but he'd soon get the lay of the land and rent a car, and then I'd leave him to his own devices. "My heart goes out to you," I said, "and I'm terrified for Ferdy."

I left him at the hotel, and with no office to go to, headed back home, first stopping at a drive-thru to pick up a large cup of decaf.

I sank onto my couch, and in a little notebook, wrote down the names of those associated with me who had met with an adversity of some kind over the last two days. Ferdy, Tony, Carrie, and Harley. I stared at the names, but didn't see any other connection – just me, as Officer Morey had suggested.

Maybe Harley would come back to work and maybe she wouldn't; I couldn't blame her if she decided not to. But I needed her now more than ever, with all of the damage control I would have to do, plus there were deadlines looming for the clients who hadn't run into trouble (yet), and I still had to find a stand-in pilot for Tony. My head hurt.

I put the list on the coffee table, curled up on the sofa, and snapped on the TV, which was still tuned to the news channel I'd been watching last night. I began to doze off as it droned on in the background, but when I heard the anchor continue the story from last night's broadcast about the bank robbery, I came awake.

A police officer, flanked by two men in FBI jackets, was announcing a $200,000.00 reward to anyone who could supply information leading to the capture of Mr. Danny Stearns, who was no longer a person of interest, but a suspect, in the brazen armed robbery of the National Bank of Rochester a decade ago. *In one day?* I thought. *He went from being a person of interest to a suspect in one day? What had happened?*

One of the other officers held up a photo of Mr. Stearns, and warned that he should be considered armed and dangerous. The camera zoomed in and my eyes locked onto the picture; I sat up straight. He looked older now, but I knew those eyes. They belonged to the man who'd run into me ten years ago; the one who'd dropped the ski mask.

Oh, God, it was him. Breathe. One...two...three...four... *Oh, God!* He'd robbed a bank and killed someone right before he'd run into me! Had he still been carrying his gun? How close had I come to being killed, too? My arms and legs prickled as though they'd been asleep. The all-too familiar feeling of trouble coming washed over me, and I knew I needed to talk to someone. Now.

I went to my bedroom and opened the top drawer of my dresser, where I'd kept the business card for the psychologist that Dr. Collins had suggested I contact; something I hadn't felt the need to do since I'd left Rochester. Black flecks clouded my vision as I tried to read the number. I hadn't paid that much attention to the card before, but now, as I tried to focus, I noticed that Dr. Karol Steele was a psychiatrist, not a psychologist, as Dr. Collins had been. Well, whatever she was, I needed to talk to her, and I dialed the number.

MARGARET BELLE

CHAPTER 4

Dr. Steele managed to talk me down in less than half an hour, which she said was a good sign, and made an appointment to see me the following afternoon. If anxiety was going to raise its ugly head, this might be the time, and I knew from past experience that I would need an arsenal to fight it. Unable to sleep, I spent the night pacing my apartment and wishing I had someone to keep me company.

In a stupor the next morning, I called my office to check messages and found one from a man named Miller Crawford, who wanted to speak with me about taking him on as a client. I jotted down his name and number on the same paper as I had written my current list of non-functioning clients. It occurred to me that if I called him back and ended up taking him on, I might be putting him in jeopardy of losing his livelihood too, at least temporarily. Well, I told myself, I could make the phone call – that wouldn't necessarily mean he'd be a good fit for the agency. But who was I kidding? If a credit check turned him up as a good pay, he'd be a perfect fit.

I made the call, and after explaining that my office was unavailable, arranged to meet him downstairs for lunch. Then I showered, dressed, and drove to the office parking lot, where I left my Jeep, Nelly, and drove Harley's car to the hospital and parked it in the garage. When I checked in on her, she was in good spirits.

"They're letting me go home tomorrow," she said. "An officer was here earlier to see if I could give him my impression of the guy –

you know, height and weight, like that, but I was too frightened at the time to notice anything."

"Did they check you for a concussion?"

"I have a slight one," she said, "but other than that, just bruises."

She ran her fingers through her hair, and I caught a glimpse of a bruise on her arm that had been covered by the sleeve of her gown; it looked a little on the green side, instead of purple, as it should have been so soon after the attack. "Promise me you'll take it easy for a few days?"

She nodded. "I'll be back in next week."

"Do you need me to check on your grandmother?"

"No, I spoke to her a few minutes ago. A neighbor is looking in on her, but thanks."

"Okay." I dug her keys and the parking stub out of my pocket. "Your car is here in the garage." I held up her tote. "Do you want me to hang onto this or leave it with you?"

"It'll be okay for one night – leave it."

I handed it over and gave her a hug. "I'm glad you're feeling better."

Next was a stop to check on Tony. When the elevator doors opened I saw a police officer speaking with a woman who I knew had to be Rose Bravada, Tony's sister. She had the same big brown eyes and salt and pepper hair as her brother. When they were done talking, I walked over and introduced myself, and asked, "How is he?"

"Terrible at the moment," she said, with tears in her eyes, "but the doctor assured me he'll be close to 100% eventually. He'll be in rehab for a long time." She wiped her nose with a cloth hankie – no tissues for this lady. I could almost see her standing at her ironing board; press, fold, press, fold again.

"Can I see him?" I asked.

"I'm sorry, but he's in no shape for visitors; he's in and out of consciousness. Both of his arms and one leg are broken, and they still have to determine the extent of head injuries. I promise to let you know as soon as he's able to have company." She took my hand, "Thank you so much for calling me. The rest of the family will be here tomorrow."

"Where will you stay?" I asked.

"I have a key to my brother's house. We'll be there."

Outside, I hailed a cab and returned to my office parking lot to retrieve Nelly. A remote check of my phone messages showed that Officer Morey had left one. He answered on the first ring. "When was the last time you spoke with Mr. Bravada?" he asked.

"The morning of the accident. Monday. We meet almost every Monday morning before he flies. Why?"

He ignored my question and followed with another of his own. "Where?"

"Same place every week – at Mike's Diner. It's close to the airport."

"Did he seem different that day? Was he feeling okay?"

"He seemed perfectly fine."

"Okay," he said, "we'll have a longer conversation about that later. I'll get back to you."

"No problem," I said, and I hung up, wondering what that was all about, and thinking he had a nice voice.

I decided to go through my files as soon as I could get back into the building, and look for anything that might be of interest to an outsider. I had records of advertising expenditures, copies of campaign schedules, and creative material for each client. I had their contact information, names of the banks they used, and in Ferdy's case, copies of applications he had made to the U.S. Patent Office over the last few years. I just didn't think anyone would want that stuff.

I drove to Krabby Kirk's, looking for my new prospective client, who was sitting in a back booth. "Miller?" I asked. He nodded, and looked surprised that I had picked him out of the crowd. "People who aren't regulars are easy to spot," I said. We ordered and got down to it.

"I'm in the security business," he explained, "alarms, cameras, that kind of thing."

"No kidding," I said, "I'm having an alarm put in my office in a couple of days. I told you that's why we're meeting here. There was an incident."

"Nothing serious I hope?"

"No, no damage," I said, omitting Harley's injuries, "and so far nothing seems to be missing." Wanting to change the subject, I asked, "So how many locations do you have?"

"This will be my third; I have a store in Watertown and one in Rochester."

"And you've been handling the advertising on your own? Or are you already with an agency and looking to switch?"

"I've been doing it, but I don't have the time to commit to it anymore, not and do it effectively. I need someone to take over that part of the business so I can concentrate on running the rest." He rattled off the names of several radio and television stations he'd used in both locations, and I tucked that information away. Tomorrow I would call each one and make an informal request for his payment history.

"I'll tell you what," he said, "take me on as a client and I'll install a top-of-the-line security system for you myself to show you how good my company is. No charge. That way you'll have firsthand experience with the product. Deal?"

"Okay, it's a deal," I said. We shook hands, and by the time he left we had agreed to meet at my office in two days. I made a mental note to cancel the other security company, signaled for my check, and asked for a receipt. That done, I made the commute home, meaning I walked up the back stairs.

I had almost two hours before my meeting with Dr. Steele. She'd been wonderful with me on the phone, and I dared to feel some confidence in being able to feel safe and comfortable with her. Since this would be our first meeting, I hadn't had a chance to fill out paperwork that would allow her to get a copy of my file from Dr. Collins, but I'd given verbal permission so she could call for some background. I kicked off my shoes and curled up on the sofa, hoping a short nap might make up for the little bit of sleep I'd had the night before.

* * *

The reception area of Dr. Steele's office was tastefully decorated with calming neutrals, not unlike the colors and tones I'd come to appreciate at Dr. Collins'. When she came out to greet me, I pegged her to be in her early 50s. She was dressed in a beige suit, medium heels, and had her hair tied back in a loose bun. Her smile and soft, even, voice were welcoming, and I relaxed and even felt a bit relieved, as I followed her into her office.

"Dr. Collins used to burn Frankincense," I said. "Do you do that?"

"My guess is that most of Dr. Collins' patients were drawn to her holistic ways, and therefore weren't bothered by lingering aromas such as incense. My patients, on the other hand, would not expect anything like that and would most likely balk at it. So, let's talk about last night's phone call."

I explained the investigations surrounding Tony's accident and Ferdy's disappearance, and told her the story of the bank robbery and my connection to Danny Stearns. "I'm not sleeping well. I can barely eat and I'm probably not going to have a business to support myself much longer."

"Are you self-medicating?"

"I've been taking over-the-counter sleeping pills and St. John's Wort because I read on the Internet it was good for stress."

"Well, actually," she said, "St. John's Wort shouldn't be mixed with other medications. I'm going to prescribe something to help you sleep – a small dose, just so you'll be able to doze off, and also something for stress. You're under a great deal of pressure, Audrey, and I know Dr. Collins told you that unless it's managed, it can – it *will*, cause your GAD to return. We don't want that." She handed me a tissue.

"I don't want to go back to those days," I said, dabbing at my eyes, "I *can't* go back to that."

She tore up one of the prescriptions and wrote another. "I'm going to increase the dosage of the antidepressant. And I'm going to want to meet with you on a weekly basis for a while; until things calm down and you're feeling better."

I signed a release form so she could get a formal copy of my file and made an appointment for the following week. I thanked her and looked forward to lighting some incense when I got home.

CHAPTER 5

The sleep medication Dr. Steele had prescribed proved way more effective than the over-the-counter stuff I'd been taking, and I'd slept soundly. Now I was energized, and felt I could take on whatever the day could throw at me.

I showered, dressed, and then ran next door to the hair salon where Lisa, the owner, gave me a quick trim and blow dry. After that, since a storm was supposed to arrive in the afternoon, I hit the grocery store for a few necessities. With the food put away, I cleaned my four rooms, those being my kitchenette, living room, bedroom, and my closet-sized bathroom. It only takes me about 45 minutes to get it all done, including a change of bed linens.

I started the dishwasher, threw my dirty laundry into a mesh bag, and turned the key in the lock on the way out. I walked six doors up (in the opposite direction from the hair salon) to the Laundromat, filled two machines with clothes and detergent, popped in a bunch of quarters, then hopped into Nelly and headed for the office to see if I could get in.

The crime scene tape was gone, and I took that as permission granted to enter. I started a pot of coffee and began picking up the mess on the floor. Within an hour I had sorted and re-filed most of the papers, and nothing had jumped out at me as being missing.

I sat at my desk and opened a file for Miller Crawford, knowing from experience that he would be bringing a shitload of promotional material and all kinds of paperwork he would want me to see, whether I needed to or not. I completed a contract for him to sign and slipped it into the file.

I looked at the birthday bag Harley had put on my desk just before I'd run out to meet Cat at Ferdy's house. *Better late than never*, I thought, and I reached for it. Inside was a beautiful crystal nameplate – large and heavy, rectangular in shape, with three words etched on it: *Audrey Dory, Separator.* I laughed at the old joke – advertising's goal is to separate people from their money.

I looked around to find the perfect place for it. While nameplates were intended to be displayed on a desk, mine was too cluttered. I went to the stairs, where a little window looked out onto the parking lot. Not a great view, but the sun came through almost all day long. I placed the heavy crystal bar on the sill and watched, as prisms of light danced across the floor beyond the stairs. Perfect.

I called SUNY Oswego and spoke to a lady about sending an intern to Carrie. Next, I cancelled the first security company and then put in a call to the airport for a list of private pilots in the area. On hold, I watched dark clouds gather; a harbinger of the storm that was predicted to hit later in the afternoon.

After approving copy for an outdoor billboard and listening to talent demos for a radio spot that needed to be voiced before the week was out, I put away my paperwork and looked at Harley's empty chair, realizing more than ever how much I depended on her.

In light of the coming bad weather, I called Harley's home number, feeling obligated to see if her grandmother needed anything. Even though a neighbor was supposed to be looking in on her, who knew how old that neighbor was and if she was capable of providing food or medication in a storm?

There was no answer. Harley had said she'd called her grandmother from the hospital, so I knew she was able to get to the phone. I waited for ten minutes and then tried again, but she did not pick up.

As the sky darkened, I decided to take a ride over there, just to be on the safe side. Once a storm hit around here, there was no telling how long it would last or if the power would stay on. I'd never been to Harley's place, but I took the address from her job application, and my GPS brought me to the front of a house in a section of the city that was more run down than my office location; it surprised me.

Harley had never really said much about where she lived; but I always assumed it was at her grandmother's house. I knocked on the door. No answer. And there were no lights on inside, which there should have been. I tried the doorknob and found it unlocked. I opened it just a crack and called, "Hello?"

MARGARET BELLE

CHAPTER 6

Pushing the door open a little wider, I called again, "Hello? Harley's grandmother?" I didn't even know the woman's name. Where was she? What if something had happened and she was hurt and all alone with no way to call for help?

When no response came, I took a couple of steps into the dark room and slid my hand over the wall, found a switch, and snapped on the light. "Hello? Harley's grandmother?" Thunder snapped in the distance++ and the first raindrops splattered against the windows.

The living room was neat as a pin, but there was no sign of an elderly woman. Maybe that neighbor had come by and invited her next door until the storm blew over. That would be a good thing. But Harley's grandmother could also be in the other room, unable to answer me; I ventured further into the space and called out again with no luck.

I moved forward, hoping with every step, that I wouldn't find her on the ground. Had she fallen and hit her head? Had a heart attack? Mixed up her medications? I spun out scenes of a little old woman meeting her Maker in a series of awful ways because no one had been around to help. *Stop!* I chastised myself.

I continued on, but found no evidence that an elderly person lived in this house. There was only one bedroom, and just one bed. Had I come to the wrong place? I looked in the closet and recognized several hippie-type pieces that I'd seen Harley wear, alongside an array of men's T-shirts and sweatshirts. Confused, and more than a little curious, I peeked into the dresser drawers and found men's jeans, socks and boxers. *What the hell?*

In the small bathroom, toiletries for both sexes crowded the top of a tiny table beside the sink, but I saw no medications one would expect to find in the home of an elderly woman, especially one who had as many doctor's appointments as Harley had led me to believe. I quickly made my way back through the house and outside, leaving the front door unlocked, as I had found it.

I was overcome with disbelief and a feeling of deep betrayal; Harley had been lying to me all this time. But why? And when she'd said she was taking her grandmother to all of those doctor's appointments, where had she actually been going? She didn't even have a grandmother – at least not one that lived with her.

As I pulled into a parking space in front of Krabby Kirk's, I noticed that the salon next door was open, and I went in hoping to find Lisa alone. She was stocking hair products, but stopped when she saw me.

"Oh, boy, what happened to you?" she asked.

"I look that bad?"

"Well, you're all wet for one thing. Don't you own an umbrella? I'll be here for a little while longer. Have a cup of tea and keep me company."

I ran my fingers through my wet hair. "No tea, thanks. I'll just sit here for a few minutes," and I lowered myself into one of the pedicure chairs and turned on the vibrating back. "Better," I said.

After telling her about Harley, Lisa said, "Come with me. I have to bring up two more boxes from the basement – it'll go faster if you help. Then we can grab an early dinner next door, if you feel like it."

I groaned, but turned off the chair's soothing vibrations and followed her. "I didn't even know there was a basement in this building."

"It's awful," she complained. "I *hate* it. It's pitch black and it takes me forever to find the chain to the light bulb."

"So that's why you want me to help," I laughed, "you're afraid of the Boogey Man." But as we descended into almost perfect darkness, I began to see her point. I reached for the back of her shirt and held on to it until she finally found and pulled the chain. The swinging bulb cast writhing shadows over the stairs and the cobweb-covered walls, and the dirt floor felt strange under my feet. "Let's get the boxes and get out of here," I said.

"It's no easier going up after the light is out!" she groaned. Since I needed both hands to carry the cumbersome box, I could no longer hang onto her shirt, but I followed as close to her as I could. "Here's the first step," she said, and up we went. I held my breath until the slight glow of light at the top of the stairs came into view. I encouraged her to hurry up and finish her work and soon we were on our way to dinner.

When we were settled at a table and had ordered, I returned to the topic of Harley. "Now I have to fire her," I whined, "and I have no one to take her place."

"Don't jump to conclusions," she said. "You *are* going to give her a chance to explain, right?"

"For lying to me all this time? What explanation could there be?" My head hurt. My shoulders ached. "I'll have to change the locks, too."

We finished our meal and said goodnight. As I watched Lisa drive away, I remembered my clothes were still at the Laundromat. I ran up the street and threw my wet duds into a dryer, plugged in some quarters, and cursed the fact that it would now be at least an hour before I could shower and change into my PJs.

Back inside my apartment, I grabbed a bag of M&Ms and headed for the couch, as rain slapped against my window. My cell phone rang; it was Sean Finnegan. "Any news?" I asked.

"No, but the police think I should hold a press conference to get the message out about Ferdy's disappearance. I'm a little nervous; would you come and be there with me?"

"I'd be happy to – when and where?

"Tomorrow at noon in front of the police station."

"I'll be there."

I turned on the TV to see if there was any news about Tony. Instead, I was treated to another pharmaceutical commercial using diversion tactics to keep the audience's mind off the list of possible side effects that included swollen tongue, stroke, gas, loose bowels, and death (watch the happy couple hike up a mountain – don't listen to what the announcer is saying). After the audience had been thoroughly warned, not to mention disgusted, the news anchor reappeared with a report on the alleged bank robber, Danny Stearns. Again, his picture was displayed on the screen and the reward for information leading to his capture was repeated.

Where was he? I wondered. Did he remember bumping into me that day? He'd stared at me just as I had stared at him. If his face, his eyes, had remained in my mind all these years; did he also have a clear mental image of me? And how much of a stretch was it to think that if he *did* remember me, and thought I could pick him out of a lineup, that he'd try and find me; that maybe he'd been trying to do just that all this time? I stood up quickly and M&Ms went everywhere, as my spin cycle revved up.

CHAPTER 7

I slipped on a rain jacket and ran to the Laundromat, loaded my dry clothes into a basket as fast as I could, and used the rear entrance of my apartment to haul it upstairs, where finally I was able to shower and put on my purple PJs. I hung up a few shirts and then dumped the rest on the bed to fold, but my hands were shaking, and I was unable to get the image of Danny Stearns out of my head.

I retrieved Officer Morey's card from my wallet and dialed him up. He was at my apartment within 20 minutes. "Nice jammies," he said.

"That's unprofessional," I bristled, tightening the belt on my robe, "this is serious."

"Are you kidding me? I've been at two crime scenes with you in the last couple of days. This is almost a date." He looked at the candy on the floor. "What happened here?"

"Just...nothing. That's not important. The thing is," I began, hating to relive the story, "I was watching the news and saw a picture of the man that the police in Rochester think robbed a bank there a while back."

"And?"

I explained as best I could about the day I left Rochester, leaving out the part about having been at my therapist's. "Now, seeing him again on TV," I said, "it occurred to me that he might remember me too, and that maybe he's been looking for me all this time. He would know I could identify him, right?"

Officer Morey looked unconvinced. "He didn't know you, correct? Never saw you before that day? Didn't know your name, or where you were from, or that you were about to leave Rochester?" I shook my head no. "Then I don't think you have anything to worry about. But since you're so upset, is there someone you can call? Somewhere else you can stay for a few days?"

I shook my head. "This is it. I'd be more afraid alone in my office."

"You know, if you're certain you can ID this guy on the day of the robbery, the DA and the police in Rochester are going to want to talk to you; not to mention the FBI."

"No, no. I'm not getting involved in that mess."

"Unfortunately, now that you've told me, I have to report it and you won't have a choice." He wrote down what I'd said and promised to ask the Camillus PD to drive by my apartment now and then. "That's the best I can do right now. If you remember anything else, let me know." He put on his hat, tugged at the brim, and smiled at me. "Goodnight now."

After he left, I wedged a kitchen chair under the knobs of both doors and checked the locks on the windows, swept up the M&Ms, and put away the rest of my clothes; anything to keep busy.

Back on the day Danny had run around that corner and slammed into me, I had not returned to Dr. Collins' office for help. She would have tried to persuade me to speak to the police and I hadn't wanted any part of that. I would have had to give a statement, look at a lineup of creepy men, and if worse came to worse, maybe even testify against him in court. I had no memory of other people being around that day, but I couldn't have been the only one on the street; someone else had surely spoken to the police in Rochester.

I went into the bedroom and pulled down a box from the top shelf of my closet. With my heart pounding in my chest, I slowly lifted the lid and stared at the black ski mask hidden inside.

CHAPTER 8

I spent most of the night listening for suspicious noises, and imagining Danny Stearns creeping up my stairs. Around 6 a.m. I gave up and got out of bed, showered, dressed, and dropped a frozen waffle into the toaster. I picked up coffee on the way to the office and wondered how open I should be with Miller, who would be installing my security system in a few hours. Should I let him know what being added to my dwindling roster of active clients could mean for him? I didn't know. I'd play it by ear.

Once in the office, I started going through Harley's desk, looking for anything that would tell me why she'd been lying to me since the day she took the job as my assistant. *Grandmother my ass!* That "grandmother" was the reason she'd given for taking the job with me, instead of at a large firm in Chicago where she'd been offered the moon. Harley was good at what she did. So if no sick old lady was holding her back, why work here, where she had no chance of stretching her wings?

And who was this guy she was living with? A husband? A boyfriend? There had only been one bed; whoever he was, he was *living* there. There were too many clothes, too many male toiletries, to be left for the occasional overnight. Was it his house? Or hers?

I stopped long enough to attach a sticky-note to my computer screen, reminding myself to meet Sean at noon for his press conference, and then checked my phone messages. The most disturbing, was the one from the airport – no names of private pilots would be forthcoming.

I began the tedious task of phoning the general managers of the stations in Tony's network to give them the bad news. By the time I'd finished I was pretty sure his career had come to an end; the stations would find another way to deliver traffic reports. It also meant that a huge chunk of my income was now just flat-out gone.

Okay then, back to Harley's desk. I pulled out her chair and started with the top left drawer. The search netted me nothing more than I would have expected; client folders, website access codes, and a list of florists, caterers, and our utility providers. In another drawer I found printer paper and a small assortment of makeup items - a tin of what looked like pancake foundation, lipstick, aspirin, and not much else. I sat back in the chair to think about what I would say to her, but within a few minutes, Miller knocked on the door.

He made two trips to his vehicle to bring in the tools and all the crap he needed for the installation. He most likely expected me to stay after he finished to discuss when I would take over his advertising, but I couldn't do that today. "You have to be done by 11:30 – is that do-able?" I asked, "I have to be somewhere at noon."

"Not a problem," he said, and he went to work, "but we need to set up a meeting pretty soon to get started on my marketing."

His credit check had been stellar. "Absolutely," I said.

At 11:30 on the dot, Miller was packed up and had launched into an explanation of the ins and outs of my shiny new security system. I put in the code, using the last four digits of the office phone number; the same code we used on everything around here, because Harley was awful with numbers and could only seem to remember the one. "The alarm will automatically react to smoke and fire," he said, "but it will also go off if the temperature in the building falls below 45-degrees. And if the glass is broken on any of the downstairs windows, the alarm will also be triggered, even if you forget to set the code at the panel next to the door here." We made an appointment to meet the next day and drove off in different directions.

When I got to the police department, the microphones for the press conference were all set up, and I waved to Sean, who indicated with a backwards wave that he wanted me to stand close to the podium. "Hi," he said. "Thanks for coming – you're the only person I know here and I'm a nervous wreck."

"You'll be fine," I said. "Just speak from your heart. The police will do some of the talking; you won't have to do all of it."

Precisely at noon, the press conference began. TV cameras from the local affiliates were there, panning the folks on and near the podium, zooming in on the police chief as he spoke. Then, flanked by two police officers, one of whom was Officer Morey, Sean pleaded for his brother's safe return.

One of the officers spoke directly to the captor or captors, stating in no uncertain terms, that letting Fergal Finnegan go was in their best interest. Sean returned to the microphone and offered a $100,000.00 reward to anyone who could provide information leading to the safe return of his brother, then, choking back tears, held up a large photo of Ferdy.

"You did great," I told him when the media had drifted away.

"I'm headed back home," he said, "but I'll keep in touch with the police and of course I'll come back if there's something else I can do to help find my brother."

After I said goodbye to Sean, Officer Morey approached me. "Listen," he said, "would you want to have a cup of coffee? Maybe grab some lunch?"

Now I have to tell you, this was something that had never crossed my mind. But how bad could it be, to be seen having lunch with law enforcement? My faithful paranoia told me that it couldn't hurt. "That sounds good," I said. "We're not going in your squad car, are we?"

"That would be a no," he smiled. "We'll have to meet at the restaurant." He had a nice smile and great Irish eyes. I hadn't noticed those features before. How could I? There had always been a crisis happening when we were together. I felt a little twinge of excitement at the prospect of sharing lunch with a handsome man, who also happened to be a protector of the people.

* * *

In the restaurant, I stared at the menu, wondering what I could order that wouldn't end up waving at him from between my teeth.

"What looks good?" he asked.

"Maybe just a salad," I said, as I polished the fork with my napkin.

"I always get beef on a wick when I come here," he said.

"Oh, that sounds good, maybe I'll try that."

"You seem nervous," he said, as he watched me rub the tines.

The word is *anxious*, I thought. I began to breathe slowly and put down the fork. "Do I? Well, I guess you're asking me out to lunch was kind of unexpected. Did you want to talk to me about the incident at my office? Or Tony? Ferdy?" Heat pickled the back of my neck.

"No, I think I just got used to bumping into you, and then realized that I was *hoping* to bump into you again. I figured you might be at the press conference, so I traded duties with a guy who was supposed to be there."

"Well, that's very sweet," I said, "but you have me at a disadvantage. You've learned a lot about me, but I don't know *anything* about you, except what you do for a living; what your first name is, where you live, you already know those things about me. You've been to my place, seen me in my *pajamas* - and don't get me wrong, you seem like a nice guy, but the way my luck is running, you're probably up to your neck in debt, have three ex-wives, and are a couple of hours away from popping out a gigantic cold sore."

"Wow," he said, sitting back in his chair, "where did *that* come from?"

I shook my head. "My life; my big, fat, mess of a life. My clients are being picked off one-by-one, in one way or another, which means I'll be out of business soon, my assistant was roughed up by some thug - she'll be okay, but now I'm wondering if she'll sue me because it happened at the office. I can't afford that. Absolutely *nothing* is going right, so it seems that the last thing I should do is get mixed up with someone who carries a gun."

"First," he said, "my name is Jack, so please call me that. Second, I live on Tip Hill. Do you know that area?"

I loved that section of the city. Tipperary Hill had a wonderful zoo, an arboretum, and Irish pubs and shops. It was the section of the city where so many people from the Old Sod lived, that its main traffic light had the green on top. I smiled, and relaxed a bit. "You must love it there."

He nodded. "So tell me," he said, "does your family live around here?"

"I don't have a family."

He looked surprised. "No one?"

I shook my head. "My father died when I was a baby, my mother when I was six."

"Aunts? Cousins? Siblings?"

"No, no, and no. No one."

"Sorry to hear that. What did your father do?"

"He was an investment banker. The only reason I have any idea of what he looked like, is because my grandmother gave me this gold locket," I said, as I pulled it out from under my shirt. "She could have put a picture of anyone inside; I wouldn't have known the difference."

"So your grandmother raised you after your mother passed?"

"Until *she* died, and then I went to live with my aunt. Money from my parents' life insurance, as I was told, went into a fund to pay for my upkeep. The money apparently followed me as I was passed from my grandmother to my aunt."

"Is she still alive? Your aunt?"

"No. Can we talk about something else, please?"

"Sure," he said, "I didn't mean to pry. Listen, I want to help you as much as I can with all of the things that are going wrong, but out of all of it, only your office break-in and Mr. Finnegan's disappearance, are within my jurisdiction."

"So when you came to my apartment..."

"It was an unofficial visit. I came because you called me; you were upset."

I smiled at him. "That was nice."

"One thing I do want to follow up on," he said, "is what you told me about Stearns himself. The robbery happened ten years ago, so how can you be positive that he was the guy who bumped into you?"

"Because I'll never forget his face – or those eyes," I said. "Never. It was him."

"Well, if that's true, you could be the only witness."

"But the police reopened the case because of an anonymous tip – that means I'm *not* the only one who knows it was him."

"Yeah, *anonymous*," he said. "They have no idea where the tip came from. It panned out, but an unknown person isn't going to be of any help at the time of trial."

It's getting hot in here, I thought, and I took a deep breath. "Look, I have what's known as Generalized Anxiety Disorder. I've had it for twelve years. I've managed to control it for the last ten, but the strain I've been under with my clients and Harley – well, I had to start seeing someone again because stress is the one thing that can bring it back full-on. I don't want that. That's why I don't want to get involved in the Danny Stearns thing."

If he was shocked, he didn't show it. I guess in his line of work, it wasn't even close to the worst thing he'd ever heard. "I'm not familiar with that," he said, "are you on medication for it?"

I nodded. "To help me sleep and to relieve stress."

"Ask your therapist, or whoever it is you see, for guidance about speaking to the police in Rochester. It's your duty to provide information that could help put Stearns away."

Again, what felt like tiny hot teeth nipped at the back of my neck, and heat built throughout my body. "They already know about me?"

"Of course," he said, "I couldn't sit on information like that."

I was suddenly fatigued and wanted to go. "I have to leave." I put my napkin on the table and stood up.

Jack reached for my wrist. "Take a day. Talk to your therapist. I don't want anything to happen to you, but you're going to have to talk to them, Audrey, so you have to find a way. "

This is not how I had envisioned our lunch going. Not having been involved with a member of the opposite sex for a long time, I'd felt the thrill of new possibilities when he'd asked me to join him; I certainly found him attractive. But now that he'd reported our conversation about Danny Stearns, fear and trepidation were thrown into the mix. I left the restaurant with my head spinning.

* * *

I wasn't in the best frame of mind to have it out with Harley, but I headed to the hospital to do just that before she was released; I wanted her in a confined space where she couldn't run. I found her still in her bed. Good.

"Hi Audrey," she said with a big smile. "I'm out of here as soon as the doctor comes back and signs my release papers; the nurse said it should be no more than a couple of hours. I can't wait. I'm going stir crazy in here."

"Not so fast," I started. "I went to your house yesterday to check on your grandmother." I watched as her smile faded. "I was worried about her because of the storm, but there was no sign of any grandmother there!"

Harley's face turned ashen. "I told you a neighbor was looking in on her. Maybe she was next door."

"No hard candy, no doilies, no old lady smell," I said, feeling mean, "no old lady at all. But there was plenty of evidence that some guy lives there. Who is he? And why have you been lying to me all this time?"

She covered her face with her hands and started to cry. "I'm sorry, I'm sorry. You don't understand."

"You bet your ass I don't understand," I said too loudly. I had to be careful. I didn't want a nurse to come in and make me leave. "Out with it."

"I had to tell you I lived with my grandmother. I needed an excuse to leave the office whenever I had to and it was the best, most logical story I could think of."

"What are you talking about?"

She dropped her eyes and fidgeted with the blanket. "My boyfriend."

"Keep going," I said, not knowing whether to believe her, wondering if this was going to be just another lie to cover up the first one.

"He's abusive. He's jealous and controlling, and when he calls and tells me to come home, I have to go. If I don't, there's always trouble. Audrey, every day he makes me to talk to him on my cell all the way home, so he knows exactly where I am and exactly when I should be pulling into the driveway."

"So you're telling me that's what you were doing when you said you had to take your grandmother to the doctor?"

She nodded. "I'm so sorry, Audrey. I hated lying to you. You've been so nice to me." She reached for the water glass on the table, and at the edge of the hospital gown's sleeve, I saw that bruise again; the one that had gone green; it wasn't new. I immediately felt like shit.

I thought about the pancake makeup in her desk drawer, and understood now that she used it to mask bruises that couldn't be covered by clothing. I got mad thinking about how little of that makeup was left in the tin. "Well, you can't go back there."

"Oh, I have to! I'm supposed to call him when I leave the hospital, so he knows when to expect me. He's probably already furious that I haven't been there to cook his meals."

"Does this guy have a job?"

"If he had a job, he couldn't control me all day long."

"How do you live? On what little I pay you?"

"You've seen the place," she said.

"He wasn't there when I went in yesterday. The door was unlocked."

"He only leaves it unlocked when he runs out for beer or cigarettes. You probably came within minutes of having him find you. I wouldn't want to think about what he would have done."

My temperature skyrocketed. "Okay," I said, "here's what we're going to do. You're going to leave your car here; don't worry about the parking charges – I'll cover those. It just so happens I want to stay away from my apartment for a while; I'll explain that later. As soon as you're released, the two of us will move into the second floor of the office. If your car isn't there, your boyfriend – what's his name?"

"Carl."

"If your car isn't in the parking lot, Carl won't know you're staying there. I just had a security system put in, so we should be okay. Sound good?"

"I don't know, Audrey, I don't want to piss him off any more than I'm sure he is already. He'll look for me at the office, and he'll kill me if he finds me."

"You can't go back to him," I said, "I won't hear of it. Has he visited you since you were admitted?"

"He wouldn't show his face around here, even though it's probably killing him not to – I'm sure he's convinced himself that I've been flirting with every doctor on staff and he's just waiting for me to get back home to punish me for it."

I gave her a hug. "I'm sorry about all this. I'm going over to the office now and get the place ready. I'll stop by my apartment and grab some things we'll need; we'll figure out how to get your stuff out of your place later. Hang in there."

"Thanks, Audrey," she sniffed.

"I'm just glad you're okay. And I'm really happy that the guy at the office didn't injure you any more than he did. It's awful that two men have hurt you like that."

She started to cry all over again. "Audrey, oh, God, there was no guy. No ski mask. It was Carl. He got angry over something stupid and came to the office when he knew you weren't there. I'm sure he'd been sitting in his truck across the street, waiting for you to leave. He pounded on the door and said if I didn't open it, he'd break it down."

In disbelief, I stared at her. *You let him in?*

She nodded. "I know it's hard to understand how he can have such a hold over me, but I'm terrified of the guy. If I wasn't, I'd have left him long ago. But he said if I did, he'd find me and kill me, and I believe him."

If there was one thing I understood, it was how a person could be controlled, either by another person, a drug, or a disorder like mine. "Don't worry," I said, "he won't get another shot at you."

Fueled by fury, I went home and loaded stuff I thought we would need into Nelly. I dug out paper plates, and plastic forks, spoons, and cups, from last year's Labor Day picnic. Harley was about my size, so I threw some extra clothes and PJs into a bag, and grabbed a bunch of washcloths and towels from my little linen closet.

As I carried my small TV out to Nelly, a sense of panic began to set in that I was taking too long. What if Carl did show up to take Harley home? Moving as quickly as I could, I packed a box with some non-perishable food, and then put everything salvageable that wasn't coming with me, into the freezer. The rest went into a garbage bag, which I threw into the dumpster on the way out. I stopped into the saloon to tell my landlord I'd be out of town, just in case anyone asked.

By the time I reached Harley's room, she had her paperwork in hand. I was relieved beyond words that Carl was not there. "I'm ready," she said. "Let's go before I lose my nerve."

Back at the office, with Harley safely inside, I began emptying Nelly. I carried the small TV upstairs and set it on a table, then pulled the sheets and blankets out of the plastic bags and made up the cots. I settled her into her makeshift bed and then gave the bathroom a quick wipe down. The place looked almost livable. Almost.

MARGARET BELLE

CHAPTER 9

By the time I was done, it was past dinnertime. "I'll hook up the cable," she said, "why don't you go get some takeout."

"You should stay in bed," I said, "and I don't want to leave you here alone."

"Better now than after Carl realizes I've left the hospital. And I do not intend to stay in this bed!"

"Okay, what sounds good?"

"Surprise me," she said.

Before I went out I checked and double checked the parking lot, vowing to park closer to the building on my return. It didn't help that I was in a neighborhood where an extra gunshot or mugging would go unreported for a good amount of time. Now, with Carl about to learn of Harley's disappearing act and Danny Stearns on my mind, I decided to have Miller add some lights in the parking lot.

A quick trip to a nearby pizzeria, netted me a large pie with everything and a six pack of soda. I nestled Nelly in close to the door, locked her up, and went inside with our hot and aromatic dinner.

We ate and watched the news. Within half an hour, coverage of Sean's press conference began. He was great – emotional, angry, and deadly serious all at the same time. But when the camera pulled back, I was horrified to see myself standing near the platform, next to the podium.

When I gasped, Harley asked, "What?"

I explained the whole story about Danny Stearns running into me, how I'd recognized him on TV, and how now maybe he'd seen me. "Do you think he'd recognize me after all this time?" I asked. "Because if he did, and he knows I could be the one to ID him, I think he'd come after me. And seeing me on the news in Syracuse would certainly narrow the search area for him."

"Why didn't you say anything about this before?" she asked, looking more upset than I'd expected her to. I didn't want to add more stress to what she was already shouldering.

"It's not exactly a story I'm fond of telling," I said. "It's one I'd hoped would stay in my past."

"So you just happened to be standing in his path," she said, almost to herself. "How does a thing like that happen? I mean, what are the odds?"

Talking to Harley made me more convinced that Danny Stearns *would* try to find out who and where I was. I could only hope that he hadn't seen the report, but these 24/7 news outlets replayed the same stories over and over for days. He would have lots of chances to see me.

I got up and examined my two medicine bottles, trying to decide which one to take. I went with the happy pill, knowing that anxiety was my worst enemy, and that I didn't really want to sleep heavily anyway. I wanted to hear any creaks or other noises that may occur during the night, and I cursed myself for having had carpeting put on the stairs.

I threw out the paper plates, took a shower, jammied up, and dropped onto my cot, facing Harley. "Listen," I started, "we're going to have to tell Jack that you were not attacked by a man in a ski mask. We can't have the cops out looking all over the place for some phantom thug. You can get in trouble for that. They can make you pay for the cost of the investigation and you can't afford that."

She put her hands over her face, shook her head, and took a deep breath. "The last thing I want to do is get myself in more trouble – especially with the police. I didn't even think about the repercussions of lying to them; I was just trying to protect myself." Then she stopped and looked at me. "Who's Jack?"

"Oh, sorry. Officer Morey. He was one of the responding officers at Ferdy's, and here too. He'd given me his card, so when I saw Danny Stearns on TV and got upset, I called him. He was also at Sean's press conference, and I had lunch with him earlier today."

"So, you're dating him now?"

"No, no, we just keep bumping into each other and like I said, we had lunch today. I mean, he's a big guy and good looking; I'd be lying if I said a little chemistry couldn't develop between us, but there's a downside too."

"Like what?"

"Like he wants me to talk to the police in Rochester and tell them I saw Danny Stearns there the day the bank was robbed. He wants me to get all involved in that, and I don't want to. And now we're going to have to tell him about Carl."

"I knew this was too good to be true," she said. "Why didn't you tell me you were dating a cop before you brought me here?"

"We're not dating! And what would you have done – gone back to Carl?"

"I don't know! You didn't really give me any time to think! I might have gone back, but maybe I would have decided to disappear, instead."

This was as close to a fight as Harley and I had ever come. Our emotions were running high and we needed sleep. "How about, first thing in the morning," I said, "we eat a big breakfast, gas up Nelly, and drive her over a big cliff holding hands – just like Thelma and Louise? Wanna?"

"That's not funny."

"It's a little funny," I said. "Come on, you know we have to tell Jack."

"Your new boyfriend."

"He's not my boyfriend! But he's the only police officer I know. Maybe he can persuade his brothers-in-blue that you were protecting yourself when you lied about the guy in the mask – that Carl is a violent person. They know all about domestic abuse and you have the bruises to prove it."

"That much is true," she said, rubbing her arm.

"Jack's already trying to figure out who's after our clients; I don't want to have to break in another cop. He can handle this for you, we just have to tell him sooner rather than later to mitigate your exposure. He can try and keep you alive and stop me from going under at the same time," I smiled.

"Maybe you don't even need Jack," she said. "You could probably stop the attacks on your clients by yourself."

"What do you mean?"

"All you'd have to do is just close up shop before anything else happens."

"Close? And do what?" I picked up the file I needed to read in preparation for tomorrow's meeting with Miller, but after fifteen minutes, realized that I was not going to be able to concentrate on it and put it aside. We tried to watch a movie, but my mind kept wandering. "I'm calling Jack, okay? You have to get this thing settled."

"Fine," she said. "I just hope you're right about him."

I picked up my cell and punched in Jack's number, realizing I was looking forward to hearing his voice. And to seeing him again. He answered on the second ring. "Jack, it's Audrey," I said. "Can you meet with Harley and me sometime tomorrow? At my office? There's something you should know."

CHAPTER 10

I opened my eyes the next morning and Harley's bed was empty. Immediately, I thought she'd decided against meeting with Jack, had called a cab, and skipped out. But the aroma of brewing coffee from downstairs brought sweet relief, and I grabbed a quick shower, dressed, and headed down for a cup.

It was already 10:30 – Jack would be here in half an hour. After tossing and turning last night, I'd given in and taken a sleeping pill; I guess I'd needed the shuteye, because I remembered nothing after taking it.

Harley had all the shades drawn and was busy working on the computer. "I had calls from six of Tony's eight stations," she said, "they're all bailing on him."

"I figured they would," I said. "Bastards. And guess who gets to tell Tony?"

"And Carrie Ashton called. She wants to know if I can go up there today. No one had an intern to spare and she's in a panic. You know, Audrey, Carrie's computer problems are probably just glitches – not connected to the others at all."

"I hope you're right, but we can't afford to lose her in any case, so go ahead; take Nelly. I'll meet with Jack and talk to him about Carl, all right?"

"Really? You'd do that for me?"

"Of course, but I'm sure he's going to want to talk to you when you get back," I said, as I tossed her my keys.

She gathered up her paraphernalia and took a good long look outside before she opened the door. I walked out with her and waited until she was safely in Nelly, then I went back inside, locked the door, and set the alarm.

Even though I was looking forward to seeing Jack, I was nervous about exposing Harley's lie, and hoped there would be no repercussions for her. She'd gone through a lot, and I completely understood her actions; I couldn't help but wonder if I would lie the way she had under the right circumstances – out of straight-up fear. I shivered, knowing that if Carl found out that Harley was living here, I'd no doubt end up in his crosshairs, right along with her.

When Jack knocked on the door, I couldn't get there fast enough to let him in. I surprised myself – and him – when I stood on my toes and kissed his cheek. "Sorry," I said, immediately embarrassed, "I shouldn't have done that." He shut the door, then turned back to me and swept me into his arms. He kissed me hard and I leaned into him. All muscles. All man. Big hands. Soft lips.

"Wow," he said. "Good ice breaker. I've been wanting to kiss you since I first laid eyes on you."

"You have?" My face got hot, and I hoped that if I was blushing, he wouldn't notice.

He kissed me again. "Good thing the other guy isn't here yet," he laughed. "He'd probably want a kiss too."

"What other guy?" I asked, trying to regain my composure.

He took off his hat. "Matt St. John. He's the Liverpool cop working Tony's investigation. He has a couple of questions, that's all. Where's your Jeep? When I drove in, I thought you might not even be here." He looked around. "Where's Harley? I thought the two of you wanted to talk to me."

"I had to send her to a client this morning, but she said I could speak for her."

"Sounds serious."

"It is. And I need you to let me tell you the whole story before you ask me any questions, okay?"

He nodded. "Come on – let's sit. What is it?"

I explained about Carl, Harley's fear of him, and how she'd made up the story about the man in the ski mask to keep from being beaten. "I understand you can't have men out there looking for a guy who doesn't exist, but she lied out of fear for her own safety. That should count for something, right?"

"Will she press charges?"

"I doubt it. She's staying here because she's scared to death of him."

"That's no good – he'll look for her car in your parking lot, first thing."

"We left it in the hospital garage. She's got my Jeep right now."

"Well, I'm telling you that he'll eventually find her. And he won't be happy to learn you're sheltering her."

A knock on the door told us that officer St. John had arrived. "We'll talk later," said Jack. "I want to ask around first and see what can be done." He gave me a wink that filled me with more than a warm feeling; it gave me hope, and I went to open the door. The two men greeted each other and then Jack introduced me.

By my guess, Officer St. John stood about six foot six; the perfect picture of someone who'd probably had his criminal justice degree paid for by a basketball scholarship. He sat down, looking like a parent forced to park himself in a child's chair at an elementary school open house. "I need to ask a few questions about your relationship with Tony Bravada, so if you don't mind, I'd like to get started." He pulled out a notebook. "How long have you and Mr. Bravada been working together?"

"About eight years," I said.

"Does he have any enemies you know of?"

"Of course not. He's one of the nicest people I know."

"How about you – anyone who might want to get to you by harming Mr. Bravada?"

"I can't think of anyone."

"So, how often do you see Mr. Bravada in an average week?"

"We meet for coffee every Monday morning before he goes up for his first round of traffic reports. We go over new contracts and the week's work."

"Where?"

"Mike's Diner on Route 11 – it's close to the airport."

"When was the last time you met him there?" he asked.

"Like I told Jack," I said, "the day of his accident."

"What time did you get there?" I threw Jack a look.

"Around 6:45."

"Did he leave the same time you did?"

"No, he stayed to finish his coffee."

"So, you didn't see him after that?"

"Not until after the crash."

"Okay, well that's it for now. I may have more questions for you later. You'll be available?"

"Of course," I said. I walked him to the door and then watched him get into his patrol car. I turned to Jack. "What the heck was that? He was asking questions I'd already answered for you."

"Just police work. It's his jurisdiction. Don't worry about it. When will Harley be back?"

"Not sure. She'll have her hands full at Carrie's."

"Okay," he said, "I'm going to take off and see what I can do with her situation. I wish you could talk her into pressing charges, but she probably knows that Carl wouldn't spend more than a few days in jail, if any, and then he'd be out looking for her. She may have to consider leaving town altogether."

"She's convinced he'll find her no matter how far she goes. She's been totally controlled by him and now that she's trying to leave, he's still there, in her mind. She'll be looking over her shoulder until the day she dies, unless he dies first."

"Keep your door locked," said Jack, as he put on his hat and headed for the door. "I don't want anything to happen to you." He took me in his arms and kissed me, leaning back until my feet left the floor. "Who would have thought I'd find someone like you at a crime scene?" he laughed.

I watched him drive away, sad to see him go. Seconds later, Miller pulled up in his van. Just as I expected, he got out carrying all kinds of crap I knew I would have to read, understand, appreciate, and figure out how to market. Business-to-business. Business-to-consumer. Suddenly I wanted to run away.

After an hour or so, Miller sat back in his chair and rubbed his eyes. My head was pounding and I reached into my desk drawer for a bottle of aspirin. "Want something?" I asked him.

"Please," he said.

My bottle was empty, so I went to Harley's desk and found that hers had only two pills left in it. I handed them to Miller without letting on that I needed them as badly as he did. He swallowed them, and then packed up the few lousy scraps of paper he was taking with him. The bulk of it would remain with lucky me.

"Everything okay with the system so far?" he asked.

"I guess so; it hasn't really been tested. But I feel a lot safer since you wired me up. I'm thinking about parking lot lights now."

"Just give me the word," he smiled.

Once he'd gone, I went back to my desk and called Harley. After I told her what Jack had said, she seemed a little relieved, but still nervous in general. "I just hope I don't get into a load of trouble over it," she said. "As for pressing charges against Carl – the answer is no; it's just too dangerous."

"That's entirely up to you," I said. "I'm in your corner, whatever you decide. Will you be back sometime today?"

"Not a chance. I've already made reservations at a hotel. I'll work the rest of today and hopefully finish up tomorrow. One way or the other, I'll see you by dinnertime."

I thought there was a chance that Carrie would try and hire Harley away from me, while she had her there. And it would make sense for Harley. A good move for her, really. A great job with a raise (anyone could pay her more than I could), the chance to use her skills with equipment and software I'd never have, and a place Carl would most likely never think to look for her.

I almost felt it was my duty to call Carrie and suggest that she hire Harley. Who knew how much longer my agency would even be viable? Jobs were not easy to come by. The more I thought about it, the more it seemed to be the perfect way out for a really nice woman who needed a serious break. It was positively ludicrous to expect her to live here at my office, even if it was temporary.

I picked up the phone and punched in Carrie's number.

CHAPTER 11

When Harley got back to the office the next day, she was livid. "You told Carrie to hire me? You really want me to leave you and go work for her? Seriously? How could you do that?"

"The question is, Harley, how could I *not* do it? Asking you to stay here is selfish. The way things are going, I won't even be able to pay you before long. You're a talented techie – Carrie would be thrilled to have you full time."

"She made that clear. But after everything you've done for me – and how I *lied* to you – I can't leave you here all alone."

"Two heads are usually better than one," I said, "but not in this case. We each have our own ass to cover and it would be too distracting to try and watch each other's as well. Besides, I think you're safer living away from me, and way better off financially working for Carrie. It's a no-brainer. Now call her and tell her you accept."

"What about Jack? What about the lie I told about Carl?"

"If the police need to talk to you, I'll tell them where you are. Jack said he was going to speak to some people and explain that you lied because you were afraid for your life. Harley, women get off of *murder* charges for that reason."

"Maybe I *should* go," she said with tears rolling down her face. "But I feel so guilty leaving you."

"Don't. Take Nelly. I'll get your car out of the garage and drive it to Carrie's. Then, on the strength of your new salary, you can take it straight to a dealership and trade it in on a new car. Get vanity plates that Carl wouldn't recognize in a million years. Keep your new location off the Internet and you've eliminated the only ways he could find you."

"But my stuff is still at the house," she said.

"Like what? Is there really anything there you can't replace? Remember, you'll actually be making some money now – get new clothes! I'm sure you can find some of that radical hippie shit you love so much in Oswego. Treat yourself! You're free!"

She laughed and gave me a hug, then called Carrie and accepted the new job. She took what she wanted from her desk (the pancake makeup went into the trash), packed a few of the outfits I'd loaned her, and all of Carrie's files (with my blessing). I walked her to the door and watched as she drove out of the parking lot for the last time.

Feeling lonely already, I called a cab and went to the hospital to get her car out of hock. Then a quick trip through a drive-thru netted me a cheeseburger and a diet soda for lunch. I was close to an hour behind Harley, as I headed north to Oswego on I-690W, a healthy forty-five minute drive from Syracuse. It was a beautiful spring day and even though there was a chill in the air, I lowered the windows a little. After driving all winter with them rolled up, it was always a thrill to hear the sound of the tires on the wet, spring pavement. It sounded loud and messy – like freedom, and it lifted my spirits.

About fifteen minutes into the trip I noticed a truck behind me; one I'd seen back at the fast food place. Not nervous, but cautious, I got off at the next exit and drove half a mile to the offices of a radio station where I often had meetings. The truck exited too, but as I pulled into the parking lot, it caught up to me and passed by. I watched until it was out of sight. *Great*, I chided myself. *Paranoid much?*

I pulled back onto the road and headed again toward the highway that would take me toward Oswego. Within five minutes, the truck reappeared in my rear view mirror. Now I knew that whoever it was, was following me, and it had to be Carl. I'd never seen him, but since I was driving Harley's car, it made sense that he would think she was behind the wheel.

It's illegal to use a cell phone while driving in New York, but I dialed Jack's number. It went to voice mail and I left a message saying I was being followed, and that I was going to turn around and head back to Syracuse to avoid leading Carl to Harley, if that was who was driving the truck.

I took the next exit and circled around to pick up the highway again, but headed in the opposite direction, toward home. The truck did the same. My throat tightened and my heart raced as the truck sped up and closed the gap between us. Was he going to drive right into me? Would he try to run me off the road? That's what always happened on TV. It was my only reference since I'd never been in a situation like this.

The truck backed off, then sped up, coming close enough that I couldn't see its headlights in my mirror, then it backed off again. It swerved into the passing lane and pulled up even with me, then slowed down and pulled in behind me again, this time ramming into my bumper. The steering wheel jerked in my hands as I felt the truck push me along the road. I swerved into the passing lane to try and break contact, but he changed lanes too, and rammed into me again. I called Jack a second time and pleaded with him to pick up, but there was no answer.

Ahead, a line of cars appeared. I sped up and pulled into the right lane, wedging myself between a sedan and a delivery van. The truck continued to follow me, but did not attempt to close in on me again.

Once off the highway, I drove on busier roads to the police station and pulled into the driveway, which was full of officers and canine units. The truck drove on by. I tried to catch a glimpse of the driver so I could give Jack some kind of a description, but the windows were tinted; something that had escaped my attention before.

I hopped out of the car and went to an officer, to tell him about the truck. He said he could look for it, but without a description of the driver or the license plate number, there was no way to prove that any gray truck he found was the right one; not even if it had tinted windows.

As I was getting back into Harley's car, Jack pulled into the parking lot. I called to him and he walked over to where I was. I explained what had happened, and how I suspected it was Carl who had been driving the truck.

"Call Harley and ask what he drives," he said.

It took me a minute to get her on the line. "A gray truck," she said, "why?"

"With tinted windows?"

"Yes. What's this about?"

"Do you know his license number?"

"No, I don't! Why do you want to know?"

I told her how he had followed me as I was bringing her car to her. "Oh, God," she said, "he's going to find me!"

"No, he isn't," I tried to assure her, "I turned around before he could possibly know where I was going. We have to figure out how to switch vehicles so you can get a new one right away. I'll call you back."

"Let me guess," said Jack. "Carl has a gray truck with tinted windows."

I nodded my head. "What are we going to do?"

"Tell me where he lives," he said. "I'll go there and park nearby. Once I'm sure he's home, I'll call you and you can head to Harley's. If he gets in the truck, I'll find a reason to pull him over."

I smiled, and the look in my eyes must have given him a hint of what I was feeling. "Don't kiss me in front of the guys," he warned. "I'm working your investigation. I could get taken off the case."

* * *

I waited there until Jack called and said that Carl had parked his truck near his house and had gone inside. I headed off toward Oswego once again and called ahead so that Harley would know when to expect me.

An hour later, I followed her to a dealership where she turned her car in on a used 4-wheel drive vehicle that she would need for snowy Oswego winters. Then off to the DMV, where she turned in her old plates and had temporaries put on. I gave her a hug and called Jack to tell him he could leave. I was on my way back to Syracuse in Nelly, and Harley now had a vehicle that Carl would not recognize. I felt like we had accomplished something big.

Instead of heading back to the office, I drove to the hospital to check on Tony. The stern day nurse allowed me into his room for "one minute and not one second more". Matt St. John was there, speaking with Tony and writing in his notebook, while Rose smoothed blankets and adjusted the pillows behind her brother's head. When she saw me, she waved me in. Tony was one big mass of tape, bandages, and plaster. His left leg was in traction, his head was bandaged, and both arms were in casts. He was conscious, but looked just awful. I went to the opposite side of the bed and gently touched his hand. "How are you?"

He shrugged. "I'll live, but the Soul of Syracuse is a goner. I've had that plane for a long time."

"Listen," I said, "I'm just glad *you're* not a goner, although I have to tell you, you had me wondering if you were going to pull through.

I've been so worried about you. Do you remember anything about what happened? Did the plane make funny noises? Or did any warning lights come on? You know the plane so well – do you have any idea what could have caused it to fall?"

"Falling" was a term Tony used when talking about planes dropping out of the air, or making emergency landings, and he'd made a few of those. Eight years ago January, during his first week of air traffic reporting, water had somehow gotten into the gas tanks he used to fuel the plane. While he was in the air, the water in the gas line froze and stopped fuel from getting to the engine. Tony had "fallen" out of the sky, but had managed to guide his plane to a stone quarry, where he'd landed safely. On another occasion, his landing gear failed and he'd flown in circles, dumping fuel, flying lower and lower, until he was able to land on the plane's belly in a grassy area. He was a fearless flier and a fearless faller.

"This time it was out of my control," he said. "Those other times I've managed to bring the plane in safely with only minor repairs necessary. But this was different."

"How?" asked Officer St. John. "How was it different?"

"I couldn't control the plane...because I couldn't control *myself*. I felt like I was falling asleep or about to faint. The doctor said there was something in my blood consistent with sleeping pills. But you know me, Audrey – I never take as much as an aspirin." I nodded. That was true. Tony not only worked out in the gym every day, but he ate healthily and didn't believe in medication of any kind; a point he and I good naturedly debated on occasion.

"Did you leave the table at any time during breakfast?" asked Officer St. John.

Tony thought for a minute. "I went to the restroom," he said, "but I don't know when. I'm sorry, things are a little fuzzy for me right now."

"That's okay," he said, as he put his notebook back in his pocket. "I'll check back every so often to see if you remember any more. Take care, Tony," then he nodded to me, and left.

"I'm going to go too," I said, "before that nurse outside chases me away." I headed toward the elevator feeling terrible, and praying that Jack was wrong; that what had happened to Tony – and Ferdy – had nothing to do with me.

Later, Jack called and wanted to have dinner. I was famished and agreed immediately, and suggested we meet at Krabby Kirk's, thinking that I might persuade him to come up to my apartment with me afterwards. I could feel infatuation for him growing into something more and wanted some alone time with him to see how receptive he would be to getting a little closer; my office wasn't going to cut it.

* * *

It was a warm evening, so we sat on the back patio while we ate. I found myself staring at him and made a concerted effort not to; I didn't want to come off as the one of us who was the most interested. My grandmother used to say that in every relationship, one person loves the other more. The person who loves the most, she'd say, is the person who gets hurt the worst. And, of course, being the person I was, with anxiety always lurking, ready to strike, that kind of hurt could do a lot of damage. It could mean years and years more therapy. More medication.

"Aren't you hungry?" he asked.

"I guess not. I thought I was, but..."

"You're okay though?"

"I'm fine. You want to have coffee upstairs?"

He smiled. "You mean upstairs, as in *upstairs*?"

I nodded. "A long as we're here, I'd like to check the place."

Jack left the money for the meal and a generous tip under the edge of his plate, and we climbed the second set of stairs that led directly to my apartment. "What's that I smell?" he asked, after we closed the door behind us. "I remember it from the night you called me over."

"Frankincense. Incense. Does it bother you?"

"Ah, incense," he laughed. "Usually when I come into contact with that, someone's trying to cover up the smell of pot."

"My previous therapist used it in our sessions to relax me."

"Previous – so you don't see that therapist anymore? I'm not prying, just wondering. You don't have to answer. I always sound like I'm in interrogation mode. Sorry."

"No, I don't see her now; she's in Rochester. In fact, I had just left our last session when Danny Stearns ran into me." *Why did you bring that up?* I chastised myself. I didn't need Jack to start talking about the bank robbery. *And don't mention you're seeing a psychiatrist now– one step higher on the mental food chain!*

"Speaking of Stearns," he said, "Rochester has pulled out all the stops to find him. They want to bring him to trial."

"I'm sure they do," I said, furious at myself for having mentioned his name.

"Your ID alone won't put him behind bars, but it will be an important part of their circumstantial case against him."

"Circumstantial because they don't have the money? Or his prints on anything at the bank? Or what?"

"All of the above. No DNA – at least not yet. But you saw him fleeing the scene."

"I didn't actually see him come out of the bank; the bank was around the corner from where I was standing. His lawyer could say he was coming from somewhere else, right?"

"And his lawyer *will* say that. But right now they can't even place him in Rochester on that day. And you can not only do that, but you saw him running with police in pursuit."

Jack was so sincere, his eyes so honest, that for the second time that day, I did something that would help someone else, even though it would make things worse for me. I went to my closet and pulled down the box that held the ski mask Danny Stearns had dropped that damnable day.

"I believe the police in Rochester will find the DNA they're looking for in here," I said.

MARGARET BELLE

CHAPTER 12

"What is it?" Jack opened the box and saw the black ski mask crumpled inside. "Where did you get this?"

"Danny dropped it when he bumped into me. I picked it up off the sidewalk and then didn't know what to do with it, so when I got back to the dorm, I stuck it in this box and it's been there ever since. His DNA will be in there, right?"

"Audrey, this is what they need, whether or not they find the money. Between this and your testimony, you'd never have to worry about running into him again."

"Take it, then," I said. "Good riddance to it."

He pulled out his cell phone. "I can't take possession of it. It's a chain of custody thing, although you've had it so long that may be a moot point."

"Who are you calling?"

"Sheriff's Department. They'll pick it up and contact Rochester."

"Tonight? They'll come here?"

"Yes – and I'm sure it'll be a relief to have it out of here." I smiled and nodded, even though what I was feeling was *not* relief. Not even close.

He explained the circumstances to someone on the other end of the phone and finally finished the call. "They'll be here in a couple of hours. You okay? Let's sit." He ushered me toward the sofa. "I'll get you some water," he said. "I'd ask where the kitchen is, but I can see every room from here."

I sipped the water and began to feel better. I liked that Jack seemed worried about me, but figured he would have done the same for anyone, until he brushed a lock of hair from my forehead and then rested his hand on the back of the sofa, near me. I felt blood rush to my cheeks, and in an effort to hide the blush, I looked down and studied my glass of water.

After an unbearable amount of time, he put his hand under my chin and lifted it up until our eyes met, and he leaned down and kissed me.

"Was that okay to do?" he asked.

"Yes," I breathed, "could you do it again please?" And this time it was a *kiss*.

"I'd ask where the bedroom is," he said, "but, well, you know." He carried me as if I weighed nothing and lowered me onto the bed, which thank God, I had made.

"Is this a good idea?" I asked, between kisses.

He slid his hand up my back and pulled me closer, and mumbled, "Is this the best time to ask?"

"What about the sheriff's deputy?" I whispered. "He's coming tonight."

"If I do this right," he whispered back, "that'll make three of us."

I couldn't get enough of his muscled arms, broad shoulders, and sturdy back. His thick wavy hair, compassionate hazel eyes, and full lips, lent beauty and wonder to an otherwise wholly masculine body, that spoke to the rigid training needed to live a life of danger. His movements in bed were focused and slow, and with great purpose: a machine with rhythm. A man who knew what he wanted, but also knew what I wanted. What I needed.

Later, as we cuddled under a sheet, he reached for my locket. "Can I see your father's picture?"

At that moment, I would have said yes to anything. "Sure," I said. He pushed the little button on the side of the heart and it popped open.

"You have his eyes," he said. "The other side, though, no photo of your mom?"

I closed the locket and covered it with my hand. "I had one, but it fell out when I was little," I lied.

"You could always replace it," he said. "You must have another one."

"No," I said, "I don't. Can we change the subject, please?"

He smiled. "Sure. It's your locket. Maybe you'll put someone else's picture in the other side someday." He raised an eyebrow, as if to say perhaps it would be his.

Instead of getting to lounge in bed, relishing our first time together, we hopped in the shower (which was fun too), and then got dressed before our company arrived.

The interview didn't take long, and I was not nervous at all, but I attributed that to Jack. After I answered his questions, the sheriff's deputy shook hands with me, then with Jack, and left with the box. I was glad to see it go, even though I knew it would be the reason my life would become even more complicated than it was now.

Jack started to pick up his things – his keys, his cell – getting ready to go. "I'm going to stay here tonight," I said, "I want to sleep in my own bed."

"I'm always just a phone call away." He kissed me goodbye, and when he went to leave, I pulled him back.

"One more," I said, and he happily obliged.

Had there ever been a time when I'd felt happier than I did at this moment? In a celebratory mood, I jammed up and threw a bag of popcorn into the microwave. I was dating a cop! A man who was putting up with me so far, and someone who could protect me; keep me safe. One who had already helped me so much, and had helped

Harley as well. I couldn't believe any harm would come to her, or to me, with Officer Jack Morey on our side.

I flipped on the news, thinking I wouldn't need any medication at all to get to sleep. The first story was a report of a crash, in which a vehicle had run off the road and sheared off a telephone pole; the scene was gruesome. A reporter was standing outside, near the scene of the accident that she said had happened yesterday. I'd turned in early last night and missed the news.

The reporter continued, "The name of the driver who perished in the crash, is Miller Crawford, owner of Miller's Security Systems, in Watertown and Rochester."

CHAPTER 13

No! This couldn't be happening! Miller was dead? I ran into the bathroom and vomited. I sat on the floor as sobs tore at my body. This was my fault. Had to be. I should never have taken him on as a client. I knew something could happen to him if I did, and I did it anyway. What kind of a person was I? Oh, God. Miller was dead.

I fell asleep right there on the floor, waking only long enough to drag myself off to bed. Throughout the night I tossed and turned, and when I couldn't lie there any longer I picked up the phone and called Dr. Steele. "Can you see me this morning? It's important."

* * *

"So what's going on?" Dr. Steele asked, settling herself into her chair. She crossed her legs, straightened her back, and held a pencil over her notebook, poised and ready to take notes like a capable secretary.

"Another client," I said. "This one died."

Her face went slack, her notebook forgotten. "Oh, my God, Audrey, when?"

"Two days ago, but I didn't hear about it until last night," I said. "The thing is, I met with him the day he died. We spent an hour in my office going over his business material. I mean, he was a new client. It was our introductory meeting, as far as his advertising went."

"What do you mean, as far as his advertising went?"

"He'd been in my office once before, and we'd had lunch together before that. He installed one of his security systems for me."

"This is most likely just a terrible coincidence," she said. "The poor man had an unfortunate accident the day he met with you, and that's the beginning and the end of it."

I shook my head. "No, there can't be that many coincidences." I jumped up. "In fact I shouldn't even be *here*. Whatever it is, I could be bringing this awfulness to you just by being here! I have to go." I grabbed my purse and ran out the door, leaving Dr. Steele sitting in her chair, apparently unable to think of anything to say that would make me stay.

Once back in Nelly, I couldn't control my panic and knew I shouldn't drive. I called Jack, explained what had happened to Miller, and told him where I was.

"I'll be right there," he said. "Hold tight."

By the time he arrived, I was hugging myself and rocking back and forth, and I let out a scream when he knocked on my window. I pushed back my seat and made an ungainly move over the console to the passenger side. He slid in behind the wheel, checked his watch, and turned on the radio.

"I knew about the crash," he said, "but I didn't know the guy was your client."

When the news began, the second story reported that Miller was found to have a drug commonly found in sleeping pills in his blood. It was assumed, barring any new findings, that he'd fallen asleep at the wheel. No skid marks were found at the scene, indicating that he had not tried to brake as his vehicle left the road, and the condition of the van was consistent with it having hit the pole while Miller's foot was still on the gas pedal.

"Sleeping pills," I whispered, "that's what they said about Tony. That he had remnants of sleeping pills in his blood."

"They also said you were the last to see Tony, but we don't know that for sure."

"I think I was the last one to see Miller, though. We had a meeting in my office that day."

"That doesn't mean anything."

"He had a headache and I gave him two aspirins."

Jack turned to look at me. "You gave him pills?"

"Yes. *Aspirin*."

"Where's the container?"

"It was empty, so I threw it in the trash can."

"Let's go," he said.

When we arrived at the office, Jack asked, "Which can? Kitchen? Or the one by your desk?"

I pointed to the one next to my desk. He took a pen out of his pocket and used it to lift out the empty bottle. "Got any plastic bags?"

I went to the kitchenette and pulled one out of a box in the cupboard. "What are you going to do with it?"

"I'm going to have the dust inside analyzed." He dropped the bottle into the bag.

"Why?"

"Because," he said, "once it's known that you may have been the last one to see Miller and you gave him pills, the department's gonna do this. We might as well do it first."

"Are you kidding me? You're telling me that I'm going to be accused of causing Miller to drive off the road?"

"I'm saying that this is the second of your clients – one who almost died, and one who did, to have sleeping pill residue in their blood, and who saw you the same day they had their accidents. We need to be proactive."

77

"Just get rid of the bottle!"

"Can't do that. You know I can't."

"Nobody else was here when Miller was. No one needs to know he met with me."

"I'm sure he has an appointment book, or a secretary who keeps his daily schedules for him. Plus, if you remember, I drove out of your driveway just as he was driving in."

"I thought dating you was going to keep me safe," I said.

"Don't panic," he said. "I won't let anything happen to you. Now come on – are you okay to drive me back to my car?"

I nodded, but in my heart I knew I was in trouble; the in-my-head kind of trouble.

CHAPTER 14

Jack called the next morning and said we needed to meet. "You don't sound right," I said. "Please don't tell me something else is wrong."

"Are you at the apartment or at the office?"

"Apartment."

"I'll be right over. I'll bring coffee."

I showered and dressed, wondering what was so urgent that he felt the need to rush right over. Maybe they'd found Danny Stearns. Or maybe it wasn't about him at all. Had they found Ferdy? Oh, God. What if they found him and he was dead? By the time Jack arrived I'd worked myself into a frenzy; the last thing I needed was coffee.

Jack walked in and handed me a large cup. "It's decaf," he said. Thankful for that, I took a sip and we sat on the sofa.

"What is it?" I asked.

"Matt St. John spoke to the manager of Mike's Diner and confirmed that you and Tony have coffee there most Monday mornings."

"Right. So?"

"He said that Tony stayed a little longer than usual that morning; refilled his coffee."

"And?"

"He knows that Tony had sleeping pill residue in his blood."

"*And?*" Jack was re-capping – leading up to a big something.

"Matt has to look at everything. He's going to ask you if you have access to sleeping pills. I just wanted to give you a heads-up."

"Are you saying that if he finds out I have sleeping pills, he'll think I hurt Tony? That's beyond ludicrous!"

"As the investigating officer, he has to look into every little thing, and I can't interfere with that. All I can do is advise you to tell him the truth. If he gets too personal, tell him you want a lawyer."

"A *lawyer*?" I excused myself, and with my anxiety meter about to blow, went into the bedroom and swallowed one of my happy pills. When I turned around, Jack was standing there.

"What was that you just took?"

"A pill. I took a friggin' happy pill, okay?"

"Sure," he said. "You told me you were on medication. I get it."

I began to pace. "No one who knows me would ever think I would hurt Tony, or anyone else for that matter! He can ask anyone. I would never do anything so awful. I don't have it in me. Tony was a client, but he was also a very good friend."

"I'm sure he *will* be asking around. People you work with, friends, like that."

"Oh, that's just *great*! I didn't mean I wanted him to talk to people! The grapevine in advertising is big enough to choke a horse; I'll never get another client. If Matt talks to even one person, I'll be done!"

Someone knocked on the door. "I'll get it," he said, and then I heard him say, "Matt."

Matt? Already? Butterflies darted through my stomach, then through my chest before making their way along my extremities. I looked at my arm, half expecting to see wings rippling under my skin.

"Sorry about this," said Matt. "I need to talk to Audrey."

"Come in, Matt," I said, and I pointed to a chair. "Have a seat." I went to the sofa and waited for him to start. I have nothing to hide, I thought, so let him have a go at me.

Matt looked toward the ceiling and sniffed. "What's that?"

"What?"

"Are you cooking?"

I thought for a second. "Oh, no – that's incense."

"Are you burning it now?"

"No, last night."

"Oh," he said. "The only time I run into that is when it's being used to cover up the smell of pot."

I rolled my eyes, "I wasn't smoking pot." But suddenly the incense was all I could smell. It seemed to get stronger and stronger, until I considered excusing myself to see if I actually had lit a stick and forgotten, but I sat tight.

"Okay," he finally said, "let's get to this."

"How can I help you?" The butterflies continued their mad flight through my body and heat prickled the back of my neck. If Jack hadn't told me this guy was going to ask me about sleeping pills, I probably wouldn't be so nervous. But then, maybe knowing ahead of time would keep my eyes from bugging out of my head when and if he did ask. What was the saying? *Forewarned is forearmed?*

He flipped open his notebook and I could see a list of questions he had prepared. With a click of his pen, he began. "So how long have you known Mr. Bravada?"

"About eight years – you asked me that before."

"And when was the last time you saw him?"

"The morning of his crash. I told you that before too."

"I spoke to the manager of Mike's Diner and he verified that you were there the morning of the crash with Mr. Bravada, around quarter to seven. Is that right?"

"Yes." What's he doing? I thought. Asking me the same questions to see if I change my answers?

"Mr. Bravada said he didn't think the plane malfunctioned. He said he felt drowsy and fought to stay awake."

"I was in the hospital room when he told you that, Matt."

Without looking up from his notebook, he continued, "Do you have access to sleeping pills?"

So there it was. "I do."

"Over-the-counter or prescription?" His voice was calm and non-threatening.

Probably a technique they used to interrogate actual criminals, I thought. "Prescription."

"Who prescribed them for you?"

"My doctor, of course."

"A general practitioner?"

I took a deep breath. "My therapist."

He looked up from his notebook. "You're seeing a psychologist?"

"A psychiatrist, actually," I said. He wrote that down. "Do you think I drugged Tony?" I asked. "You can't possibly think that."

"I have to cover all the bases," he explained. "You were the last known person to see him before his accident."

"So?" A trainload of agitation chugged toward the section of tracks I was tied to.

"Audrey," he said, "at this point I have to pause and Mirandize you, because your answers might be incriminating."

Jack spoke up, "Do you want a lawyer?"

"Why would I need a lawyer?" I asked, hearing the exasperation in my voice. "I haven't done anything wrong!"

Matt read me my rights and then continued. "So, the doctors found no physical ailments or disorders that would cause Mr. Bravada to become drowsy. That means it was caused by an outside source, in this case sleeping pills, which he does not have in his possession. So, at this time I have to ask if you put sleeping pills in his coffee that morning."

"To what end?" I asked. "He's been a client and a friend for years. His sponsors provided a huge portion of my income. I would have no reason to do anything to him from a personal or a business standpoint."

"Another client of yours, Miller Crawford, had the same drug in his blood when he crashed his car," he said, "and it's come to my attention that you may also have been the last person to see him before his accident."

I shot a look at Jack that said, *you told him?*

"Also," Matt continued, "I have reason to believe that you gave Mr. Crawford pills while the two of you were together, just before his accident. Is that true?"

I looked again at Jack, only this time, I felt tears running down my face. He looked stricken, and I knew he had told Matt. "Yes, that's true," I said, "but I thought they were aspirin. They were in an aspirin bottle, so why would I have thought they were anything else?"

"I was going to tell you," Jack whispered.

"I don't have any more questions for you," Matt said, and he stuck his notebook into his back pocket and headed toward the door. "Listen, Audrey," he said, "better me than someone you've never met, right? I know you didn't do any of this. But the process is the process. I have to ask you not to leave town."

Jack followed him. "It's your job, man. I know that."

After the door closed, I turned to Jack. "Why did you tell him about Miller?"

"Take it easy," he said.

"Don't tell me to take it easy!" I shouted. "You betrayed me!"

"Hold on. Remember when you told me you had given Miller the aspirin? And we went to your office to retrieve the bottle? I said it was because I knew that the police would eventually know you were with him before he died, and had given him those pills. And what did I tell you was the reason for picking the bottle out of your trash?"

"To analyze the contents before the police did."

"Yes. To be forthcoming about everything, so it didn't look like evidence was piling up against you. We told *them*. So when Matt came to me with the results of Miller's blood analysis, and it was the same as Tony's, I told him the rest – that you gave Miller the pills. We were working together."

"Against me!"

He held up his hands. "No, not against you. I would never do that. You know better."

"I need you to leave, Jack."

"Okay, I'll go. But first tell me you understand why I told Matt what I did."

"I know you had my best interest at heart. I just wish I'd heard it from you, before I heard it from him."

"I'd fully intended to tell you, Audrey, but then he showed up at the door before I had a chance. Look, I have to go to work." He kissed my forehead. "I'll see you later."

I paced the floor, going over the interview, and realized I'd been so nervous that I'd already forgotten much of what was said. I needed something to occupy my mind and decided to drive over to Mike's Diner. I wanted to know what Mike had said to Matt; what questions he'd been asked.

When I arrived, the place was packed with the lunch crowd; not the best time to get and keep Mike's attention. I waved at him and caught his eye. He was working the counter, but was willing to sit with me for a minute.

"I'm sorry to bother you," I began, "but I'm freaking out. The police are asking me questions about the last morning I was here with Tony. Officer St. John told me he talked to you. What did he say?"

"He asked me how often you two came in, was it always about the same time, were you here that morning, and did I see anything weird happening between the two of you."

"Anything else?"

"Wanted to know did any customers get sick that day, which insulted the b'Jesus out of me, and he asked who else was working the counter that morning – I said it was just me. That was about it. Listen," he said, "I have to get back to work," and he started to get up.

"So after I left, Tony was still here, right?"

"For a few minutes. Some guy who was sitting at the counter, a fan I guess, recognized his voice. He stopped by the table, and come to think about it, he sat in the booth for a minute or two."

"You didn't tell that to the officer?"

He shook his head. "I just answered his questions. I was busy."

"That means I *wasn't* the last person to see him that morning! Do you know who the man was?"

"Never saw him before. I'm pretty sure he came in after you and Tony had already been here for a while; he sat at the counter. But then the place started getting busy and I really didn't pay any attention after that."

"Thanks Mike!" I said, as I got up to leave. I burst through the door feeling relieved and pissed at the same time. And so ready to tell off Matt. He should have asked more questions – gotten Mike to remember more. I jumped into Nelly and headed to the police station to find him.

MARGARET BELLE

CHAPTER 15

Better judgment prevailed. When was it ever smart to ha-ha a cop, especially when you wanted him on your side? So instead of driving to the police station all worked up, I sent Jack a text and asked him to come to my apartment when his tour ended; he could pass the information along.

He said he'd come for dinner, so I put in an order downstairs and then went up and aired out my apartment. A swish of a cloth took care of tabletop dust and I ran the vacuum.

With time to spare, I ran next door to the hair salon and found Lisa finishing up her last appointment for the day; a teen who was mooning over her newly-dyed pink hair. Lisa had given her a short cut, jagged on the sides, while the hair over her eyes hung straight down like a starched flag. How could she even see herself in the mirror? Lisa winked at me, knowing exactly what I was thinking.

While the girl paid, I lowered myself into one of the massage chairs and turned it on. *Oh Lordy.* One of these would definitely be in my letter to Santa this year. I kicked off my shoes.

"Well, *you* look happy," said Lisa, as she dropped into the chair next to mine. "What's up?"

I gave her an abbreviated explanation about the conversation I'd had with Matt and the subsequent talk with Mike at the café. I also told her I was moving back into my apartment now that Harley was gone. I was alone here, or I was alone there. What was the difference?

"No wonder that chair feels good – you've had a crazy day." She reached for the remote and hit the heat button on my chair. "Want to have dinner tonight?"

I shook my head. "Jack's coming over after work. I can't wait to tell him all of this."

"Seems like I hardly see you anymore since Hunky Man entered the picture! I'm glad for you. As for me, I'm taking this weekend off," she said. "A much needed R&R. I'll be back on Monday. As long as you're back in your apartment, will you keep an eye on this place for me?"

"Sure. And good for you for taking a break. You deserve it." As much as I hated to leave the vibrating chair, I had to pick up my dinner order and head upstairs. "Relax this weekend," I said, "and try to forgive yourself for what you did to that poor girl who just left here."

"It's all the rage," she laughed, as she twisted her door key off its ring and handed it to me. "Hang on to this just in case."

"Well, don't ever try that color on me," I said, "or that cut." I left her shaking her head at my lack of hair fashion savvy.

My landlord handed me my order and I asked if he'd mind putting deadbolts on my doors.

"Sure thing, Aud," he said, "something up?"

"I'd just feel more secure."

"I'll put it on the top of my list," he said. "You have a good night."

Upstairs, I lit a stick of Frankincense and flopped on the sofa, needing to loosen up before Jack arrived. I was happy to be home, and looked forward to sleeping in my own bed. There were only so many nights I could take tossing around on that cot like a kid at summer camp.

I revisited my talk with Mike and smiled, anticipating Jack's reaction to the news. I was beginning to think he was right. Danny

Stearns didn't know where I was. He had to be busy staying ahead of the law's long arm. Flying under the radar. Hiding in the weeds.

By the time Jack arrived I was ravenous. Over dinner, I filled him in on everything, but spent the most time on my conversation with Mike. "That's *great*," he said. "I'll have Matt talk to him again. This is a big deal, Audrey, not to be the last one to see Tony. A very big deal. He'll send an officer to Mike to get a description of the guy."

"A sketch artist."

"We don't have an actual artist on staff; it's done with a computer program now. Any officer can do it. It's just a matter of mixing and matching different shapes of facial features."

"And this will get Matt off my back?"

"He'd have no reason to follow up with you. You have no motive, and now you weren't even the last one to see Tony, so there's no case to be made."

My cell phone rang and I recognized the number as Sean Finnegan's. "Sean?" I asked, "Have you heard something?"

"No. In fact, that's why I'm calling. I'm flying in tomorrow. I want to talk to the investigators on Ferdy's case, and I want to do it face-to-face. I don't like asking people questions on the phone when I can't see their eyes. Are you going to be around? Maybe we could meet for lunch?"

"Sure. Absolutely. Do you need me to pick you up at the airport?"

"No, I'll rent a car. Can we meet at that restaurant — the one you live above?"

"Sure. I can meet you there around 11:30, before the crowd gets bad. Will that work?"

"Great. See you then, Audrey. I'm hoping for some good news. Even one lead. Something."

I turned to Jack. "You heard."

"Was he summoned? Or is he coming on his own?"

"No one called him – he just wants some answers. I feel so bad for him. I mean, how does someone just vanish into thin air like that?"

"It happens."

My phone rang again. *What now?* I did not recognize the number. "Out of town," I said.

"What's the area code?" Jack asked.

"585"

"Rochester."

I fought to keep down what little I had eaten. "Hello?"

"Audrey Dory?" a deep voice asked.

"Yes?"

"This is officer Donaldson, Rochester PD. I need to talk to you about Danny Stearns. I understand you can place him in Rochester the day the bank was robbed."

"Yes...but,"

"I'd like to do it tomorrow. Is 10 a.m. good for you?"

What was I going to do, say no? "I guess so, sure." I gave him my address and directions.

I hung up and looked at Jack, who had poured us decaf while I was on the phone. He put two mugs on the table and took our plates to the sink. "So?"

"So it was the Rochester police department. They want to talk to me about Danny Stearns."

"Of course they do. When?"

"Tomorrow. Should I be nervous?"

"Why would you be?"

"An officer's coming *here*; do you think he'll be in an unmarked car?"

"Why," he laughed. "Are you worried about what your neighbors will say?"

"If he *is* in an unmarked car, how will I know he's a real cop?"

"He'll have a badge."

"You can buy those on-line. What if it turns out to be someone Danny Stearns is sending?"

"Audrey, for Christ's sake! You have to stop imagining these whacked-out scenarios!"

Dr. Steele had said something similar to me, but in kinder terms. "I know I obsess, Jack – it's a symptom of my disorder, and I can't stop just because you want me to. It doesn't work like that!"

"Take a pill then – really. If they're supposed to help, *take* one for God's sake." He handed me one of the mugs. "Go get one. Take it with this."

I went to get a pill, recognizing the weariness in his voice. I'd heard that tone before, and it was not something I wanted to hear from Jack. I didn't want to lose him, yet I knew it was only a matter of time before he would get sick of my histrionics; only so long he would be able to watch me fear things I thought were worth fearing, but in his eyes were unsubstantiated. It had happened before.

There was Luke in my sophomore year of college: *Look, Audrey, you're great. I thought we had a shot, but the truth is, I just can't put up with your crap any more.*

After that was Rob in my junior year: *What the hell's wrong with you? I've hung in there for almost a year, but shit Audrey – life is just too short.*

Then there was Eddie, the love of my life during my senior year. I'd ended things two months after we'd become engaged, because I realized I just couldn't put him through a lifetime of me. He was a wonderful guy. He'd calmed me when I needed it, and made excuses for me when I couldn't be calmed. Every day he went before me, paving the way, making sure I would experience as little stress as possible. He did it willingly. But I couldn't have watched him do it forever. It was too much to ask any man to be the husband – no, the caretaker – of someone like me.

Eddie was talented, and smart, and people loved him. He needed a life free of me, so he could pursue his own dreams. I would not only have held him back, I would have ruined him. I'd had no family to approve or disapprove of my decision to end things with him, but his family had been ecstatic over the cancelled engagement. I believed to this day I abandoned Eddie because I'd loved him so much.

I looked at Jack. "Want to stay here with me tonight?"

"Absolutely. But I should leave before Rochester gets here in the morning."

"Oh, then you'd better go right to sleep. No fooling around."

He unbuttoned his shirt. "Let's go to bed and see how that works out."

The deadbolts hadn't been installed yet, but not wanting another display of insecurity in front of Jack, I fought the urge to wedge a chair under the doors. After all, I had 9-1-1 right here.

Still, dreams pursued me the whole night through. I was next door, sure that something was amiss at the salon in Lisa's absence. I trudged along, carrying a key as long as my arm and as heavy as a brick, ready to unlock the door and take care of whatever might be wrong. Seeing nothing unusual on the main floor, I left the huge key on the reception desk and went to check the basement.

The darkness was as absolute as it had been the day Lisa and I had descended the rickety stairs. It smelled old, felt damp, and I recoiled as a spider web brushed my face and got caught up in my hair.

As my foot hit the rough dirt floor, I reached out one arm and extended my fingers, trying to remember where the chain to the light was. I felt around in search of it, but to my horror, when I found it, someone else's hand was already wrapped around it.

I turned to scramble up the stairs, but whoever was down there with me, grabbed my ankle and dragged me back. I awoke, clutching my throat, unable to scream; the feeling of that hand on my ankle so real, I yanked back the covers to look.

Jack slept, unaware of my middle-of-the-night trauma. I went to the kitchen to get a drink of water, and not knowing whether to take a sleeping pill or a happy pill, I took one of each.

MARGARET BELLE

CHAPTER 16

Jack kissed me awake around 8 a.m., and I struggled to pull myself out of what felt like a coma. "I made coffee," he said. "You were really out, so I let you sleep. But Rochester's going to be here at 10, so you'd better hit the shower."

"Yes *sir*," I answered. "Are you always this pushy?"

He shrugged. "I have to get home and pretty myself up for work." He put his hand on my shoulder. "Don't be nervous, okay? Call me when it's over."

"Call you at work?"

"Yeah, it's okay. I left my number on the kitchen table. If I'm busy I just won't answer, but you can leave a message."

I hated being left to meet with the detective by myself, afraid that his questions and my answers were going to poison the air in my little dwelling, my sanctuary. Just the thought of law enforcement traveling from another city to talk to me about Danny Stearns, whose image wouldn't leave me, made me nauseous.

I went to my computer, signed on, and Googled the Rochester bank robbery. Several newspaper articles, photos of the bank, and videos of interviews appeared as choices, and I clicked on the first one.

About halfway through the article, I learned that police had interviewed all of the bank's employees, whether they'd been at work the day of the robbery or not. Because of the unusually large amount of money stolen, an inside connection was originally suspected. That theory, however, was later dropped. The robber, it seemed, had simply chosen a day when a big haul was available.

An inside job, I thought. I wondered why the police had dismissed that theory so quickly. I glanced at an old group photo of some of the bank's employees, who had been herded together in front of a police officer for a PR story several years before the robbery. The caption read, *Tellers at the National Bank of Rochester receive robbery training from the local police department.* This type of training, according to the story, occurred twice a year, particularly around holidays when robberies were apt to increase.

At 10 sharp, Officer Donaldson knocked on my door. I offered him coffee, which he declined, and he stood for a moment just inside the door gazing around the room. I waited for him to sniff the air and ask if I'd been smoking pot.

"Lived here long?" he asked, instead.

"For years," I said. "It's pretty small, but I don't need a lot of room. It's just me."

"Can we sit?"

"Oh, of course, sorry." I indicated the sofa with a Vanna White wave of my hand.

"So let's go back about ten years," he said. "You were living in Rochester at that time?"

"I had just graduated from college."

"Exactly where were you when you saw Danny Stearns?"

"On Franklin Street, waiting for a taxi. I was going back to my dorm to pick up my things and go to the airport to come home."

"Where did you go to school?"

"Nazareth."

"What did you study?"

"Marketing Management. Excuse me, but I thought you wanted to talk about Danny Stearns."

"Just trying to get a clear picture. What brought you to Franklin Street that day?"

"An appointment."

"Business?"

"Personal."

"What time of day was this?"

"Around 10 a.m. I guess."

"So walk me through it," he said. "You were waiting for a cab..."

"Yes, and a man ran around the corner and slammed into me."

"Danny Stearns?"

"Yes, but I didn't know his name at the time."

"When did you learn his name?"

"When it was on the news recently. There was a story about the case being reopened and they showed a picture of him."

"And you recognized him?"

"Yes. I'll never forget his face. His eyes in particular."

"So you got a good look at him?"

"I did. He grabbed my shoulders when he bumped into me and he stared at me for a couple of seconds."

"Then what?"

"He shoved me against the building and ran. Police cars came screeching around the corner right after that."

"Now this ski mask. You think it was his?"

"He dropped it when we collided. I picked it up."

"And kept it all these years?"

"Yes."

He looked at me thoughtfully. "Why didn't you take it to the police?"

"For one thing," I said, "I didn't know a bank had been robbed."

"It didn't seem strange?" he asked. "A guy runs around the corner, drops a ski mask, and police cars head in the same direction?"

"I just wanted to go home."

"Why did you keep the mask?"

"I couldn't let go of it at the time. I was upset at the whole incident and I just couldn't let go of it."

"I never heard of that happening. You *couldn't* let it go. Why would that be?"

I took a deep breath. "I have an anxiety disorder. I don't know, maybe that's why. I couldn't let it go; my hand wouldn't open. My taxi came and I got in. That's it."

He considered that for a moment. "Did this man have a weapon with him?"

"Not that I saw."

"No gun, no knife, nothing?"

I shook my head. "That's really all I can tell you."

"The ski mask has been sent to a lab," he said. "Hopefully some of his hair, or dried sweat, or saliva will be in it. They'll run any DNA they find through the data base to try and get a match, but as far as we can tell, Stearns has had no prior arrests, so it's a long shot that there'll be a match.

So you see, Ms. Dory, without you, Mr. Stearns most likely won't even be arrested, assuming of course, he's found. And if they do find him, his lawyer will say that the suspect could have worn the ski mask at any point in his life, not necessarily on the day the bank was robbed, rendering any DNA of his inside of it useless to the investigation. Only you can put the mask and the man together in Rochester on that day."

I pictured one of the old wartime posters, with Uncle Sam pointing at me and exclaiming, *I want you (to ID Danny Stearns!)* "I get it."

"Do you remember what he was wearing?"

"I couldn't even tell you what I was wearing that day."

"But you remember his face and his eyes 100%. No doubt at all."

"I wish I didn't, but I do."

"Okay then," he said, and he stood up and looked out my front window. "I'll get back to you if I need anything else. In the meantime, be real careful. You're an eye witness. Nobody knows that yet..."

"Except Danny Stearns," I cut in. "*He* knows. He saw me."

"Okay, well, that's true, and there may come a time when you'll need to be put into protective custody. But not yet." We said goodbye, and he left.

I called Jack and left a message, asking if he would have dinner with me and assuring him I was fine after my interview with Officer Donaldson, even though I was anything but fine.

The interview had brought back all the stomach-knotting, brain-numbing fear I'd felt on that day. And now I was a known witness – perhaps the *only* witness – someone who may need police protection in the near future. I was going to have to talk to Dr. Steele again. I took a happy pill and headed downstairs to meet Sean for lunch.

MARGARET BELLE

CHAPTER 17

I waved at Sean when he walked through the door. I'd arrived early, needing some quiet time between my meeting with Officer Donaldson and this one. He looked worn out.

"Hi," he said, as he slid into his side of the table. "Thanks for agreeing to see me."

"Did you talk with the police yet? Or is that after lunch?" Our waitress brought over water glasses, silverware, and menus. "Thanks, Lyn," I said. She smiled, and said she'd be right back to take our order.

Not needing to check my menu, I waited quietly while Sean perused his. I eyed the manila envelope he'd brought with him; the word PHOTOS was printed on the front.

"I'm meeting with them at three o'clock," he said. "I need to look at their faces when they tell me where they are in the investigation. Or where they aren't. I can't detect bullshit over the phone – excuse my French. But I *can* look someone in the eye and tell if they're full of it or not."

"What's that?" I asked, pointing to the envelope.

"Pictures of Ferdy. I thought it would help if they had some different shots of him. The one they had at the press conference was of him all shined up for a friend's wedding."

"It's almost impossible that no one has laid eyes on him after all this time," I said. "I mean people fake their deaths and get found, and I assume they put a lot of thought into how to stay gone. Ferdy just up and disappeared!"

"Ferdy was taken by someone, or more than one person, who did a lot of planning before they ever went to his house to get him," he said. "The condition of his house that day was a huge clue for me. He's a total neat freak."

I smiled, remembering how he would tidy up things on my desk when he came to the office. "I would try to have things organized when Ferdy came to see me," I said, "but he would always fidget – it was like he couldn't sit still until he had my folders in a perfect pile or my pens arranged according to ink color. I used to tell him he would be impossible to live with."

"Trust me – he *was* impossible to live with. He was the same when he was a kid." We ate our lunch while Sean shared fond memories of his brother.

"I'm sorry I haven't kept in closer touch," I said. "There's something going on with me that's dividing my attention and most days I don't know which way to turn."

"Don't feel badly. There's only so much you can do when it comes to Ferdy."

"Can I see the pictures?"

He pushed the envelope across the table to me. "Be my guest."

I went through the stack, pausing at each one long enough for Sean to explain how old Ferdy was and where the photo was taken. I had to admit he was right. Ferdy did look different in these then he did in the formal shot. "I'm glad you thought to bring them," I said, "they should be very helpful." I stopped at a shot of Ferdy playing basketball with Sean. They both looked a lot younger, a nice memory of brothers having a great time shooting hoops.

"That one was taken at the old house," he said. "We'd have a game of pickup before Mom's Sunday dinners."

"Where was that?"

"Rochester."

"Rochester, New York?"

"Yeah," he said. "We grew up there. Eventually I moved to Pennsylvania for a job and Ferdy moved here to open his company."

"How long ago did Ferdy move to Syracuse?"

"Oh, jeez," he said, "has to be eight years now. Maybe a little longer."

"Did he work in the software business in Rochester too?"

Sean shook his head, "No, software was a hobby for him. Ferdy was always a numbers man. Nerdy sort. But he took some courses in software development and loved that too. He got so good at both, he decided to open his financial planning business. He held several patents on software he'd developed for his and other companies."

I nodded. I had marketed two of them for him. "So what did Ferdy do for a job before he opened his company?"

"He was a teller at the National Bank of Rochester, why?"

MARGARET BELLE

CHAPTER 18

As much as I wanted to tell Jack about this epic revelation, I also wanted to be compassionate toward Sean. After all, he was tortured by the fact that his brother was missing; I couldn't just leap up and run out of the restaurant. But as soon as it was possible to get away gracefully, I bolted.

I called Jack and told him that Ferdy had worked as a teller in the bank that Danny Stearns had robbed. "I read on-line that police thought the robbery had been an inside job because so much money was taken," I said, "but then they talked to the employees and ruled out the theory. You don't think that Ferdy..."

"Ferdy what? Was in cahoots with Danny Stearns? Anything's possible, but we need to know exactly when Ferdy worked there. Why didn't you ask Sean?"

"I couldn't do that. He's already a basket case over his brother's disappearance. I couldn't lay this on him too. I'm going to the office to do a search."

I could tell Jack was thinking from the silence on his end of the line. Then he said, "I'm going to call Matt and see if he's had someone from the department talk to Mike at the café about a description. If he has, I'll come get you and we'll go take a look. If it hasn't been done, I'll light a fire under him."

"You don't think it could have been *Ferdy* at the café? And that he drugged Tony? No. What would be his motive? He had no connection to Tony other than they were both clients of mine. I don't think they'd even met!"

"That we know of," he said. "But before today, we didn't know that Ferdy and Stearns were connected by a bank, whether it was an innocent connection or not. I want to follow up on it."

"But *why*? It makes no sense!"

"Because," he said, "a lead is a lead."

* * *

Back at the office, I unlocked the door, closed it behind me, and re-set the alarm; the new normal that would remind me of poor Miller every time I repeated those steps.

I booted up my computer and went to the page I'd bookmarked. I scrolled through the grainy black and white photos of bank employees; some had only a few people in them, others whole groups. I saw nothing in the first few, but then there was one of a dozen or so employees standing in the bank's newly remodeled lobby. I searched the faces, one by one, staring at each much too long. But it paid off. Face #10 was Ferdy's. No doubt about it. The date on the newspaper was November, 2000. Thirteen years ago. I printed out the page and called Jack.

"I found a photo of Ferdy as a bank employee 13 years ago. Jack – he was most likely still there at the time of the robbery, three years later."

"Print it out..."

"I did," I interrupted.

"Let me finish what I was saying," he said calmly. "Print it out and put it in a safe place. But also send me a link to the page."

"Okay, I'll do that right now." Harley could have done it faster, but I finally clicked SEND. "There. Did you get it?"

"Yes, but keep the page bookmarked on your end, just in case."

Adrenalin washed through me. *Ferdy*, I thought. Then I snapped back to reality; Ferdy was a nerd of epic proportions. Nerds don't rob banks. It would take them too long to explain the intricacies of their mission to a teller. I dismissed the thought of Fergal Finnegan doing anything unseemly.

I turned off the computer and looked around my office, wondering if there was a future for me here at all. This building had been my salvation for so long – a place to come where I had specific things to accomplish each day, and deadlines to keep me on track. Would it be fair to me if I closed the doors permanently? Would it be fair to my clients if I didn't?

The rent was paid until the end of the year, so I had some time to figure it out, but questions persisted. Could I even find another Harley? Did I have it in me to bring on new clients to replace the income I'd lost from Tony and Ferdy, not to mention Carrie? Did I dare find another Miller, knowing that something could happen to him too? Jack would tell me I was over-thinking, but I didn't know how else to make a decision this significant. Maybe closing was too large a response for the actual problem, like burning down a house because it had ants.

After hours of debating with myself, I decided to go halfway, and close my doors temporarily; the clients I had left would have to fend for themselves for now. I called them all and explained that I was taking some time off; that I would be in contact when I returned. I offered to recommend another small agency in the area and a couple of them took me up on it. I then called each of my media reps and told them I would be out of touch for a while.

Realizing that this place would feel like an empty shell in another couple of days, I decided to start clearing things out. I went to my filing cabinet and started pulling folders, artwork, scripts, and billboard designs; anything I was working on for new campaigns, and copies of old as well as newly-paid invoices for each client. It all went into neat piles on my desk, on Harley's desk – excuse me, on Harley's *former* desk, and on the floor. It took three hours to get the padded envelopes and boxes stuffed and addressed. I hauled them out to Nelly and piled them in the hatch. Finally, I went back into the office, grabbed my purse, locked up, and headed to the post office.

Once that was done (to the tune of $247.00), I headed back to the office for my printer and filled an empty box with ink cartridges, paper, and my Rolodex. I left my letterhead, envelopes, and business cards, for another time. Done for now, I was too tired to clear out the kitchen or go upstairs and pack my clothes and remaining personal items.

Before I left the building, I put in a call to Carrie Ashton's office to tell Harley I had taken her advice to close, at least temporarily.

"Hi Carrie," I started, "this is Audrey. I'd like to speak with Harley, if she's free."

"Oh, hi there, Audrey, Harley's not here."

I looked at the clock. "She left early today? Well, I'll try her cell. If I don't reach her, I'll call back tomorrow."

"No," she said, "that's not what I mean. Harley's not here *anymore*. I assumed you knew. She called yesterday and quit. Just like that. And she's not answering her cell."

Oh, Lord, I thought, did Carl find her? "Did she say why?"

"No explanation whatsoever."

"Did she say where she was going? Another job maybe?"

"Nope. I can tell you she sounded like she was in a hurry, though. I asked her if she wanted me to send her the check she had coming, or if she wanted to pick it up, but she said no, that I should donate it to Vera House. Any idea what that's all about?"

I do, I thought. Vera House was the agency in the city that provided shelter for victims of domestic violence. Carl must have tracked Harley down, and she had fled. I didn't believe I'd ever see or hear from her again. I grabbed a tissue and wiped my eyes, imagining the hopelessness she must be feeling. So alone. And terrified. She would have to find a place safe from Carl, and how far away would that take her? I said goodbye to Carrie and hung up.

I supposed Harley could be here, under the protection of Vera House; after all, she had donated her last paycheck to them. Maybe she'd done that as a clue to me, either to let me know where she'd gone, or that she'd left because Carl was on her trail. Only a handful of people knew the location of the shelter; not even the police knew where it was. So if that's where she'd landed, there was nothing I could do to help her. I tried her cell, thinking maybe she'd pick up for me. Nothing. Not even voice mail. I felt my own world shrink in the wake of Harley's disappearance, and I put my head in my hands and sobbed.

MARGARET BELLE

CHAPTER 19

Jack called. "Hey, can you come down to the police station? We've got a composite of the guy who spoke with Tony at Mike's Diner. Like you to take a look at it."

"I'll be right there." I grabbed my keys and headed toward Nelly, wondering if I would recognize the man. Was it someone I knew, or had at least met? As upset as I still was over the conversation I'd had with Carrie, a sort of nervous excitement bubbled up in my chest at the anticipation of seeing this composite. I pulled onto the street and drove away.

"So?" asked Jack. I was sitting in a chair next to Matt's desk, staring at his computer screen. "Have you ever seen this guy? At the diner? Anywhere else?"

I shook my head in disappointment. The guy in the sketch looked so plain, so unremarkable, that I stared at the rendering, wondering if he could even be real, or if Mike was just not good at giving descriptions. This was a rendition of a million guys rolled into one; dark shaggy hair, mustache, glasses. A run-of-the-mill Joe. Try as I may, I could not see Ferdy in it.

I felt relieved at that, but wondered if it was possible I'd seen this guy at the counter and not remembered; if I worked at it, would the memory of him come to me? Right now, the answer was no. "Sorry," I said.

I went from the police station to the hospital. I wanted to see what Tony remembered about Diner Guy. Why hadn't he mentioned him before? The trauma of the accident, I guess, could have overshadowed many details and I wondered what else Tony might have forgotten.

Rose was at her brother's bedside when I arrived. She waved me in and introduced me to her sister Bella, and brother Nick. "Look how good our boy looks today," she said.

Tony indeed looked more like his old self. The bandages that had covered the top of his head had been removed, and a lot of the facial swelling had gone down. He smiled at me. "They haven't given me a mirror yet," he said. "Do I want one?"

"You look wonderful to me," I said, and I went to the side of the bed opposite Rose. "I can't tell you how happy I am to see you making so much progress."

"We'll leave you two alone," said Rose, as she motioned to the others, "and go get something to eat."

I waited until they were gone to ask, "Tony, do you remember a man at the diner who came to your table the morning of the crash? Someone who shook your hand – maybe said he was a fan? Mike said he sat down at your table."

"Yeah, the police already asked me about him. He came over to me and said he recognized my voice. Said he'd listened to my traffic reports for years and was happy to meet me."

"Did they say why they were interested in him?"

"No," he said, "but they asked if there was anything strange about the way he walked, or moved, you know, like a limp. Or if I remembered something different about the way he spoke; if he had an accent or a lisp or anything like that."

"Did he?"

Tony shook his head.

"They think he put sleeping pills in your coffee," I said. "They're trying to figure out who he is."

"Why didn't they tell *me* that?"

"They probably didn't want to upset you. They don't know you like I do; don't know how strong you are. The police talked to Mike and created a composite," I said. "I saw it but didn't recognize the guy. Did you see it?"

He nodded. "I meet a lot of people," he said, "and usually have a good memory for faces, but nothing about the printout they showed me looked like the guy I saw that morning. In fact, they're sending over a sketch artist – someone from out of town. They're supposed to be more accurate than the cut-and-paste computer programs. They want to compare Mike's memory with mine."

"I'm just glad Mike remembered the guy at all. The police thought I was the one who put something in your coffee."

"You! Why on Earth would anyone think that?"

"I know, right? They were going on the fact that I was the last one to see you that morning. But now they know I wasn't – Diner Guy was. So they need to find out who he is."

Tony looked up at the ceiling. "You remember when that cop asked me if I'd left my table?"

I nodded. "You didn't get up while I was with you. Why?"

"Because I did use the restroom right before I had my last cup of coffee – not just before I left, like I first thought."

"So you came back to the table and then ordered another cup?"

"No, I ordered it before I went to the restroom. I was just getting up when the guy came over and shook my hand. I asked him to join me, told him I'd be right back. He sat down and I left, but I was only gone a few minutes."

"And your coffee was there when you got back?"

He nodded. "Yeah."

"That has to be when he slipped the pills into your cup. Mike said it was busy after I left. No wonder no one saw him do it."

"I didn't even remember the sequence," Tony said, "until just now."

"I can't wait to tell Matt St. John. I'm sure he'll come to take a formal statement."

"Listen, Audrey, I'm getting tired. Do you mind?" he asked.

"Of course not. I'm sorry I stayed so long. Get some rest. I'll be back."

After picking up a decaf at a drive-through, I headed to Harley's house. I had only caught a glimpse of Carl's face through the truck's tinted window, which was as good as never having seen him at all. I wanted to see this guy who had hit Harley and made her so fearful she'd had to disappear. It would be good to be able to recognize him, in case he decided to show up at my apartment or at the office.

I parked down the street, because he knew Nelly. There were a lot of Jeeps exactly like her on the road, but I didn't want him to have even an inkling that I was nearby. I hadn't finished half of my coffee when a man exited the house. It had to be Carl. He walked quickly and gave me the impression that he was prone to jerky movements; about as laid back as a squirrel. Just the sight of him upset me. I looked at his hands; the hands he'd hit Harley with.

Heat built at the back of my neck and my heart rate picked up as I imagined myself revving up Nelly and ramming into him, pinning him against a building, waving at him through the windshield, and then gunning the engine and driving further into him until he squished like a bug. I felt flushed as adrenalin pumped through me, and I realized that in the excitement of the moment, I'd put down my coffee and was clutching the steering wheel with both hands.

As my heart rate slowed, I watched him enter a little grocery store just a few doors down. Harley said that he almost never left the house, except to pick up beer and cigarettes. He wasn't in there very long, and as I expected, he came out carrying a six pack. It was not only nerve-wracking seeing him, but even from this distance, I realized there was something familiar about him. But what was it?

Having had enough of this day, I headed home. I ordered dinner at the bar and hiked my sorry behind up the back stairs to my apartment. I juggled the food, my purse, and the Styrofoam cup that held the cold remains of my coffee, and unlocked the deadbolt, cursing it, yet grateful for it. Everything went on the table.

I ran back downstairs to grab my mail, then back up to lock myself in and wedge kitchen chairs under the doorknobs. I showered and donned a pair of flowered PJs, poured a diet soda, grabbed some silverware, and set my feast in front of the TV. Oh, the grace of tiny living.

As usual, before I dug in, I turned on the tube to see what was on the news. Half an hour of local stuff reported nothing about Tony. He was old news now, I guessed, and until something formal came down from the FAA, or whoever else was involved, he would be off the radar. No pun intended.

A short piece about Ferdy's disappearance reported that the police had no leads, and mentioned again the $100,000.00 dollar reward. This time, instead of the one formal shot of Ferdy, the screen was filled with a compilation of the photos Sean had brought.

Where are you, Ferdy? I thought. *Are you involved in this Danny Stearns thing? Did you know him? Did you tell him when the bank would have that three million in the vault? Was it you? And did Danny come get you? Did he kidnap you or kill you because you could confirm his part in the robbery? What did you do, Ferdy?*

The national news came on and the first story was the capture of Danny Stearns. The FBI had delivered him to Rochester, where he was shown being led into what I assumed was the police station there, his hands bound behind him in cuffs, or zip ties, I couldn't tell. My food forgotten, I stared at the screen. Breathe 1.....2.....3......4...5...6. Breathe 1...2...3...4...5...

Now it would begin, I thought. He was in police custody. They wouldn't have arrested him without reason. They wouldn't jeopardize their case against him with a flimsy arrest. Did they find DNA in that ski mask? Did it match something in that data base they talked about? Now they would come for me. They'd want me to pick him out of a lineup. How long would it be before they brought him to trial? I would have to sit in that witness chair and see him. Up close. He would stare at me with those eyes of his and try to intimidate me. I knew he would.

I ran to my bedroom and shook not one, but two happy pills out of the bottle into my palm. Without hesitation I swallowed them both with the dregs of the cold coffee. I put my dinner in the fridge and climbed into bed, not wanting to prolong this day any longer. I yearned for the solace of unconsciousness – for the escape sleep could afford me. But it wasn't to be.

Danny Stearns haunted my dreams. He was at my door, in my kitchen, getting closer and closer to me as I slept. He waved a ski mask in one hand, a gun in the other. "You want my DNA?" he shouted, his eyes burning with fury. "I'll give you all the DNA you can handle."

I woke drenched in sweat, quaking like an Aspen leaf – my legs hardly held me as I got out of bed and made my way to each of my doors. My shoulders, aching with tension, relaxed a little as I saw that both deadbolts were in place and the kitchen chairs were still wedged beneath the doorknobs. Sobbing, I sank to the floor, hands over my ears, eyes closed, and rocked back and forth to comfort myself.

My cell phone rang. I crawled to the table near my sofa and retrieved it; the readout flashed "unknown caller." Who would be looking for me in the middle of the night? Fearing it was Harley in a panic, or that something had happened to Jack, I pressed the Talk button.

"Hello?" I whispered.

"Did you get a good look at me today?" The voice was deep and raspy. And angry.

"Who is this?" I asked. But I already knew it was Carl.

"Did you? While you were parked down the street from my house? What – are you watching me now? Holding your own little stakeouts?"

"I," I started.

"Let me tell you something, *Audrey* - I don't know where the hell you've stashed Harley, but I'll find out. So why don't you smarten up and just tell me where she is?"

"I didn't stash her anywhere," I said, "I don't know where she went." I couldn't loosen my grasp on the phone. *Lord, help me!*

"I want her back here now!" he shouted.

"I can't help you, Carl."

At last I was able to hang up, expecting him to call right back, but he didn't. He knew where my office was, but did he know where I lived?

It was 4 a.m. and with no way to go back to sleep, I made a pot of coffee, lit a stick of Frankincense, and kept watch on my kitchen chairs, expecting one of them to shift and the door behind it to fly open.

MARGARET BELLE

CHAPTER 20

I opened my eyes just after 7 a.m. Somehow, I'd drifted off on the sofa and was thankful for the sleep, even though it had only been a couple of hours. At eight, I called Jack and told him about Carl's call. "Can you come over?" I asked.

"I have to testify in court this morning," he said, "but I should be out by lunch."

"I'm pretty much of a mess," I said, hearing a tremble in my voice. "I can't believe he called me."

"Keep your doors locked. Meet me at Heid's at noon, okay?" he asked, referring to a popular hotdog stand.

"I'll see you there."

I showered, and did what I could to make myself presentable. I looked tired and drawn in the mirror; my skin so pale that the blush I dusted onto my cheeks looked like blood stains in snow. I re-washed my face; pale was better than looking like a clown.

When my cell phone rang, I saw Tony's face smiling up at me. "Hey! How are you doing?" I asked.

"A lot better. I'm actually getting out of here later today."

"Seriously? You're okay to go home? Is Rose going to stay with you?"

"Rose and everyone else."

"Listen, Tony," I said, "I've spoken with the GMs of your stations and..."

"No need to say another word. There's no way I'll be in shape to fly for a long time. I know they can't wait for me."

"You're quite a guy, Tony."

"I also wanted to give you a heads-up," he said. "I met with the sketch artist and he wants you to take a look at my version of what that guy looked like; compare it to the one Mike did. They do look different. He'll probably call you today."

"Thanks," I said. "You take care. I'll be in touch."

I wanted to run away. The number of police who wanted something from me was only going to grow. Maybe looking at another sketch of Diner Guy wasn't that big of a deal, but how long would it be before the FBI agents who'd captured Danny Stearns and more members of Rochester law enforcement would be knocking on my door?

Not five minutes after I'd hung up from Tony, my cell rang again. This time it was the sketch artist and I agreed to meet him in half an hour; it beat sitting here, hiding behind locked doors. It looked like rain so I grabbed my umbrella and headed outside. As I unlocked Nelly, I wondered what would happen if I just drove away and kept going. How long would it take for them to find me? Harley had disappeared, why couldn't I?

At the police station, the sketch artist, who introduced himself as Officer Fields, offered me coffee, but I declined remembering how Jack had referred to precinct coffee as swill. He showed me the sketch of the man Tony had described, and I saw immediately that his description differed from Mike's. While the man's hair was shaggy, as it had been in Mike's sketch, and the mustache and glasses were similar, the eyes, nose, and mouth were different enough to make me stare at the image. A dark something wiggled in my stomach.

"Do you mind if we change this up a little?" I asked.

"Let's do it," he said, "what did you have in mind?"

"Can you get rid of the glasses?" I asked.

He erased the lines from around the eyes and across the bridge of the nose. "Anything else?"

"How about the mustache. Can you get rid of that?"

He worked for a minute or two and then asked, "How's that?"

"The hair," I said, and I realized my voice had gotten louder. "Get rid of the hair." Heat built inside me and my arms prickled.

"How's that look?"

"Make the lips a tad thinner."

When Officer Fields was done, I found myself looking at a somewhat skewed picture of Ferdy. It wasn't perfect by any means, but it was him. "I know who this is," I said.

Officer Fields stared at me. "Are you sure?"

I nodded. "It's not dead-on, but it's him. It's Ferdy. Fergal Finnegan."

He waved over another officer and asked him to locate Matt, who arrived within ten minutes. "You're saying you can positively identify Mr. Finnegan from this sketch?" he asked.

"The eyes and nose were different enough in Mike's version that it didn't click before, but seeing Tony's version, it was obvious once Officer Fields made the changes."

Matt called a detective over to the desk and introduced me to him. "Miss Dory has just identified the man in this sketch as Fergal Finnegan. Put an APB out on him right now. I don't believe he was kidnapped; he just made it look that way. I think he took off after he drugged Tony Bravada, and I want him found *yesterday*!" The officer turned and left, walking fast, excitement clearly hastening his pace.

"What about his brother, Sean?" I asked. "He held that press conference and offered the reward – he's tortured thinking Ferdy has been kidnapped. Shouldn't he be told?"

"No, no, no," he said. "Sean could warn his brother if he hears from him. If Mr. Finnegan saw the press conference, he'll think we're still looking for him as he appeared in those pictures. If he finds out we suspect he disappeared on purpose, and that he's using a disguise, he'll go deeper underground, change the disguise, and make it that much harder for us to find him. So keep it zipped until I tell you otherwise."

"Jack can know, though, right?"

He nodded. "Of course."

I looked at my watch. "Are we done here then?"

"Yes, we are. Thanks for coming in. Good job."

I headed for Nelly, having just enough time to make my lunch date. Old Liverpool Road took me along the shores of Onondaga Lake, the scene of Tony's crash, and I began to wish Jack had chosen another place to eat. The image in my head of my friend being floated to shore and loaded into an ambulance, his plane in ruins, depressed and saddened me.

Noon wasn't the best time to go to Heid's, the lines would be long – but standing with Jack would take the sting out of it. I thought about the feel of his skin, the color of his eyes, the touch of his hand. Yum. He was already in line when I arrived. "Why don't you tell me what you want," he said. "I'll get the food and you go get a table before they're all taken." I gave him my order and then, because the rain clouds had dissipated, headed toward the picnic tables instead of the inside seating area.

As soon as he put the food on the table I brought up Carl's call. "My phone doesn't have a record feature so I couldn't capture it for you," I said. "But he was mad as all hell and he's sure I know where Harley is, which I don't. If he calls again, can I report him?"

"Depends on if he threatens you, or if he calls often enough for it to be deemed harassment – but with his history of abuse, he may not do that, if only to keep from calling attention to himself. Abusers are basically cowards; they know where the legal lines are drawn and they'll go right up to them, but not over."

Between bites, I described how I'd had the sketch artist make changes to Tony's description of Diner Guy, and how that had turned the picture into something I could positively identify as Ferdy.

"That's great news, Audrey. Now we need to see if we can tie him to Danny Stearns."

"First we have to *find* Ferdy," I said.

"They'll find him, don't worry. And remember, we don't know for sure if he has ties to Stearns. We can only be suspicious because he worked at the bank. Right now they're chasing Ferdy down in connection with Tony. But my gut tells me that he's in the robbery up to his neck, even though he didn't seem to be living a lavish lifestyle."

"He didn't, I mean, you saw his house; it's in a very nice neighborhood, but a mansion it's not. He ran a successful business. He made legitimate money from his patents and had a new one ready to go. If he *was* in on it though, maybe he and Danny split the money after the robbery, and they've each been sitting on their half, waiting a good long time before they dare spend any of it."

"I can't imagine anyone having the patience to sit on that kind of money for a decade," he said, "but then I can't imagine being stupid enough to rob a bank and believe I could get away with it."

"Well, it took a whole ten years to arrest Danny. And he still has to be convicted. I know from TV that he could go through a trial and still go free."

"I think once we get both of them in custody, one of them will sing if, in fact, they were in on it together. And you, Audrey, watch entirely too much TV."

MARGARET BELLE

CHAPTER 21

"Will I see you tonight?" I asked, as we tossed out our paper plates.

"Sure. I'll bring dinner."

"Actually, I have a barbeque meal in the fridge that was supposed to be my dinner last night. There's plenty for two."

"So I'll bring wine."

"Stay over?"

"As long as you don't try and ply me with my own wine and take advantage of me," he smiled.

As soon as I arrived home I checked the mail and found a small bubble envelope amongst the bills and junk mail. I tore open the top of the package and found a single key inside. There was a piece of paper with Warners Post Office Box #281 printed on it. No indication of why the key was sent to me or who it was from. I put it on the kitchen table. The more I looked at it, the more I wanted to try it out. Finally, I put the damn thing in my pocket and drove to the post office, a tiny two-room building which was only a five-minute drive from my apartment.

I started to call Jack, but then decided to keep the key a secret for now. Well-meaning or not, he'd dragged me into the Danny Stearns case when I confided in him, and I had no idea what this key was for, or where it would lead. I pulled into the post office driveway, wondering what I would find.

I entered the tiny room of mail boxes and looked at the rows and rows of them. Most were rented by normal people who simply received their mail here. But what about the others? Like the box for the key I had? How many of these innocuous little boxes held secrets, surreptitious messages, covert instructions, or even facilitated illegal goings-on? With shaking hands, I opened the box and found something so unexpected, it took me a minute to comprehend what I was holding. It was a letter from Harley. I tore it open.

Dear Audrey,

First, please don't tell anyone I've contacted you. Not even your Jack. I really need to speak with you. It's time I explained some things. I will try and Skype with you at noon on May 3rd E.S.T. Hopefully you will have read this letter before that date. I can't tell you where I am, but I can tell you I am NOT in New Orleans, as the postmark on this envelope suggests. Forgive me, but I have to keep my location a secret. H.

I stuffed the letter and the key into my purse and headed for home. Jack would be there shortly and I would have to act like nothing amazing had happened. I had heard from Harley! She was apparently fine, just in hiding.

I wanted to tell her all I'd learned about Ferdy and how Danny Stearns had been arrested, although depending on where she was, she may have already heard about it on the news. I could tell her I was in love with Jack, that I'd moved back to my apartment, and about the call from Carl. I envisioned our Skype as two old friends on a catch-up call, but I knew it would be way more serious than that. I was almost exhausted from the excitement that was pinging around inside of me and the trepidation that was pounding away at my brain at the same time.

When Jack knocked on the door at 6:30, I had the table set and the food warming. "I'm a little later than I thought I'd be," he said. "It smells good in here."

"Did you bring the wine?"

"Right here," he said, as he held up a bottle. "It's okay for you to have wine when you're taking medication?"

"I haven't taken any today," I said, keeping to myself the fact that last night I'd doubled the number of pills I was supposed to take.

"Okay then," he said, and he proceeded to remove the cork from the bottle and fill the glasses I had set out. Over dinner we talked a little more about Ferdy and bet each other a nickel on how long it would take to catch him. "I'm stuffed," he said, as he got up from the table and began clearing. "Your landlord makes a mean barbeque. It's some of the best I've ever had."

"I know. This apartment always smells like great food. It makes me want to eat all the time. Really, it's a miracle I'm not having trouble squeezing through the door."

Jack continued to clean up, scraping and rinsing the dishes. "Just leave it," I said. "I mean it. I'll take care of it later." He smiled at me. "Or tomorrow's good," I added.

"Want to watch a movie?" he asked. "It's still pretty early. We could go for a drive, or a walk if you want."

"I've been waiting to be alone with you all day," I said. "I want to stay right here, if you don't mind." *Don't sound desperate. You'll chase him away.*

"You have a little TV in your room, right?"

I shook my head. "It's still at the office."

"Well, I could tell you a bedtime story. But we'd have to be, you know, in bed."

"I don't know if I should trust you," I laughed. "I think you're just trying to take advantage of me."

"No, seriously," he said, as we walked into the bedroom, "I think you'll like it. It's the story of this Swedish guy, Hans Downerpantz."

I laughed at the ridiculousness of it. "So?" I asked. "How does it go?"

"The real question," he said, "is how would one illustrate the title in a game of charades?"

Who needed a TV? Jack and I spent the entire night in each other's arms. His powerful hands explored, massaged, until I felt like the most desired woman in the world, instead of the craziest woman in Camillus. Exhausted, we faded into a drowsy bliss. "Night Audrey," he murmured, as he cuddled close.

I smiled and cuddled right back. "Night, Hans."

No horrid dreams invaded my sleep. Jack's steady breathing regulated my own, and even though my bed was small for a man of his size, neither of us tossed and turned. We fit together perfectly and sailed through the night, waking wrapped in each other's arms, just as we had started.

"I could get used to this," he said, as he smoothed the hair away from my face. "You're so beautiful in the morning."

Never one to take a compliment graciously, I gave my usual, "Oh, sure."

"I hate to move, but I have to get up," he said. "Mind if I shower here?"

"Not at all, if I can come too."

We soaped each other up and Jack washed my hair. He leaned down so I could do the same for him. His hair was so thick it took a while to rinse out the lather. "I'll use less shampoo next time," I laughed. We dried each other off and I wondered how long couples did this kind of thing; how long before they showered separately and even slept in different bedrooms. I couldn't imagine feeling any differently about Jack than I did right this minute, as I finished toweling off his muscled back. "I don't want you to put your clothes on," I whispered. "I love looking at your body."

"Oh, God, Audrey, you're going to make me late for roll call, aren't you."

He swept me up and carried me back to bed and I closed my eyes as he brushed his lips over my stomach. "Absolutely," I breathed.

MARGARET BELLE

CHAPTER 22

One more day until I spoke to Harley! I could barely contain my excitement. But as the morning wore on, I thought about Jack and wondered if maybe I should let him listen in on the conversation after all. Who knew what Harley was going to say? If she talked about Carl, she might unwittingly give Jack a reason to arrest the creep and give me one less person to worry about.

Carl was nothing more than a thug, and with his history of abuse, he might also be a petty thief, or into selling drugs. Jack could sit on the other side of the computer so Harley wouldn't know he was in the room.

I thought again about how much I'd enjoyed my vision of pinning Carl to the wall of a building with my Jeep, and wondered if I would really do it if I had the chance; I felt giddy at the thought. *Don't mention it to Jack. You don't want him finding out what kind of stuff run through your head.*

I tapped out a text asking Jack if he could meet me at my apartment at 11 a.m. the next day, adding that it was important. Half an hour later he answered that he would come, but he had pulled an extra shift, so he wouldn't see me until then. To keep busy, I wrote out bills, did some errands, and then drove to the office to see what else I could do to get it ready for my hiatus.

By noon, I'd packed up the remaining paperwork and office supplies, cleaned the kitchenette and vacuumed the downstairs. I headed to the second floor and stripped the two cots, packed up the sheets, blankets, towels, and all of the things I'd brought for the time Harley and I had stayed up there.

I folded up the first of the two cots and in doing so, caught a wheel on the edge of the carpet and pulled it loose. Cursing, I pushed the makeshift bed out of the way and stepped on the slightly frayed edge, securing it back down under the molding. Just shoving the cot around made me realize I wouldn't be able to get it down the stairs by myself; I'd have to ask Jack to do it for me. For an encore, I filled three garbage bags for the dumpster, and packed my personal items into Nelly.

I thought again about Carl and wondered what it was about him that had seemed familiar; it was something I'd noticed the day I'd watched him walk back home from the store. I tried to capture the image in my mind; maybe it was the way he walked, the stoop of his shoulders, or the shape of his head. I tried to place him, but no matter how hard I tried, I couldn't come up with where I might have seen him before, like the grocery store, the drug store, or hell, maybe it wasn't that at all. Maybe he resembled someone I knew. Oh well, it would come to me eventually. Right now I was hungry and had a full Nelly to unload.

I headed home feeling like I'd accomplished something, and enjoying the sense of calm I'd found in the busywork. It was a good feeling. I turned on the radio and began to sing along, aware that I was smiling.

I slid onto a barstool at Krabby Kirk's to order lunch. "An iced tea and a bison burger please."

"Sure, Audrey," said Dick, as he wiped down the bar. "But listen, there's something I need to talk to you about."

"Oh, yeah?" I asked, knowing that nothing good ever followed a sentence like that. "What's up?"

"It's your apartment," he started.

"Does the incense bother you?" *It couldn't be that after all these years.*

"Incense – no, it's nothing like that. We're going to turn the upstairs into a billiards room, so we're gonna have to give you notice to find another place. I'm sorry. You're a good tenant. We just need the space for our customers."

Well, that was about the last thing I had expected. "Cancel the tea," I said. "Bring me a beer."

"Oh, hell, Audrey, I'm *really* sorry. It's just business." He put a frosty bottle on the bar.

"How long have I got?" I asked, sounding like I'd just been diagnosed with a terminal illness.

"A couple of weeks after Memorial Day."

"That soon? Really?"

"That's the downside of being on a month-to-month – but it's what we agreed on, remember?"

Of course I remembered. At least I'd get to enjoy one more parade from my window. "This just sucks," I told him.

"I know. I'm really sorry."

I spent the rest of the day unloading Nelly, all the while thinking that I would soon be loading her right back up with everything I owned. Where would I go? Once I'd finished stacking the boxes in my apartment, I gathered up the sheets, towels, and blankets from the office, and threw them all into a giant front-loader at the Laundromat. Then I walked to the corner newspaper box, dropped in four quarters, and removed a copy, thinking I should start looking at what kinds of rentals were available these days. Soon my wonderful little apartment would be full of beery men, shooting pool, passing gas, and telling dirty jokes. I trudged up the stairs, mad, and determined to make my mark on the place.

I pulled a paring knife from one of my two kitchen drawers and walked into my bedroom, where I proceeded to carve my initials into the molding around the door where I didn't think anyone would notice. I *lived here, damn it. It was my home. My tiny space.* It was where I felt most in control.

I would look for another little apartment; a place where I could see every room by taking a few steps in one direction or another. I'd preferred to live in tiny spaces for as long as I could remember, certainly since the age of six. *Hurry up, Audrey! Run!* Those words had echoed in my mind almost every day of my life.

Outside my mother's room, the hospital had seemed as big and as busy as a city. I'd been sitting in a plastic chair in the corner of the room, next to a metal table that rolled on little wheels. I'd pushed the table out and back with my foot, over and over, as my grandmother and my aunt stood beside my mother's bed, blocking her from my view. I didn't mind because the tubes, the blinking lights, and the needle stuck into the back of my mother's hand frightened me. I heard my grandmother say, "How many times did I tell her not to smoke in bed?" and remember how my aunt had hushed her and told her that my mother might be able to hear what they were saying.

At some point, I'd fallen asleep in the chair, and woke to my grandmother yelling my name. "Audrey! Run and get a nurse! Hurry up! Audrey! Run!" Half-awake, I'd struggled off the chair and stumbled into the long hallway, looking frantically up and down, but I didn't see a nurse. In my picture book at home, they'd all worn little white hats, but none of the women I saw that day had one on.

I'd stood there in the hallway and wet my pants, as the light over the door to my mother's room blinked on and off. Fearing repercussions for not "holding it" at my big girl age of six, I'd taken off the soggy pink panties and kicked them as far away from me as I could. I'd heard my grandmother and my aunt cry out and several people ran into the room as I stood outside the door, terrified of what it all might mean.

My grandmother had finally come looking for me. She said my mother had died, and I could tell she thought it was my fault, because I hadn't been able to find the one person – a nurse – who could have saved her. Through the door I saw a woman cover my mother's face with a sheet. My grandmother took me by the hand and we'd left the hospital, and with me went the knowledge that I, at the age of six, had killed my mother.

I wiped my eyes with the back of my hand, then took a deep breath and sent Jack a text, telling him that I'd just been booted from my apartment. I was starting to lose track of the problems that had piled up in my life and I couldn't imagine how annoying it must be for him to listen to me go on about them; and now I was adding a new one to the heap. When would he say it was enough – as in, *enough already!* When would he dump me like the others had and leave me to fend for myself?

I grabbed a bag of M&Ms, headed to the couch with my newspaper, and turned to the rental section. The available apartments were double what I'd been paying and seemed too big. The ones I could afford, and were in decent neighborhoods, were in two-family homes, where I would have to put up with people living above or below me; that wasn't going to work. I needed a place where no one would complain about my burning Frankincense, and where I wouldn't be bothered by other people banging around, noisy kids, or late-night domestic fights. I didn't think that made me picky. So my place smelled like barbeque most of the time. So what? That never bothered me. And what little noise that came from downstairs had never been anything more than the pleasant sounds of people enjoying themselves.

I reminded myself that I had the lease on my office building until the end of the year, so if worse came to worse, I could lug everything back there until I found something. It would be my last choice, but it was better than being homeless, and cheaper than any of the places listed in the paper. After all, I was officially out of work and my savings weren't going to last forever.

I decided that the sooner I went to bed, the sooner tomorrow would come. I showered and jammied up, brushed my teeth, and picked up my bottle of sleeping pills. Nope. No more pills. I didn't need them now that I had Jack. Not the happy pills either. I would call Dr. Steele and tell her I was stopping both of them, right after I spoke to Harley.

CHAPTER 23

Jack was at my apartment door precisely at 11 o'clock, and I knew it was him by his knock.

"Hi," I smiled, as he walked in. "I'm glad you're here."

He gave me a quick kiss as he took off his hat and put it on the table. "So what's this all about? Your lease here is up?"

"I've been on a month-to-month all these years. They need the space for a friggin' billiards room."

He pointed to my laptop on the kitchen table. "Looking for apartments?"

"Sit down, Jack." I poured him a cup of coffee. "At noon, Harley is going to contact me. I'm going to Skype with her."

"No kidding," he said. "What's she want?"

"I don't know. She sent me a key to a post office box. There was a note inside saying she'd contact me at noon today. She also believes I'll be alone, but I thought it would be better if you were here."

"Why?"

"I'm pretty sure she took off to hide from Carl," I said. "I thought that if she talked about him, she might say something you could use to arrest him. I need him off the street; I don't feel safe after he tried to intimidate me on the road and with that phone call. I mean, what's next?"

"Okay, but you'll have to record the conversation in case you need proof of something she tells you."

I rummaged through my dresser until I found a voice-activated cassette player. It had a tape in it, but a quick check told me that there was nothing on it I needed. I erased it and set the recorder near the laptop, where Harley would not be able to see it.

"You sit behind the monitor," I said to Jack, feeling guilty that I was betraying Harley by letting him listen. "Do you mind that I want you to stay?"

"No, it's okay," he smiled. "But I need to eat. I'm going downstairs to grab some food. I'll bring lunch for us up here."

"Well, keep an eye on the time. You can't be coming in while I'm on with her."

"Don't worry – I'll be right back."

The clock seemed to tick louder and louder. Would she call before Jack got back? Seconds seemed to stretch into minutes until I knew – just knew – that she would call early and hang up when she heard the door open and close. *Come on, Jack!* I turned on the laptop and clicked on the Skype icon. I was ready. Where the hell was Jack?

I found a sheet of paper and scribbled on it – DO NOT COME IN – YOU'RE TOO LATE AND HARLEY WILL HEAR YOU. *Nice work, Jack.* I found a piece of tape and was headed to the door when he walked in. Feeling foolish, I wadded it up and threw it in the trash. I thought about what Dr. Steele had said about overreacting, and tried to calm myself.

We ate quickly, and by five 'til noon were seated at the table, with Jack behind the monitor. Precisely at twelve, there was an alert on my laptop that someone was trying to contact me. I clicked on the YES button and suddenly, I was looking at Harley.

"Hi Audrey," she said with a big smile, and the tape began rotating in concert with her voice.

"Harley!" I said, "How are you? *Where* are you?"

"I'm fine, but I don't want to say where I am. You understand, don't you?"

"I guess so," I said, "but did Carl find you? Is that why you left so suddenly?"

"I'm sorry I took off without telling you," she said, "I really am. But I don't want to talk about that either."

"Then what *do* you want to talk about? Why did you send me the message?"

"I sent it so you'd know exactly when I was going to contact you, so you could make sure you were alone. You're alone, right?"

Oh, God. "Of course."

"Is Carl still living in the same house?"

"As far as I know. He called me the other night and demanded to know where you were. I told him I didn't know, but I doubt he believed me."

"I'm sorry he did that." After a pause, she asked, "Are you still staying at the office?"

"No, I moved back into my apartment."

"How's the agency doing?"

"I took your advice and closed."

"It's probably for the best," she said. "What are you doing about money? Did you take another job?"

"I'm living off my savings at the moment. I've just been given notice that I have to be out of my apartment soon, so things here are unsettled."

"I saw that Danny Stearns was arrested," she said. "You must be happy about that."

"Except that now I'll have to testify against him. Harley, we also learned that Ferdy may have been in on the robbery. He worked at that bank as a teller."

"I know," she said.

"What do you mean you know? How could you know that?" I felt Jack come awake.

"That's why I wanted to talk to you, Audrey. You've been so great to me, and now that I'm fairly safe, I want to help you."

"How?" I asked, as a chill went through me.

"By telling you what I know about Danny Stearns."

"*Danny Stearns!* What are you *talking* about? What could you possibly know about him?"

"Something I've known for a long time."

"Well, let's have it," I said. My heart thrummed like a tuning fork.

"I can tie Danny to the robbery."

"What? How?" I was flabbergasted, and on my way to irate. I wanted to look at Jack, but didn't dare.

"Because Carl and Danny were friends."

"What!" I felt lightheaded. "You knew how terrified I've been that Danny would look for me – how could you not tell me this before? What do you know?"

"They met in a bar years ago. They were a lot alike – sick of having crap jobs and no money."

"So let me guess – they decided to rob a bank?" This was unbelievable. I wasn't sure I could handle hearing any more.

"One night, Carl brought his cousin to the bar with him – Ferdy."

"Ferdy is Carl's cousin?" I couldn't believe what I was hearing. *So that's why Carl looked familiar.*

"Ferdy was just a kid and had just started a job as a teller. Kind of a nerdy type, but he liked being one of the guys, and eventually Danny and Carl were able to talk him into helping them. I was living with Carl, so I used to hear the three of them talking about it at our place."

"And you never called the police?"

"I was as afraid of Carl then as I am now. And Danny was there too – are you kidding? You couldn't have paid me enough to say anything."

"So what happened?"

"They each had a job to do; Carl's was to drive around a few different cities and find a good place to hide the money, and a house to live in. Ferdy was supposed to find out when a big amount of money was due at the bank and develop some kind of software that would delay the alarm or something. Danny's job was to do the actual robbery.

The plan was for Danny to hand off the money to Carl, who was parked just outside, but the gun accidently fired and hit one of the customers. I guess everything went to hell from there."

"*Carl* drove the getaway car?"

"Yes. But as I said, things got hairy. Whatever Ferdy did to the alarm, didn't work, and it went off. Danny was supposed to get in the car too, but the police showed up. Carl drove off with the money and Danny started running."

"Which was when he bumped into me." Oh, my God. It was surreal hearing the backstory of that day. And it was my dumb luck to have been standing right there in Danny's path. If I'd have met with Dr. Collins the day before, or even stayed in her office ten minutes longer, I wouldn't have been there at all when he ran around that corner, and none of this would be happening.

"They were going to keep the money hidden for a few years before they split it up," she said, "thinking that at some point the investigation would lose steam. They were willing to wait it out."

"How did Carl get three million dollars into the car by himself?"

"They knew that one million, the way banks bundle money, would weigh twenty-two pounds. So the whole thing only came to about sixty-six pounds. Not a problem. Believe me, they planned and researched every aspect. And if Ferdy's alarm thing had worked, there wouldn't have been any hitch in the plan at all."

"What else?"

"That's all I'm prepared to say right now, Audrey. I just felt I owed you this much."

"So where's the money? Does Carl have it?"

"I don't know, either him or Ferdy. But hang onto the key I sent to you. I may be able to contact you again, depending on where I end up. I sent you the envelope from the last place I was, just before I got on a plane. Believe me, Audrey, I don't intend to be found. I'm not stupid enough to testify and get myself killed."

"Wait - what about Ferdy? He was at the bank. Why wasn't he caught?"

"I don't know for sure, but Carl used to ride him about wetting himself that day. He didn't know Danny was going to bring a gun. When he saw it − and then when the customer was shot − well, I guess the wet pants made him look innocent."

"So where is he?"

"I have no idea," she said.

"I think it was Ferdy who put sleeping pills in Tony's coffee that morning. The manager of the café and Tony both did sketches of the guy, and I'm sure it was Ferdy in disguise. I just don't know why he'd do that. Do you?"

"I've said enough. I have to go. Thanks again for being so nice to me. I won't forget you. Bye, Audrey."

"Harley, wait!" I pleaded. But she was gone.

I shut off the laptop and the cassette player and looked at Jack. "I can't believe this. I'm so glad you were here − I never would have thought to record it."

He stood up and rubbed the back of his neck. "Unbelievable."

"I wish she'd known where Carl had put the money. Wouldn't that be something? It sounded like it's probably still where he hid it all those years ago. Do you think it's in that awful house of his?"

"I don't know, but the department will search the place from top to bottom. Come on," he said, "let's get this to the station."

"Should I meet you there?"

"Nope, you get to ride with me this time. You're officially in this up to your pretty little neck."

MARGARET BELLE

CHAPTER 24

"So you recorded this conversation with your former assistant?" asked Matt, after he'd listened to the tape.

"Not more than an hour ago," I answered.

"And she worked with you for how long?"

"Around two years."

"And no problems with her in all that time? Nothing ever came up missing? She never displayed odd behavior?"

"She lied about living with her grandmother, but she never confided in me about Carl's violent behavior until I confronted her in the hospital. I don't know if I'd call that odd; given the circumstances, I'd call it survival."

"And all this time she knew about Carl and Danny Stearns and Mr. Finnegan, and never said a word? Even though she knew you were afraid of Stearns?"

"I'm telling you she was *terrified* of Carl – and throw Danny Stearns into the mix and I can't blame her. She obviously felt badly enough, though, to call and tell me about it today."

"But not bad enough to say where she was or where the money is hidden."

"It didn't sound like she knew about the money." I looked at Jack who winked at me and nodded, as if to tell me I was doing a good job.

"It doesn't smell right to me," Matt said, "there's more to this."

"I agree," said Jack, "it can't be a coincidence that the bank robbery and Tony's plane crash are tied to Ferdy – who's tied to Danny and Carl – who are all tied to Harley – who's tied to you, Audrey. It's all connected. We need to find Ferdy to see what we can get out of him. Of the three men, I'd say he'd cave the quickest."

"Another thing," said Matt. "The pills you gave to Miller Crawford came from a bottle in Harley's desk, and the bottle tested positive for the drug found in his blood. And Tony's. So where did she get them? From Carl? Or Ferdy? Whoever it was had to do some research to find pills that looked so much like aspirin. That alone spells premeditation."

"And," said Jack, "*why* did she have them? Miller getting them had to have been an accident; there was no way Harley could have known that he was going to get a headache."

"Unless," said Matt, "she was supposed to put them in someone else's drink."

"Whose?" I asked.

He shrugged his shoulders. "Maybe yours."

I shook my head. "She would never have done that."

"Think about it," he said, "the woman was holding on to a ton of secrets. It wasn't impossible for something to slip out. She would have needed to be prepared for a scenario like that."

"So she could what, drug me before I got into my vehicle?"

"Three million bucks is a boatload of motive, Audrey. And so is fear."

"You know, if I were Harley," I said, "I'd turn the three guys in, testify against them, and collect the reward money."

"That's exactly what she did with the conversation on this cassette," said Jack, "except she screwed herself out of the reward money by admitting to aiding and abetting, and interfering with an investigation. So, that little lady is in a lot of trouble, and they'll be looking for her too, now."

This was not the outcome I'd been hoping for. I wanted the men caught, but I didn't want to bring any more trouble to Harley; she'd had enough in her life. We'd truly gotten along from the first day we met and I couldn't have asked for a better assistant or friend.

Now I'd betrayed her by having Jack listen to our conversation and made her a wanted woman. I felt awful. If I ever heard from her again, I'd warn her. I'd confess that we hadn't had a private talk at all; that Jack had heard everything. I wanted the opportunity to tell her to stay away – that if the reward money was on her mind, to forget it; that thanks to me, she could never, ever, collect it.

"Well, I'll turn the cassette over to the Rochester D.A.," said Matt, "and it will become part of the prosecution's case."

"Does this mean I won't have to testify?"

"Just the opposite," he said. "It means you'll have to testify about making the recording."

Well, wasn't this day going just super. In trying to do the right thing, I'd screwed myself six ways to Sunday and dragged Harley along with me. I looked at Jack. "If we're done here, can we go? I've had enough for one day."

Once we were back in the car, tears streamed down my face. "I don't know what to do," I said. "Every time I turn around something's going from bad to worse, and now I'm causing even more problems for myself and for Harley."

"Audrey!" he said, "Will you please get over Harley? Write her *off* for Christ's sake. You have to stop thinking of her as a friend. She's not! You have enough to deal with without feeling guilty about her. Now stop it!"

Frustration. It was as bad as hearing weariness in his voice. Jack didn't understand my inability to let go of the things in my life I saw as being positive. Like Harley. My anxiety aggravated him, and I knew he was at the end of his rope.

"I'm sorry, Jack."

"You don't have to be sorry," he said. "I know you have issues, and just because I don't understand them – because I'm not a therapist or a psychologist – doesn't mean I shouldn't be patient with you."

"I'm going to call Dr. Steele and set up an appointment for as soon as she can see me."

"That's probably a good idea," he said. He held me tight and pressed his lips to my forehead. "I've never kissed someone in my patrol car before. Better not start now."

"I'm going to spend the rest of the day looking at apartments," I said. "At least that's productive."

"Oh, I think you've been plenty productive today," he laughed. "See you tomorrow?"

"The earlier the better," I said, and I waved goodbye.

Lisa's car was parked outside the salon, so I decided to pay her a visit; I needed a few minutes in her magic chair. When I walked in, she was winding up the last rod on the head of a woman who had to be two hundred years old. The odor of permanent solution filled the air as Lisa squeezed it over the rods, and I couldn't understand how the lady's ancient lungs could take it. The stuff smelled God-awful.

Lisa set the woman up with a cup of coffee and a magazine and came to sit next to me as I vibrated along with the chair. I told her I was losing my apartment.

"Oh, Audrey, you've been up there for so long! It never crossed my mind that you'd be gone someday."

"Just one more thing for me to worry about," I sighed. "I already have way too much on my mind."

"So I noticed." She went into the coat area and brought out my laundry basket full of the sheets, towels, and blankets I'd taken to the Laundromat. I'd completely forgotten they were there. "This was sitting empty in front of one of the big washers – it has your initials on it. It's your stuff, right?"

I nodded. "I can't believe I did that. Thanks for drying them for me."

"Not a problem, but I'm getting worried about you; should I be? Are you all right? I mean, really all right?"

"No, I'm not. I should go." I picked up my laundry basket, walked next door, and climbed the stairs to my apartment, wondering if I would *ever* be really all right.

Needing something to occupy my mind, I drove to the office, determined to round up everything still left that pertained to my agency, and maybe even take a stab at wrestling one of the cots down the stairs. If I could manage to lug it that far, I could roll it out to Nelly and hoist it into the hatch.

I backed up close to the door, opened Nelly's hatch, and started fishing in my purse for the door key. Not paying attention to my surroundings, as Jack had warned me to do, I failed to hear the approach of the person who stuck the business end of a gun in my back.

"Open it," a man said, and I knew from his phone call, that it was Carl. I froze with the key in my hand, unable to insert it into the lock. "Give me the damn thing," he ordered, and I placed the key in his outstretched hand.

"Carl," I started. "I told you, I don't know where Harley is." He pushed me inside and kicked the door closed behind him while his grip on my arm tightened. "She's not here. I swear!"

Keeping me with him, he searched every room and closet on the first floor before he waved the gun toward the stairs, "Let's go."

"Are you serious?" I cried.

"Shut up and go!" he ordered, as he pushed me forward, poking the gun in my back for emphasis.

Suddenly I remembered Miller saying that the alarm would be triggered by breaking glass; surely it wouldn't matter if it was broken from the inside or outside. I moved toward the stairs and the window where my nameplate rested on the sill. As we got to the window, I pointed to the crystal piece. "Harley gave this to me."

"Keep moving," he ordered.

Adrenalin coursed through my body, providing speed and strength that surprised even me, as I grabbed the heavy piece and rammed it into the window. The glass shattered and the alarm sounded. *Thank you, Miller!*

Startled by the noise, Carl lost his focus and I was able to push him off balance; he tumbled backwards onto the floor. "Son of a bitch!" he shouted. He landed hard and the gun skittered away. He'd only fallen from the fifth step, but that left enough space between us to let me run the rest of the way up and lock myself in the small bathroom.

I didn't think he'd follow me with the alarm blaring, knowing that the police would arrive at any moment, but I stayed where I was, having seen enough TV to know that sometimes a bad guy waits to draw the innocent person out. I sat tight until the sirens became so loud it sounded like the patrol cars were going to drive through the wall of the building.

I cautiously made my way to the first floor with my hands in the air, just in case. Two uniformed officers were in the parking lot, handcuffing an irate Carl, while two more, with weapons drawn, moved toward the stairs. I recognized Matt, and better yet, he recognized me.

Matt asked, "Was he alone?"

I nodded, and answered, "Yes," at which point, he and the officer next to him holstered their weapons.

"You hurt?"

"No, just rattled." But as I said that, I felt what I can only describe as an electrical short in my head. *What the heck was that?* It almost had a sound to it – *ffft!*

I explained what had happened and answered Matt's questions as he wrote in his notebook. Within ten minutes, Jack arrived. "Was that

Carl they put into a squad car?" I nodded. "Are you okay?" I nodded again. "Thank God you weren't hurt. Why he was here?"

"I guess he thought he could force me to tell him where Harley went," I said, and I explained how I'd broken the glass with the gift she had given me. "Without that, I don't know how I would have signaled for help."

"Why were you even here?" he asked.

"Among other things," I said, "I came to move one of the stupid cots."

"Lord, Audrey, you know I'd do that for you!" I could tell he was trying to control his frustration with me, but he soon realized how upset I was and backed off. "Do you have your medication with you? You're shaking."

"I stopped taking it," I said, as another *ffft!* buzzed through my head. It didn't hurt, but it felt like someone had poked the end of a live wire into my brain. There. And then not there. What was happening to me?

"Why?"

"What?" I asked, having lost his voice for a second.

"I asked why? Why did you stop taking your medication?"

"I didn't like the way it made me feel." I looked down, not wanting to see concern, or worse, judgment, in his eyes. "I don't need it when I have you."

"You'd better mention that to Dr. Steele when you see her."

"I will." I'd fully intended to tell Dr. Steele, and hoped she would understand. Even if she didn't, it was my life. She was my therapist, but she didn't own me. I was able to take her advice or ignore it. I wanted so badly to be able to declare myself to be my own woman; a fully capable, anxiety-free, human being. I was still holding on – my GAD had not fully returned, as far as I could tell, but then I hadn't known it had a hold on me when I was in college either; not until I'd been told I was fully in its grasp.

Jack said, "I'll call you tomorrow. I'm working overtime tonight."

I nodded. "I'll be fine. I'm going to call a glass service and wait for them to come fix the window, and then I'll head home. You be careful, okay?"

"I always am." He winked at me and left, along with the other officers.

I called the glass company's emergency number, made a mental note to have the land line in here disconnected, then sat at my desk to wait. Half an hour later the van from the glass company pulled into the driveway and within twenty minutes the window had been replaced. I thanked the installer, and asked if we could walk out together; I set the alarm, turned out the lights, and we left. My shoulders were stiff and my head was pounding. Maybe a hot shower would help clear out the cobwebs.

* * *

Clean and jammied up, I made a call to Dr. Steele's office, which netted me an appointment for the following Wednesday. Suddenly, another zap to my head – *ffft!* like a lighting strike – and I knew I had lost a split second of consciousness. Did I have a brain tumor now? Is that how I would wind up this crazy-ass life of mine? As if the universe wanted to answer, a vision materialized.

I saw myself in a hospital bed, a doctor standing nearby, telling me the tumor was inoperable and that the end of my life was near. Would I have enough time to come back to my apartment? Or would I have to remain in the hospital until the end? If I came home to die in my beloved apartment, would I live long enough that I would still have to find a new place and move? Or would my landlord take pity on me and let me stay, even if my lease expired before I did? Another zap. I went to bed, but did not sleep. How could I?

CHAPTER 25

Wednesday came, and I was in Dr. Steele's office, wondering when to tell her I thought I had a brain tumor; I had already fessed up about ditching my meds. She leaned forward in her chair. "Audrey, you can't stop taking your medication just like that. You need to be weaned off of it. When did you last take your antidepressant?"

"A few days ago."

She shook her head in dismay. "We can start reducing the amount if you're determined to get off them, but cold turkey is not the way to go. There can be severe side effects to that."

"Is loose bowels one of them?" I asked, thinking of those dreadful pharmaceutical commercials. "Or boils?"

"Sorry?"

"Never mind," I said. "So, what could happen?" As I asked the question, another zap pierced my brain. I must have winced, because Dr. Steele asked what was wrong. "Are you all right?"

"I don't know. I just had what felt like a lightning strike inside my head. I think I have a brain tumor."

"No, you don't have a tumor," she said softly. "That zap was a withdrawal symptom. That's what happens when you just stop taking your antidepressant instead of getting off gradually."

"It's happened before," I said, waiting for it to happen again.

"And it will happen again. And it will get worse. Other symptoms will accompany the zaps."

I leaned back in my chair and cried. "I feel so helpless. Carl's arrest should have bolstered me. Danny is off the street. Only Ferdy is on the run, and I doubt he'll want to come anywhere near me. But none of that makes me feel any less vulnerable."

"There's still a lot up in the air," she said. "Nothing has been resolved. Well, you must see that this is not the time to stop your medication. When all of this is over, *that's* the time to begin weaning you off. Not now, for heaven's sake. Please listen to me."

I rubbed my eyes and leaned my head back. "I can't think any more."

"Which is why I think it might be a good time for you to consider letting me admit you to the hospital for a week or two, to get you away from the stress."

"You mean a psych ward?"

"I'm talking about a therapeutic, in-patient environment."

"So, a psych ward."

"I have a lovely place in mind," she continued, "a peaceful facility near here where you can get your mental balance back. I'm worried that your GAD will get out of control and lead you into more serious problems, if it hasn't already."

"Are you kidding? *No way!* Jack would never stay with me. What do you think *that* would do to my so-called mental balance?"

"I don't need your permission, Audrey, if I think you're on a dangerous path."

My temper skyrocketed, maybe out of fear and maybe out of disbelief; she'd said it so quickly it was obvious she'd been thinking of that as her Plan B before today. "Go to hell!" I said, and I grabbed my purse and left, slamming the door behind me.

I drove erratically all the way home and was shocked that I hadn't been pulled over. *What nerve she has*, I thought. *How arrogant to say that she could decide for me!* I would not be admitted to any psych ward. That was the end of Dr. Steele.

A vision of me choking the daylights out of her flashed in my head. I saw myself squeezing that scrawny bird-neck of hers, as her face reddened and contorted. I could feel my thumbs pressing harder and harder on the soft flesh of her throat, until her trachea collapsed and her tongue lolled out of her mouth, like a dead dog I'd seen once on TV.

Shaking and sweating, I pulled into the parking area behind my apartment, managed to gather up my mail, and climbed the stairs. I tried to put the key into the lock but my hands wouldn't be still; I could almost feel Carl's gun in my back. I dropped the key and it fell through a crack in the decking, down to the gravel below. I wanted to scream, but diners were seated on both levels. Clenching my teeth, choking on my fury, I went back down the stairs, dropping and recovering two pieces of mail along the way. I finally retrieved my key and went back up; this time I was able to let myself in.

I threw everything on the couch, wanting nothing more than to tear off the clothes that were strangling me. Piece by piece, I ripped them off and flung them aside, like a pissed-off exotic dancer, then ran through the kitchenette, into the bathroom, and into the shower, all the while hearing Dr. Steele's voice in my head, threatening to put me away. As I turned on the water, I was overcome with a feeling of abject helplessness, wretched enough to weaken my knees. I sank to the floor, hugging myself and sobbing; I rocked back and forth until the water turned cold and forced me out.

Naked and wet, I paced my small apartment, wringing my hands, until I spotted the mail I'd dumped on the sofa. A bubble envelope, like the one Harley had sent to me before, lay partially covered by junk mail and bills; I picked it up and tore it open. The note inside read: *May 13, same time. Like before, just you and me. H.*

Harley wanted to Skype again. In two days. Already on overload, I stared at this new communication from her. What would she reveal this time? What new piece of the puzzle would she provide? I paced back and forth, faster and faster, tugging at my hair, so unfocused, that when someone knocked on the door, I just opened it.

"Whoa!" said Jack. "What are you doing? Back up so I can close the door."

"What?"

"You opened the door in the buff, that's what!"

I looked down at myself, horrified to see I was naked. "Oh, my God!" I grabbed the afghan from the sofa and wrapped it around myself.

"What's going on?" Concern wrinkled his brow. "What if it hadn't been me?"

"I, I don't know," I stammered. "I had a very upsetting session with Dr. Steele – she wants to admit me to a psycho ward!" *You weren't going to tell him that!* I screamed inside my head. *He'll leave you now!*

"She said that?"

"She claims it's to get me away from this God-awful stress so I can gain back my mental balance, but I know what she means," I said, unable to shut myself up. "She thinks I need to be put away. She said she doesn't need my permission to do it!"

"Okay, calm down. You know I'm on your side, right?"

I nodded. "But you have no say in it. If she wants to go to court and get me put away, she can. With or without you."

"Listen, go put something on and then come back and we'll talk."

I let the afghan fall to the ground. "Make love to me, Jack. Prove you love me."

He took me in his arms and held me. I hadn't realized how cold I was until the warmth of him seeped into my skin. He kissed the top of my head, and then whispered, "Not like this. Now go get dressed."

When I returned, he was holding the note from Harley. "Another one? When did this come?"

"Today. Just now."

"I'm on security detail that day," he said. "She never gives you much notice, does she."

I shook my head. "I'll record the whole thing and play it for you. Listen, Jack – I'm so sorry about –"

"About what?" he smiled. "Answering the door in your birthday suit?"

"I'm so embarrassed," I said. "I was in such a state."

"I'm not complaining; I could look at you naked all day long. I just need you to ask who's at the door before you open it – you know," he chided, "to be sure it's me and not the luckiest-ever Jehovah's Witness, or some impressionable little Girl Scout selling cookies."

"It's just that Dr. Steele," I started.

"Obviously I don't know her, never met her, but I'm sure she has your best interest at heart. She probably didn't mean she was going to send the men in white coats after you, she probably meant she wants you to get away for a while."

"So you're taking her side now?"

"Of course not – and you need to stop and think before you say something like that to me."

"You'd better leave, Jack."

"Audrey!"

"I mean it. I want you to go."

He opened the door, but stopped and looked back at me. "You'd better consider going back on your medication. I can only do so much for you, Audrey, and I sure as hell can't do that." He left, slamming the door as he did.

No, no, no, no, no! Now I was turning Jack against me and there would be no one left – no one but Harley.

* * *

157

For the next day and a half, I bided my time looking for an apartment, and finally found a complex of efficiencies under construction not too far away. Units would not be ready for a couple of months, and the deposit required to reserve one, was thankfully an amount I could afford.

When Monday arrived, and I was mentally preparing myself to talk to Harley, I realized I'd forgotten that yesterday was Mother's Day. I dug through my kitchen drawer for a marker and then proceeded to black out the entire day on my calendar, making sure no white showed through. It was something I did every year. The tradition had almost slipped by me this year with so much else on my mind. That done, it was time to set up my laptop; in an hour Harley's face would appear on my monitor. I'd picked up a new pack of cassettes and loaded one into the recorder, and just to be sure, put in new batteries. Then I placed it on the table, just out of the monitor's range.

My phone rang, and Jack's picture appeared on the screen. I had ignored three other calls from him, so I decided to answer this time. "Hello?"

"Audrey, it's me."

"I know. What do you want?" My heart ached. I missed him so, but I couldn't take a chance that he would not only agree with Dr. Steele, but might work in concert with her to put me in some institution where I'd never get out.

"You may not want to talk to me," he said, "but I wanted to give you a heads-up. Danny Stearns' trial is about to get underway and you'll be called to testify. Someone from the Rochester PD will be getting in touch with you in the next day or two. I didn't want it to come as a shock."

"I appreciate that. Thank you."

"Also," he said, "it was confirmed that Danny Stearns' DNA was inside that ski mask, but you knew it would be. Are you okay?"

"I'm fine, Jack, thanks. But I have to go now." I clicked off and his face disappeared from the screen.

I turned on my laptop and the recorder, wondering how I would be able to mask the anger I still felt toward Harley after our last conversation. I was hoping to get new information from her, and I knew that being pissy was not going to help my cause. I did some slow breathing and waited for the Skype tone to tell me she was calling. Within a few minutes, she was there.

MARGARET BELLE

CHAPTER 26

She had changed her appearance. Her long, smooth, dark hair was now shorter than mine, and choppy. And red. I thought of Lisa and wondered who had done the job on Harley.

"Hi Aud," she waved.

I waved back, "Wow, do you look different!"

"Like it?" she giggled.

"I was surprised to get your note," I said. "After the last time, I didn't know if you'd ever get back in touch or not. I'm glad you did, because I wanted you to know that Carl came to the office. He had a gun." Out of the corner of my eye, I could see the wheels in the recorder turn.

"Oh, no! What did he want?"

"I guess he wanted to see if he could scare me into telling him where you were. I told him over and over that I didn't know, but then he tried to make me go upstairs with him and it scared the crap out of me. I was terrified!"

"Oh, God, Audrey, he didn't hurt you did he?"

"No, in fact, I grabbed the crystal nameplate you gave me and put it through that little window on the staircase. That sucker is heavy; it smashed the glass all to hell and set off the alarm."

"So he ran?"

"He tried, but the police arrested him. He's in jail, just like Danny Stearns."

She paused for a moment, then asked, "Do you remember when I was in the hospital and you told me that I was going to come stay with you in the office and you wouldn't take no for an answer? Remember how in charge you were?"

"Yes. And I think that was the last time I felt that way."

"Well, now I'm going to return the favor. I'm going to send you a one-way ticket. I'll send it to the post office box. Do you still have the key?"

"Of course, but..."

"No buts about it – I'll overnight it to you. You can stay with me."

"Where are you?"

"Let it be a surprise. But pack light. We aren't going anywhere cold."

"I don't know how I'd pull that off – what I'd do with all my things."

"Audrey, what did you tell me? You said, leave it and get new stuff! It's a new life! Start over!"

I didn't know what to do. As angry as I was with her, she *had* separated herself from the three men, and she did seem to genuinely want to help me escape this life that was so overwhelming. I stopped for a moment to think of what I'd be leaving behind if I took Harley up on her offer. Sadly, the answer was not much. Nothing I couldn't replace. My landlords could sell off the contents of my apartment and ditto for the guy I rented the office from. And Jack? Well, in the long run, Jack would be better off without me, just like Eddie.

"You don't want to testify, do you?" she asked, "and you don't want to end up in that booby hatch, right?"

"Right."

"So *come on* - I can tell by your face that you're thinking about it. I'll overnight the ticket. It'll be there tomorrow."

"I'll do it," I said, with hope bubbling up in my chest. "It's the perfect way out for me."

We said goodbye and I closed up the laptop, wondering if I should take it with me. I'd heard a hard drive contained everything, even deleted material, and I thought Jack could probably find my conversation with Harley on it. I didn't know what a hard drive looked like, let alone know what to do with one. I had an idea and slid the machine into its case.

I carried the laptop next door to the salon and set it on Lisa's desk. "Hey Girl," I said. Lisa was in the middle of giving a man a Telly Savalas – in other words, shaving his head. While Telly's head was beautifully shaped, smooth, and the same color as his face, this man's skull was small, pink, and wrinkled. Not a good look – but you could tell he thought he was hot.

After he left, Lisa pointed to the laptop. "What's this?"

"I want you to have it!" Excitement at escaping my life had overtaken me to the point where I was giddy. I could feel my face stretch into an absurd smile, but seeing the confusion on Lisa's face brought me back with a thud. "I'm leaving, and I can't take much with me."

"You're moving already? Why can't you take your stuff?" I started to cry and Lisa went to the door and locked it. "Audrey! You're up, you're down, what's the matter?"

"I can only tell you if you promise not to breathe a word. Not even to Jack."

"Of course, you know I wouldn't."

"I'm going to meet Harley. I have to leave. Danny Stearns' trial is coming up and I cannot – I mean I *cannot* – testify. My therapist wants to commit me. Jack and I are on the outs, and I've just had it. I can't take any more."

"Harley? I thought she flew the coop? You know where she is?"

"No."

"Oh, Audrey, you are not making any sense! How can you go with Harley if you don't know where she is?"

I explained how Harley was sending me a plane ticket. "I won't know where I'm going until I see it."

"Well, did she tell you to bring a passport?"

"No, and I don't have one."

"Then she's still in the country somewhere."

"I can get into Canada and Mexico with my driver's license – she could be in one of those places, I guess."

"This does not sound like the greatest idea," she said. "Are you sure this isn't just a gigantic knee-jerk reaction? I mean, what about Jack? You're ready to just leave this guy you're so crazy about?"

"Don't try to talk me out of it, *please!* I've made up my mind. You've got my spare key. Go through the apartment after I'm gone and help yourself to whatever you want. I'm taking only a few things with me." I pulled a key out of my pocket and pressed it into her hand. "This is my spare to Nelly. And here," I said, as I pulled paperwork out of another pocket, "is the title and registration. I signed it all over to you. Take good care of her, okay?"

Lisa started to cry. "I can't take your Jeep, Audrey."

"You have to. Otherwise she'll get sold, and I want to know she's in good hands."

"Are you ever coming back?"

"I don't know," I sobbed. "But remember, not a word of this." We hugged for a long time and then said goodbye.

I went back to my apartment and popped two happy pills, then pulled the tape of my conversation with Harley out of the cassette and cut it into little pieces.

CHAPTER 27

Jack called, and not wanting him to remember me angry, I invited him over. By the time he arrived, I was in a better frame of mind, and fixed him dinner from food I had in the fridge; less to throw out before I went to meet Harley.

After we ate we sat on the sofa, my head on his shoulder. "So what did Harley have to say?" he asked.

"No big revelations this time."

"Huh," he said. "So, where are you going?"

Startled, I sat up and looked at him, "What?"

"You found a new place, right? A new apartment?"

"Oh, yes," I breathed, and settled back.

"I'll help you pack up when it's time." I didn't respond. "At least we'll get to watch one parade from your window together," he said. "You made it sound like fun."

"It is."

"You're quiet tonight – one or two-word answers and no enthusiasm. You feel okay?"

"I'm fine Jack. Can you stay tonight?"

"That's more like it," he said. "I was hoping you'd ask." I turned to him and stared at his wonderful face, taking in every laugh line and worry wrinkle. His Irish eyes and ruddy skin – he was everything I'd ever wanted. And I was going to walk out on him in a matter of days. I wrapped my arms around his neck and kissed him – a lingering kiss that I could remember.

Taking the kiss as a signal, he stood up and unbuttoned his shirt, untucked the ends, and pulled it off. He tossed it on the sofa beside me. "Now you," he whispered.

I was amazed, as I always was, at the well-defined muscles in his arms and shoulders, and the spectacle of them brought me to my feet. I pulled my T-shirt over my head and dropped it next to his. He unbuttoned his jeans, pushed them to the floor, and stepped out of them. I did the same. With one swoop, he picked me up and carried me to the bedroom, where we scrambled out of our underwear and fell onto the bed.

He slid his hands and mouth over me, igniting a hunger that I'd not yet experienced. I fought to lay still, resist the urge to give in to my yearning for him, and let him continue to press his lips and fingers into my flesh, but I couldn't wait – I reached for him and brought him down on top of me.

We spent the night moving in concert, rising and falling together, calling to each other, responding to each other. He breathed, I moaned. He whispered my name, I whimpered. At last we rested, tied in a human knot. No one dared to move, for fear of triggering a reaction that would motivate us to go again, when neither of us had an ounce of energy left.

The next morning we woke to find that during the night, one of us had pulled up the covers. "Wow," Jack said.

"I know," I smiled.

"I had no idea you had that much passion in you, Audrey. I mean every time's been incredible, but last night...wow. I hate to get up, but I have to go to work."

"How about a shower?" I said.

"I'm sure I need one," he laughed. "I just hope my legs are strong enough to walk into the bathroom. You really took it out of me, young lady."

"I was planning on joining you."

"Ah, well be gentle. If I had to run after a thief right now, I'd have to shoot him to catch him."

* * *

After Jack left, I broke down. I didn't know when I was leaving to join Harley, but I assumed it would be in the next day or two and I might have just seen the last of him. I dried my eyes and took a deep breath, got dressed, filled a travel mug with decaf, and headed down to Nelly.

On the way to the post office, I patted my pocket to be sure I had the key. Though my heart was full of grief at the thought of leaving Jack, a feeling of excitement built within, as I wondered if the plane ticket had arrived; I wanted to know where I was going.

I fit the key into the lock and opened box #281. An envelope was there. In it was a one-way ticket to LAX, via Philly, for tomorrow. *Tomorrow!* Harley was in Los Angeles. Where would she take me from there? There was also a note, instructing me to use the layover in Philly to go to the airport salon and do something to my hair that would change my appearance. I felt like I was in a movie, or a play – that nothing was real – except now one thing was. I was leaving tomorrow.

Once back in Nelly, I re-read the ticket. The USAIR flight would leave here at 1:25 p.m. and land at 6:38 in Philly, where I would have the 90-minute hairdo layover. From there I would fly again with USAIR, and because of the change in time zones, I would arrive in Los Angeles at 7 p.m. I wondered how long it would take Jack to start looking for me.

167

I made a stop at the bank and cleared out what money I had left. I would take my own advice and buy what I needed when we reached whatever destination Harley had in mind. There was precious little I couldn't leave; not one belonging I could think of. How sad was that? I headed back to my apartment to figure out what I could pack into just a duffle bag, and trying not to think about how much I would miss Jack and Lisa.

CHAPTER 28

Even with pills, I'd tossed and turned all night and finally got up and showered around seven. I sat by my window, knowing I'd never watch another parade through it, and sure that I would never be back in Camillus again. My stomach was upset and the beginnings of a headache had already started. Was I doing the right thing? I didn't know. I dug my bottle of happy pills out of my purse and swallowed one, hoping that, if nothing else, it would keep my stomach and head from getting any worse. At least the brain zaps had stopped.

My duffle, packed and ready to go, waited by the front door. On top, was an envelope I would leave downstairs for my landlord, informing him that I was going out of town and that Lisa would be using my Jeep. I'd tossed all perishables into the dumpster outside, and cleaned the entire apartment.

Jack would expect to see me tonight, but not before. I thought about writing a note and leaving it for him, but what would I say? I certainly couldn't tell him I was going away with Harley, but I didn't want him to think I'd been kidnapped, or like characters on TV, had come down with amnesia and wandered away.

He would be beside himself with worry and would no doubt organize an all-out search for me. Maybe I could think of something to say that would convince him I'd taken off of my own free will. But he'd never believe it; he would think my abductor had forced me to write the note. It was all too much.

At 11:30, with my taxi on the way, I hadn't written a word to Jack, so I gave up and stuck the one I'd written to my landlord in the restaurant mailbox. Then I went back upstairs to take a last look at my apartment. Small as it was, it had been mine. I rounded the corner to where I'd carved my initials into the woodwork and ran my fingers over them. *Enough!* I picked up my duffle and checked to be sure I had the plane ticket, my phone, and my medicine. Mentally ready to go, I straightened my shoulders and opened the front door to find Jack standing there.

"Hi," he said. "What's up?"

"I" – I stammered, "I was just going out."

"Where to?"

"What are you doing here? I wasn't expecting you until tonight."

"Obviously, now where are you going?" He walked toward me and I backed up into the living room.

"Jack – what are you doing?"

"Okay, look," he said. "I know you're on your way to the airport, and you're going to meet up with Harley. Am I correct?"

Lisa! "Lisa promised she wouldn't say anything!" I couldn't believe she had betrayed me.

"She thought about what you were doing and couldn't let you go through with it. She called me this morning."

"She had no right to do that!"

"She was worried about you," he said. "So you were going to leave me? Run off with Harley?"

"I can't stay here!" I said. "I hated the thought of leaving you, but I cannot testify in that trial and I will not let Dr. Steele commit me! I won't! And you can't stop me!" Then I had an awful thought. "Please don't tell me you have a warrant, or a subpoena, or something with you."

"Of course I don't."

"Then I'm leaving, if you will kindly get out of my way."

"I'm sure you have one minute to talk to me before you go."

"So you won't stop me?"

"No, in fact, I want you to go."

I sat on the sofa, thoroughly confused. "What?"

"I want you to go meet Harley, so we can arrest her."

"You want me to set a trap for her?"

"If that's the way you want to put it, yes."

"I can't do that!"

"Think about it, Audrey, Harley is every bit as much a fugitive as Ferdy. She will be found. And if you're with her, you will be charged with interfering with an investigation, aiding and abetting, and who knows what else? You can't put yourself in that position."

I covered my face with my hands. Jack made sense; I'd been about to put myself in the middle of yet another disaster. The booby hatch was looking better and better.

"One way or the other, Harley is going to be brought in," he said. "Now you can be with her when that happens, as her accomplice, or you can work with law enforcement and keep yourself out of trouble."

"I should have realized," I said.

"So you'll do it? You'll work with us?"

I hated myself for agreeing to set a trap for Harley. No matter what, I had this soft spot in my heart for her, and sympathy for the life she'd led. But I agreed. "I'll do it."

He produced a cell phone from his belt. "You'll take this along because Harley will want you to give yours to her. She's not going to take any chances that you might be able to give her location away."

"Just leave it on? How am I supposed to charge it?"

"It'll stay charged for a few days. You'll be back by then. Don't call me unless you feel you have to; just text. It's permanently set to vibrate – no beeps or rings will come out of this thing. Got it? Texts only. Don't *offer* her your phone, but if she asks for it, give it willingly. It'll convince her you're on her side."

"I feel like a spy."

"All you have to do is get on the plane and meet Harley in Los Angeles. Undercover officers will be watching for you at LAX. The moment you meet her, they'll move in and arrest her. They'll hand you a return ticket and you'll fly right back here. I'll be waiting for you at the gate."

I threw my arms around him. "I'm sorry, Jack – I'm so glad I don't have to leave you. I didn't know how I was going to handle that. I think it would have killed me."

"When you get back," he said, "I hope you'll put this on." He took a small velvet box out of his pocket and opened it. Inside was an engagement ring with an exquisite, square-cut, solitaire diamond.

"Oh, my God, Jack! This is the last thing I expected!"

"After the other night, I knew I wanted to spend the rest of my life with you."

"Was that the only reason?"

"No, it's you. Everything about you," he smiled. "But I have to tell you, after that night you could have had my badge and all my credit cards."

"How long have you had this ring?"

"Not long; when Lisa called me, I was in the jewelry store, buying it. Want to try it on?"

"No. If I put it on, I won't want to take it off. It's the most beautiful ring I've ever seen! But Jack, we've only known each other a little while. Don't you think this is too fast? You might regret tying yourself to someone like me."

"Audrey, you are the strongest person I know. For so many years you've managed your anxiety, and the problems you're having now are external. Not internal. Once this crap you've had hurled at you goes away, you'll be totally fine again. I know you will. I *believe* you will. Besides, I've wanted you with me since the first time I saw you."

"Still...,"

"It'll be here when you get back." He closed the box and tucked it back in his pocket. "By the way," he said, as he pulled some papers out of another pocket, "here's the title and registration to your Jeep; Lisa wanted me to give them back to you. Now you'd better get going."

"Will you drive me? I can cancel my cab."

"No, you can't be seen with me at the airport, but an officer will be watching in case Ferdy is in the vicinity keeping an eye on you for Harley."

We kissed goodbye – a wonderful kiss that I wouldn't forget. The last kiss before I wore his ring. The last kiss before I walked Harley into a trap. Probably the last kiss before lost my mind.

MARGARET BELLE

CHAPTER 29

When the cab arrived, I climbed in, pulled my duffle in after me, and headed to Hancock Airport. The plane was on time, and after I went through security I settled in at the gate and waited to board.

Second thoughts plagued me, but Jack's words played over and over in my head, and by the time my flight was called I knew I had no choice but to go through with his plan. I focused on the flights to Philly and Los Angeles and the return flight that would bring me back here, and not so much on what was going to take place in the hours between. It was going to be a long day.

In Philly, I went to the airport salon and had my hair stripped of all its color. Since it was already on the short side, there wasn't a lot the stylist could do with it, but she moussed the curls into spikes and sprayed the hell out of it. I also subjected myself to a makeup session with a young lady who lined my eyes with black and smudged my lids with a shade of charcoal. The combination of hair and eyes left me looking like a punk raccoon, but it did the trick; I didn't even recognize myself.

The plane ride to Los Angeles was long, but I managed to entertain myself with a couple of magazines I'd purchased in the airport gift shop, when I wasn't envisioning all the ways this could go wrong. My feet had barely hit the ground at LAX, when my cell rang. "Change of plans," said Harley.

"What do you mean?" The first thing that could go wrong, just did. I glanced around in search of uniforms, but then remembered Jack had said the officers looking for me would be undercover. Shit.

"I'm not in the airport," she said. "I'm outside. Leave through the USAir door so I can see you. Did you go to the salon in Philly?"

"I did," I said, hoping I sounded normal. Where were the police? Then it hit me – they would be looking for me as I appeared in the photo they'd been given. And I'd forgotten to tell Jack that Harley had instructed me to change my appearance, let alone that she'd changed hers.

"What color?"

"Well, I guess you could say platinum, but they really just had time to strip the color out."

"Wow."

"Yeah, and it's all spiky." Did I sound nervous? Could she hear distraction in my voice as I searched for people who looked like they were searching for me?

"Okay," she said, as I exited the terminal, "I see you. Now take the shuttle to Parking Lot B. I'll meet you there."

"How will I find you?"

"I'll find you," she said.

Sure that she was still watching, I didn't dare text Jack to tell him of Harley's change of plans or of my new look. I followed the signs to the shuttles, where one was loading up. On the ride to Parking Lot B, heat built at the back of my neck and my muscles tensed, as I wondered if someone on the shuttle was watching me for Harley. Paranoia like mine allowed no leeway, and I could easily believe she had hired the driver, the acne-riddled boy in front of me, or the old lady sitting next to me, as easily as not. I'd known I would screw this up and now I had. It looked like I would be leaving the area with Harley. I wanted to cry.

I got off the shuttle and waited until the vehicle rolled away. Five minutes passed with no sign of her and I began to get nervous. Was she watching me? Waiting to see if it looked like I'd brought police with me? I didn't think so. She wouldn't have asked me to come if she didn't trust me.

A black Cadillac Escalade ESV with tinted windows pulled up to the curb; one of the back windows whirred down. A red-haired Harley waved me into the back. "Audrey!" She was fairly wiggling with excitement. "I'm so happy to see you! I'm so glad you came!"

I threw my duffle into the enormous vehicle and chose a seat directly across from her. I would be riding backwards, but that was okay. I wanted to see her eyes when she talked to me. I thought I would be able to tell if she lied, even though so far she'd managed to do just fine in that department.

"Oh my God," she said, "you look so different!"

I put my hands on my head. "I know - can you believe this makeup?" While we talked, a totally different conversation played in my head and I hoped that I wouldn't confuse the two and blurt out the wrong thing. Soon we were on the road. "Where are we going?" I asked.

"For a long ride," she smiled, "so settle in."

"Seriously? You're not going to tell me after I took this incredible leap of faith? I left Jack, my apartment, the one friend I had besides you, screwed up my entire appearance, and flew across the country!"

"You also left the possibility of being committed and the certainty of testifying against Danny. And you said you were *losing* your apartment."

"That's true, but I still want to know where we're going." I was no longer Harley's boss, and not even on an equal footing with her now. Hippie Harley was holding all the cards.

"Okay," she said. "We're going to drive up the coast to the place I've been staying. It's right on the beach, it's secluded, and it's so beautiful, Audrey. You won't even believe the sunsets."

"Good," I said, "I was afraid we might be heading to Mexico and I really wasn't keen on that. But you didn't have to hire such a luxurious car just to pick me up!"

"I didn't want to drive that far."

"So what have you been up to?" I asked.

"Happily living without fear, especially now that Carl has been arrested – honestly, Audrey, that was the best news you could have given me, although I'm sorry it happened the way it did."

"How did you stand him all those years?" I asked. "He's so mean. Whatever made you fall for a guy like that?"

"He wasn't like that until well into our relationship. It was like he was hiding that part of himself until he was sure I wouldn't leave. I guess he saw a vulnerability in me that made him think he could dominate me, and that if he slowly put the fear of God into me, I'd put up with his abuse. And of course, he was right. I'm still afraid of him, even knowing he's behind bars. People escape."

"I doubt he could find you now."

"I don't ever take safety for granted," she said.

All I could think of was Jack. He would have heard by now that no one matching my description had gotten off the plane. He'd be out of his mind with worry. As soon as I could, I'd text him. I was carrying two cell phones and Harley hadn't yet asked for mine, which comforted me. Being able to keep them both would be helpful in case one of them lost its juice.

As if on cue, Harley put out her hand, "I'm gonna need your phone, Aud. Sorry."

"My phone? Really?"

"Yeah, I can't take any chances, you know? Pings and all that?"

I dug it out of my purse and handed it over. "Wow, Harley, this feels serious."

"It is, believe me."

As the night wore on, we talked ourselves out. Harley fell asleep and I quickly got bored not being able to see much of anything out of the heavily tinted windows; I eventually dropped off too. Harley shook me awake around 4 a.m. and announced that we had reached our destination. "You were really out," she said. "You slept right through a fuel stop."

She looked like she wanted to say something else, but didn't know how. "What's wrong?" I asked. "What is it?"

"It's...," she said.

"What? Come on! You're scaring me."

"I don't mean to," she said. "But I'm going to need you to let me explain some things without interrupting me, okay?" The driver got out and shut his door.

"Yes, yes, okay! Out with it!"

Just then the car door opened and the driver reached for my hand to help me out. I slid to the end of the seat and looked up at him. It was Ferdy.

MARGARET BELLE

CHAPTER 30

"Ferdy!" I couldn't take it in! "What the hell are you doing here? You were driving this car?"

He held both hands up defensively, "Don't be upset," he said. "Don't be mad."

Harley said, "That's what I need to talk to you about."

I couldn't catch my breath. "What the hell are you two *doing* together?" I stared at Harley. "You're with *Ferdy*? Oh my God – are you in on all of it Harley? With the three guys?" Behind me, waves pounded the shore, sounding cold and dark – a warning perhaps.

"Yes," she said.

She reached for me, but I pulled away. "Don't touch me." I turned to Ferdy, "And you!" I screamed. "I thought I knew you, and I worried so much when I thought you'd been *kidnapped!*" I spun around again to Harley. "And all the time you knew nothing had happened to him! You saw how devastated I was, and how his brother" - I spun back around to Ferdy. "Do you even know or care how distraught Sean has been? Do you?"

Harley took my arm, and this time I had no strength left to fight her off. "Let's go inside," she said. "We'll tell you all about it." Ferdy picked up my duffle and led the way. I followed them inside, all the while staring at the back of Ferdy's head and the stupid driver's cap he was still wearing. It was like being in a dream – a really bad dream. I looked back at the car, hoping I was still inside sleeping. But, no.

The beach house was full of bamboo, glass, ceiling fans, potted palms, and casual furnishings, done in turquoise and white stripes. And Ferdy. "This just doesn't play right," I said. "Why would you two be living here together?"

Ferdy took off the cap and poured himself a drink. He held the glass up in my direction. "Want one?"

I ignored him, unable to stop the flock of questions that were flying through my brain, most of all the question of how I could have been so stupid. Would I never learn?

Harley pointed to an overstuffed sofa. "Sit," she said, and she folded herself onto the other end of it. "I was unhappy, and afraid of Carl; you know that. Ferdy was around a lot, and eventually a client of yours, and we just became close."

"I'm guessing you didn't become a client because you'd heard how talented I was," I said to him. "And," I said, as it dawned on me, "*you* were the one who recommended Harley to me!"

He nodded. "Audrey, you are talented. But you're right. Carl had me contact you."

I envisioned a wounded animal, separated from the herd, with jackals closing in; a perfect analogy for what had happened to me. And here, in front of me, were two of the jackals.

I looked at Ferdy, "Why would you want to kill Tony? How could you have done that?"

Ferdy said, "I wasn't trying to kill him. He'd made emergency landings before; I thought he'd do it again."

"His career is over!" I shouted. "And you almost did kill him! And when you disappeared the same day we all thought you'd been kidnapped – do you know what hell you've put all of us through?"

"The consequences were devastating for a lot of people," he said. "I regret that."

"Regret? Are you serious?" I stood up and looked at Harley. "I can't stay here with him. I thought I was coming here to be with *you*. Why didn't you tell me?"

"Because you wouldn't have come, obviously," she said.

"You walked out on your job at Carrie's after I helped you to get away from Carl, and when you left without a word, I thought he'd found you. But what – you were just running away with *Ferdy?*"

"Yes," she said, "he had to hide."

I began to cry, and knew that hysteria was only a gasp or two away. "I have to go."

"Go where?" asked Ferdy.

"Anywhere. I have to get away from the two of you."

"You're certainly not in any danger," Harley said, "Please, just get some rest. Come on, I'll show you to your room. You can get some sleep and we'll talk later."

I didn't know what else to do. I didn't even know where the hell I was. I followed her down a long hallway, into a room filled with more bamboo and wicker.

"Audrey, please don't pass judgment until you hear everything, okay? I know this is not what you expected to find when you came here, but I promise, you won't be unhappy if you just wait until I get a chance to explain. I'll send Ferdy out and we'll talk alone, okay?"

I did not respond, but sat down on the bed. One side of the sliding glass doors was open, and a warm breeze stirred the gauzy strips of cloth that made up the drapes. It was a stunning home but Hell on Earth to me; I wanted nothing more to do with it, and wondered how long it would be before I would be rescued.

"I'll see you later," she said. "We all need to sleep. It's only 5 a.m. – sleep till noon if you can. I didn't answer, and she left. I went to lock the door and found that I couldn't. Scrapes and scars from an old, larger door knob were visible on the wood around the new, smaller one they must have put on especially for me.

I went into the bathroom where the door did have a lock, and sent a text to Jack: *I'm in a house somewhere on a beach about eight hours from the airport. Harley had a car waiting at LAX. Ferdy is here!*

Almost immediately a text came back: *What happened? No one saw you get off the plane. Thank God you're okay. Do you feel safe for the time being?*

I texted back: *I'm pissed but I don't feel threatened. Harley had me change my appearance in the Philly airport so the police in LA wouldn't recognize me.*

Take a pic of yourself, he wrote, *and email it to me so I can forward it.*

I held up the camera and snapped the photo; the first two words of his quick response came back: *Holy shit.* Then he continued: *We'll find you. Just hang in. Be nice, understanding, whatever you have to do. Carl confessed, hoping for leniency. Before you moved into your office, he hid the money under the floorboards in one of the bedrooms. There's a team in there now, pulling up the floors trying to find it. The plan was to put your largest clients out of business so you'd lose so much income you'd have to close and they could retrieve the 3 mil. Ferdy – wow! I love you.*

I looked in the mirror, then quickly stripped and got into the shower. I scrubbed my face clean and shampooed until I'd removed all of the product from my hair. As the water pounded down on me, I wondered how I would ever be able to sleep here under the same roof as these people, who had hidden stolen money in my office and tried for years to figure out how to get at it. At least I'd screwed them up by moving in and running my agency for so long.

Actually, I realized, my being there had worked to their advantage; no one would have thought to look inside my office building for the money. But eventually, tired of waiting me out, and wanting to get their mitts on their ill-gotten gains, they'd come up with a way to *force* me out. Poor Tony. Poor Miller. All because they did business with me. I soaped up and rinsed off, but remained under the spray, letting it wash away the tears that kept coming.

Jack and Matt and I had wondered how everything tied together with me in the middle, and now it was all becoming clear. So many details, so many people, so much secrecy. I pictured the officers pulling up the floorboards and wondered what they'd find.

Suddenly, I remembered that when I was folding up the cots, part of the carpet had come loose. A chill went through me. I got out of the shower, wrapped a towel around myself, and sent another text to Jack – *Have them look in the front bedroom. The carpet was loose in the far right corner.*

Could the money already be gone? I put my dirty clothes in my duffle and hung up my towel. Now, feeling more than a chill, I dressed and got into bed, pulled up the covers, and hoped that Jack would get back to me before Harley and Ferdy woke up.

Half an hour later another text came in: *Money gone. Floorboards right where you said showed evidence of being removed and then replaced.*

So, who had it? And when had it been taken? Circumstances suggested that Ferdy had ended up with the money. It was probably where got the funds for that car. And this beach house. Harley had referred to him as the money guy, and certainly, career-wise, that was true. Perhaps he was having the last laugh.

Another text came in: *Take a pic of the outside of the house. They're working on finding it.* How was I supposed to do that without being seen? At last the warm breeze got to me. Comfy on the plush bed, I felt myself slip away.

I dreamed I was outside, on a beach so dark I couldn't see where the sand met the ocean. But waves lapped at my feet, and soon the water had risen to my knees. Jack ran toward me with his hand extended, hoping to keep me on the shore, but a rip tide that turned out to be Danny Stearns, dragged me out deeper and deeper, until the water swirled under my chin. Jack's grasp slipped until he was only holding onto my fingers. I turned to look at Danny, and saw that

Ferdy and Harley had formed a human chain behind him, tugging, pulling all of us further and further into the black water. Lights flashed, as if someone was taking pictures of us for some gruesome photo album, and I shouted to the unseen photographer, "No! Take a picture of the house! That's what I'm supposed to do!"

But the cold, salty water filled my mouth so that only gurgles escaped. I could see the horrified expression on Jack's face as the ocean continued to cover mine.

I sat upright in bed, sweating, my lungs expanding and deflating as fast as my heart was beating. I fell back onto the pillow. Breathe... one... two... three... four... five... six. Eventually my breathing and my pulse returned to normal, but the traumatic dream had left me with a pounding headache. I went to the window and took in the spectacular view. The ocean, unlike in my dream, was a beautiful blue, and waves rolled gently onto the shore.

I ran my fingers through my hair, smoothed my shorts and shirt, and made the bed, then went to listen for voices at the door. Hearing none, I headed toward the sliders, hoping to get at least one shot of the side of the house for Jack.

I jumped at a knock on the bedroom door. "Audrey?" called Harley. "Can I come in?"

"I don't feel well," I said. "I'm going to rest a little longer." I shoved the phone into a pocket and hopped back into the just-made bed. I wasn't ready to face her yet.

"I want to talk to you. You don't have to get out of bed."

"Please, Harley, later."

She opened the door a crack and stuck her head in. "Pretty please?"

Before I could answer, she was in the room and had closed the door behind her. "I won't bother you, I promise," she said. "I'll be quick and then you can rest. I just didn't like the way we left things earlier."

"And I don't like that you put me in a room without a door that locks so you can walk in whenever you want."

"We didn't do that, Audrey. Whoever lived here before must have. Honest. All the bedroom doors are like that. Maybe they were swingers," she smiled. "Anyway, I feel bad about how you're taking this. I know it's not easy."

Anger built quickly inside of me. "Taking what? How you made a fool of me? Or that you got me down here without telling me that Ferdy was with you? No, you're right. Not easy."

She sat on the edge of my bed, and in my mind I had a vision of police creeping up on the place with their guns drawn. How was I going to get rid of her? "I'll tell you what," I said. "Let me sleep now and you'll have my full attention later. Can you please just leave me alone in here?"

"I have the money," she whispered.

"What?" I sat up and stared at her, wondering if she'd actually said what I thought I'd just heard.

She looked at my shirt. "You're already dressed."

"I thought I'd feel better," I said, thinking fast, "if I showered and dressed, but I didn't, so I got back in bed. You have what money – from the robbery?"

Excitement fairly exuded from her. "I overheard a phone call between Carl and Danny, and Carl told him where he'd hidden the money. I just waited them out, same as they were doing to you."

"So you *did* know." Another lie. "And Ferdy?"

She shook her head and gave me a wicked grin. "Nope. He took care of all this," she said, as she waved her arm around at the house in general. "The guy is loaded. He thinks the 3 million is still hidden in the office."

"Where is it?"

"The money? Right here, divided up in three of my suitcases."

"And Ferdy has no idea?"

"He could care less about my luggage; how much I unpack and how much I don't. We're never in the same place long enough for me to unpack everything anyway."

"So that's why you escaped by car. Airport security."

"I could eventually have found a way to move the money, but it would have taken me too long to figure out how. That's not my strong suit. I don't know about off-shore accounts and that stuff. Ferdy does, but he'd want a cut."

The minutes were ticking away in my head. How close were the police now? How soon before they broke into the house? "Where's Ferdy?" I asked.

"Sleeping it off on the lanai — that's what they call a patio down here," she said. "He didn't realize how hard it would be to face you and he drank way too much, way too fast. I tried to tell him you'd be fine once you had some time. Anyway, Aud," she continued, "I want you to come with me. Tomorrow I'll send Ferdy out for something. He'll put on one of his disguises — he does it all the time to buy food and stuff. Then the two of us can take the money and go! We can leave every damn thing here and just go." She took my hand. "I've been *waiting* for you. I'm willing to share the money with you. What do you say?"

"Why would you do that?"

"Because you're the one person in this world I've always been able to trust — even though I was deceiving you in the worst way — I could always depend on you."

If Bizzarro Land was an actual place, I'd swear that I was in it. "If you sent Ferdy out, how would we leave?"

"There's another car out back," she said. "I can leave him a note saying we went for a drive to talk. We can ditch it somewhere, then take a bus wherever we want and get another car. By the time Ferdy figures out something's up, we'll be gone!"

I pictured the two of us on a bus, carrying that amount of money. It was almost comical. "Harley," I said, "you can't run forever. Don't you watch TV? People always get caught. *Always!*"

"I *won't!* Listen, I put up with these guys for all these years, listened to them, cooked for them, got beat up by one of them – but then, after all that, I stole their stinking money right out from under their noses! Audrey, we can do this!"

I got up and went to my purse. "I need a pill," I said. I rooted around, removed items from my bag and then put them all back. Rubbing my forehead, I turned to Harley. "I left one of my medications at home. What am I going to do?"

"What kind? Maybe I have something."

I shook my head. "It's a prescription. For stress. I *need* it Harley. There's an over-the-counter product I could substitute to take the edge off, but hell, I'm sure you're not going to drive me to a pharmacy."

"I can't send Ferdy in the shape he's in, but I'll go for you." She pulled a sheet of paper and a pen from a drawer and handed them to me. "You write down the name. I'll go and be back in a jiff. Are you okay till I get back? I didn't mean to cause you so much stress, Aud. Everything will be fine. I swear."

"What if someone recognizes you?"

"No one is looking for me – they're looking for Ferdy. Besides, you're the only one who's seen my hair like this," she said.

I wrote St. John's Wort on the paper. "Aren't you afraid I'll run away while you're gone?" I asked, wanting desperately to change the subject.

"There's nothing around here for miles, Kiddo. Nowhere to go. I've got the keys to both cars, your cell, and there's no land line in the house, so..."

"Okay, I get it; I'm going back to bed. But Harley, we're not done talking about this."

"And I'm not done trying to convince you to run away with me." She winked. "Now go ahead and lay down. I'll be right back." She closed the door behind her just as my phone vibrated.

It was a text from Jack: *Local police think they have your location narrowed down. Do you know if F. or H. has access to a weapon?*

I typed back: *Don't know. How long 'til they come?*

It seemed like a lifetime before he answered: *A couple of hours. Where are you now?*

Me: *In a bedroom. Harley just went out to the store. She should be back before then. She has no idea anyone is looking for her. And FYI, her hair is short and red.*

Jack: *Stay in the room. The police have your new photo. You'll be okay. I love you.*

Me: *I love you too, Jack. I'll do my best.*

When Harley got back, I would look at the receipt, which would give me the name and location of the pharmacy. I could pass that information along to Jack; maybe it would help the police find me faster. I went back to my bag, took out my bottle of happy pills, and swallowed one.

So, Harley was not concerned that I'd run while she was gone. What she didn't understand, was that I couldn't have anyway; I was working with police to locate *her*. And now Ferdy. The police needed me to stay with them, here, or anywhere else they went, until they were caught. I felt like one of those double agents I'd seen on TV, and hoped I was up to the task.

CHAPTER 31

As I waited for Harley, I wondered how much Danny Stearns knew; how much contact he'd had with the others over the years. It might not have been safe for him to be in touch, but among thieves, would it ever be smart *not* to be in touch?

It seemed that thieves did trust each other, at least initially, maybe during the planning and execution stages of a crime, but once that was over, how many times had I seen on TV, where one crook shot the other to eliminate having to divvy up the spoils? And here was Harley, who was planning on dumping the last man standing. That wouldn't have boded well for me if I had actually agreed to go on the run with her.

Harley returned, thankfully before I'd heard Ferdy moving around. "Here you go," she said, as she tossed the bag onto the bed.

"Thank you! How much? I'm happy to pay you for it," I said, as I headed for the bathroom. I took out the medicine but there was no receipt in the bag. Harley had gotten rid of it. Shit. I had to give her credit for that move. I opened the box and dropped it into the wicker trash basket, opened the bottle, and turned on the water at the sink. After a few seconds, I turned off the water and popped the top back on the bottle, in case she was listening at the door.

"The last thing I need is a couple of bucks from you!" she whispered, as I came back out. "Weren't you listening to me before? I have all the money we will ever need. Come outside. I want to tell you my plans."

She led me through the sliders and we walked down the deserted beach, but stopped dead in our tracks, as a loud *bang!* came from inside the house. Thundering voices yelled, "Get on the ground! Get on the ground *now*!"

"Come on!" she whispered. She grabbed my hand and pulled me along at a dead run, and I wondered how she thought she could avoid being seen without so much as a beach umbrella to hide behind.

"What are you doing?" I yelled. "They're going to see us! Harley! Stop! This is no good!"

"We can't stop," she said, "they're still in the house! Ferdy won't even tell them I was here. He loves me!"

A police cruiser started up and headed toward us, its wheels throwing sand in all directions. "Oh, God," Harley cried. "This can't be how it ends; not after all my planning, all my work." She turned and ran toward the ocean.

"Harley, *no!*" I yelled, as I ran after her, but visions of the dream I'd had of being pulled into the water stopped me; I could feel salt water rising in my throat, as my mind screamed, *don't go in!* I fell to the sand and watched as she continued on - now knee deep in the water, now waist deep, and then, toppled by a breaking wave, she disappeared. The officer stopped his patrol car, jumped out, and ran into the ocean after her.

He pulled her up and they scuffled, flailed in the water, and I heard Harley choking, heard the officer yell for her to stop fighting him, and finally, finally, he dragged her out. She collapsed on the sand, coughing, vomiting up seawater. Two other officers approached on the run. One assisted his dripping brother-in-blue get Harley into the back of his vehicle. The other approached me. "Audrey Dory?" I nodded. "Come with me, please."

"Gladly."

"Are you okay?" he asked.

"I guess." I looked up the beach to where Ferdy was standing next to one of the other patrol cars; the one carrying Harley pulled up to it and parked alongside. By the looks of it, the officer standing with Ferdy was reading him his rights.

When I reached the house, both Harley and Ferdy were watching me, and I was sure, wondering why I hadn't been cuffed as they had been. But then I saw reality hit in Harley's eyes, and she yelled from inside the car, "Audrey? What did you do?"

I wiped tears from my face and turned to the police officer. "I know where the money from the bank robbery is."

"Show me."

"Harley said it was in three suitcases. You just have to find those."

As the patrol cars pulled away, I followed the officer into the beautiful beach house and watched, as he pulled on Latex gloves and began rooting through closets and looking under beds. He carefully moved furniture and opened doors until he found the three pieces in the fourth bedroom. He put them on the bed and tried to open them, but they were locked, and the locks had keypads for which he had no codes. "Well," he said, "we'll get the prints off the bags and then have someone break the locks. Until then, we can't be sure what's inside."

"Try 5-0-9-5." I said. "Those are the last four digits of my agency's phone number. We used it for everything – our security system, passwords, literally everything, because Harley's so bad with numbers she could never remember more than one."

He turned the suitcase on its side, punched in the numbers, and the lock popped.

"Well," he smiled, "you called that one."

Inside the bag was money. Bundles and bundles of money. "Bingo," he said. He closed it back up and pulled out his phone. "I need to get a crime scene unit over here. And tell the Feds the money's here. Tell 'em to come get it." Then he turned to me. "A helicopter will be landing shortly to take you to the airport. You don't need another 8-hour drive back to LAX before you start your trip home. Now if you'll excuse me." I listened, as he instructed two officers to start "bagging" as soon as the ETs had done their work. "There's a lot more than money to confiscate," he told them.

That's right, I thought. Ferdy had disguises here that would tie him to this place, and in turn to the robbery, and maybe even Tony's plane crash. I called Jack on my Mata Hari phone, and he picked up right away. "Audrey?"

"It's me – I am so glad to hear your voice." I started to cry as the tension began to leave my body. "It's all over. Harley and Ferdy are in custody and Jack – we have the money!"

"The *money!*" he shouted. "Now it's my turn to cry. Are you kidding me? They had it with them? All of it?"

"Not they – *Harley* – she's the one who took it from my office. Can you believe that?"

"How? When?"

"Didn't have time to ask her."

"Wait 'til Carl hears that," he laughed.

"And Ferdy!" I said. "He's been driving all over the country with it, and probably still has no idea!"

"Come home to me," Jack said, suddenly serious.

"A helicopter is on its way to take me to LAX. Not sure yet how long it will take me to get home."

"I'll be waiting for my punk rocker," he laughed.

"I'm hoping Lisa can fix me."

The helicopter I'd heard in the distance rapidly drew near and landed, its rotors blowing sand with a mighty force. The pilot helped me board and I stowed my duffle behind my seat. "Buckle up," he said, and I watched the beach house, which was now surrounded by flashing lights, disappear as we flew away.

* * *

I thanked the officer who escorted me from the airport helipad to the security line; he handed me a ticket, just as Jack said he would.

"It'll be good to get home," I smiled. We shook hands and he went on his way.

I woke up back in Philly, having at last slept soundly, and later, when I landed in Syracuse, I spotted Jack right away and ran to him. "Don't ask me to wait," he said, as he pulled the ring box out of his pocket. "Will you put this on now? Will you say yes?"

I threw my arms around him. "Yes, yes, yes!" And I held out my left hand.

He slipped the ring on my finger; it was more beautiful than I'd remembered. "I love it," I said, as tears made their way down my face. "And I love you."

I turned at the sound of applause, and realized that our impromptu engagement had attracted a small group of spectators. I curtsied and Jack took a bow, then to cap off the performance, we kissed.

MARGARET BELLE

CHAPTER 32

On the ride back to my apartment, I filled Jack in on what had taken place at the airport and the beach house, and how Harley had told me that she was the one who'd taken the money.

Jack said, "After all you did for that little shit. When I think of how she covered up for those thugs – honestly, that's an alliance I would not have expected. It's not how I thought this would turn out."

"That's because Harley was such a pitiful figure, to me anyway, at least after I found out how badly Carl treated her. And she always made such a point of telling me how much she appreciated my friendship and the help I gave her, I mean, I never would have suspected her."

"Well at least your reputation is still intact in the world of advertising. Have you thought about reopening your agency?"

"I don't know. I'm going to need some income, and fast. And honestly, the amount of billing I've lost will be hard to replace, especially in time to keep the agency afloat."

"You may have to put it off anyway," he said. "Stearns' trial has started. You'll be heading to Rochester before long."

I felt like banging my head on the dashboard. "You know, I could probably avoid the whole thing if I let Dr. Steele put me in the nut house for a while."

"Maybe. Or they could just postpone the trial till you got out. But I think you're stronger than you give yourself credit for being. I think the woman I know and love would want this thing behind her for all time, and not want to take even the smallest chance of Danny Stearns going free on some technicality. She'd want the tightest possible case against him."

"Me, right?" I smiled.

"Of course you. And then life can go back to normal."

"I don't even know what normal is any more."

"Well, to start your journey towards it, why not move in with me?"

"Really?"

"I was thinking we could go to my place; stay there for a while. Your landlord thinks you're out of town anyway, so why not?"

"I don't have much with me."

"We can go to your place and pick up whatever you need in a couple of days. What do you say?"

"Actually, that sounds really good. After all, we're engaged and I've never even seen your place. Maybe I'll pick up some clues to the inner you," I teased. "You know, if your apartment is full of taxidermy, or if there's a pool table in the living room, mirrors on the bedroom ceiling, that kind of thing."

"Sounds reasonable."

"Actually, Jack," I said, "the fact that I've never been to your home points up the fact that we haven't known each other that long. Are we rushing into this marriage?"

"We aren't rushing. We're in love."

We drove to Tipp Hill and pulled into the driveway of a huge brick home that looked to be a circa 1800 colonial, not far from the zoo, and across from the arboretum. "Which floor do you live on?" I asked, knowing that many older homes in this area had been converted into two-families.

"Both," he said, "I own it."

"You're kidding," I said. We entered through a side door and I wandered through room after room, in awe of the original pocket doors, woodwork, wide-plank hardwood floors, a butler's pantry, two fireplaces, and high ceilings. "Jack," I said, "this is spectacular!"

"Thanks. I did most of the restoration myself. There's still more to be done upstairs."

"I can't wait to see the rest!" We climbed the stairs and he pointed the way to a bedroom that had been fully restored. "So stately," I said. "Looks like a bedroom Lincoln would have slept in." A four-poster bed dominated the room. "It's just beautiful. So different than the tiny spaces I spend most of my time in."

"Reflects the inner me," he laughed.

"Show me your room." He pointed again, indicating we needed to go to the other end of the hall. The room was enormous. "I didn't realize these homes had such large bedrooms," I said, feeling a little unsettled.

"I knocked down a wall between two smaller ones," he said.

A cherry four-poster stood in the center of the space, with a chest of drawers against one wall and a highboy against another, both in the same rich wood. He'd managed to keep a sense of the bygone era, without the fussiness that can accompany that décor. Royal blues and burgundies on the bed and walls fairly screamed the fact that a man slept in this room; his service weapon, holstered and hung on a chair, fortified that.

"My whole apartment could fit in here!" I said, "I love the color palette. I'm really impressed!"

"So was I, when the decorator got done," he laughed. "I did the construction, the woodworking, the windows, and all that, but I'm no good with color. I thank the Lord every day that I wear a uniform to work, so I don't have to think about it."

"Do we get to sleep in here?"

"We do. I'll go down and lock up. Help yourself to a bath or a shower. Unwind."

"I'll go with you and get a clean pair of pajamas out of my duffle."

"Oh," he smiled, "you won't be needing those tonight."

CHAPTER 33

By the time Jack came back upstairs, I was soaking in the clawfoot tub. "You've modernized this with all the conveniences of a spa, yet still managed to make it feel like you're stepping back in time."

He handed me a glass of wine, and pulled a wooden stool to the side of the tub. "You look relaxed," he smiled, and took a sip from his own glass.

"I am."

"Good. Soak. I'm going to grab a shower." As part of Jack's remodeling project, he'd installed a three-sided glass shower. Five water jets protruded from the walls at various levels, and a huge rain showerhead extended from the ceiling.

I watched as he stripped the clothes from his perfect body and while he turned on the water and waited until it reached temperature. I took another sip of wine, unable to pry my eyes from the muscles of his arms and legs that flexed with every move. He seemed not to notice me staring. Men. They weren't self-conscious about their bodies like women were. Of course there was no reason Jack should be worried about anyone seeing him naked. He was beautiful.

He stepped into the shower and the water glistened on his skin. I stayed put while he washed his hair, but a girl can only take so much. By the time he'd rinsed out the shampoo, I was standing with him under the spray, wrapped in his arms.

Every inch of him was like granite pressed up against me; the very definition of a hard body. As he leaned down to kiss me, he slid his hands slowly down my back until he reached my bottom, where he massaged and probed, until I pleaded with him to get on with it. Obligingly, he reached further down, to the backs of my thighs and picked me up. I wrapped myself around him, pleased that he seemed to be exerting no effort to hold me exactly where he wanted me. I stroked the back of his head, whispered to him, and in a single move, we were one.

Later, as we snuggled under the covers, I glanced around the room; my eyes came to rest on Jack's service weapon. "Why did you become a police officer?"

"Lots of reasons," he said. "I was bullied in school as a kid."

"You? Seriously?"

"I was scrawny, not terribly athletic back then, and my family didn't have much money. I was the awkward kid in old clothes the other boys made fun of to make themselves feel better."

"That's awful!" I cuddled in closer.

"Without my parents knowing it," he said, "I stopped taking the bus and started walking to school. And before I left in the mornings, I ate as much as I could get away with so I could skip lunch and not have my tray dumped in the cafeteria. It was a constant struggle to stay out of harm's way."

"Did you tell anyone?"

"My parents didn't want to hear about it, and there was no way I was about to talk to a teacher, so I tried to avoid the kids that bugged me, and when I couldn't, I suffered through it."

"When did things change?"

"Not until after I graduated. But I believe that our past dictates who we become, and because I was bullied, I had this hope that one day I could be there for someone else who felt they had no one to turn to."

"That's noble," I said, knowing that what he'd said was true: our past *is* responsible, at least to a large degree, for who we become.

"That's why a lot of people join the force," he said. "Unfortunately, that feeling gets worked out of you pretty fast, once you see what the job really entails."

"Is that what drew you to me? You thought I needed someone to turn to?"

"I didn't know anything about you when we first met, except that at the time, you thought one of your clients had disappeared. I saw such compassion and worry in your face. I knew you were someone who cared about people. Plus," he smiled, "you were hot."

"I was a mess shortly thereafter," I said. "You've seen me. I can be a problem. In fact, I've been thinking about making an appointment with Dr. Steele," I said. "I'd like to try and convince her that I'm in pretty good shape, and get her off my back."

"Worth a try," he said. "Show her the new you." That should be easy, I thought, since she's never met the old me. "I'll tell you what I want," he continued, "I want to see Harley testify against Ferdy."

"Do you think they'd let me see her?"

"Harley? I don't know. Why would you want to put yourself through that?"

"I didn't get to talk to her much in California. Maybe, if she's cooled down a little, I can get more information out of her."

"It's not common practice," he said, "but I'll see what I can do."

He handed me my freshly topped-off wine glass, then retrieved his own from the bedside table. "Cheers."

I held up my glass. "To my future husband. You know, back in the day, when this beautiful house was built, we'd never have been allowed to drink wine in bed together before we were married."

"Naked. Don't forget naked."

"Bless the passage of time," I said.

He held up his glass and touched it to mine with a little clink. "To the passage of time. Know what else we wouldn't have been allowed to do?"

"Pray tell."

He put his glass back on the table and disappeared under the covers.

"Oh," I breathed. *"That!"*

CHAPTER 34

I fidgeted in my chair and waited for Harley to appear. The windowless walls in the visitor's room were cement and the furnishings, if you could call them that, consisted of an oblong table that was bolted to the floor, and two uncomfortable plastic chairs - one on either side of the immovable table. An officer stood outside the door.

Harley walked in, handcuffed, and wearing a prison jumpsuit; her outwardly calm demeanor was betrayed by the anger that flashed in her eyes. She took the chair opposite me and put her bound hands on the table. "I can't believe you called the police on me."

"I didn't have a choice, Harley. If I had done what you wanted, I'd have been as guilty as you. And anyway, what did you *think* I would do – you lied to me from the moment we met!"

"Well, I didn't have a choice, either. You have no idea what my life was like."

"So when did you take the money? In the middle of the night?" I asked. "Then what? You just showed up for work the next day, like nothing had happened?"

"What difference does it make now?"

"And who did you hire to install the carpet?" I asked. "There are no receipts or checks for the work."

She sat back in her chair. "Is that why you came? To interrogate me? Because if it is, you might just as well leave."

"All right," I said, "then tell me what you plan to do now. Testify against Ferdy and Danny, and try to get immunity in return? Be a jailhouse snitch?"

"I have a public defender, not some big-shot lawyer like Ferdy," she said, "so I don't know what will happen. But I'll make any deal that will get me out of here."

"You mean Lover Boy isn't going to spring for a lawyer to represent you? What does that tell you? You're almost as stupid as I am, Harley. Now are you going to testify against Danny, or not?"

"What do you care? You should just be happy he's in jail."

I stared at her, and noticed a little twinkle in her eye. What was that? Not a happy twinkle – but one that spoke of cunningness. And then it hit me. "It was *you*," I said. "You were the one who turned in that anonymous tip about Danny, way back when."

"Of course it was me – *duh*, Audrey – I needed him to be arrested so he wouldn't try to get the money, and find out it was already gone. What do you think – I didn't plan every little thing? The only mistake I made was to trust you."

"I should have realized it was you when you said those very words to me the first time we Skyped. You said you could connect Danny to the robbery. I just didn't put it together until this minute."

"Don't sell yourself short, Audrey, you put Carl in jail for me, although it was unintentional on your part," she smiled, "it saved me from having to do it. I got one of them arrested, then you got one of them arrested – it was like we were working together for a common goal. It was almost cosmic!"

"Yeah," I said, "it was magical. So then, all you had to do was dump Ferdy, the non-violent one - the only one who was never a threat to you, and off you'd go, with three million dollars. That was the plan, right? To pick them off, one-two-three?"

"Except it happened faster than I'd thought it would," she said. "That night, when I was sitting on that damn cot and you told me the story of how Danny had bumped into you, and how afraid you were that he might have seen you on TV and recognized you, I freaked out. Right then I knew I had to get out of there in case Danny *had* seen you. He would have tracked you down and sent Carl after you! And let me tell you, it would not have gone well for me if they'd found me hiding in the building with you!" She shook her head. "I kept trying to wrap my mind around the fact that Carl had hidden the money in the building *you* moved into. How the hell does something like that happen?"

"So you took the job at Carrie's to get away from me?"

"I figured it was a chance to get away from Carl *and* you – two birds, one stone. But when you told me Carl had followed you in his truck, I knew I hadn't gone *nearly* far enough away."

"So you took off."

"I took off."

We sat in silence for a minute, then I said, "Look, I don't want to testify against Danny – I don't want to ever look at him again. The least you could do is testify against him *for* me after all the crap you pulled – and after all I've done for you."

"So that's it? That's why you drove all the way here? To get me to agree to keep you from having to look Danny in the eyes again?"

"Yes."

"Well, let's see," she said. "You ruined my life – it's your fault I'm here – so *no!*"

"Don't be stupid," I said. "You'd have been caught sooner or later. You might be good with a computer, but you're not as smart as you think you are; I got the police into your suitcase with the office phone number."

She raised her hands and shook them, causing the handcuffs to clink together. "I think it would be good for you to see Danny again. Maybe the little reunion would be so awful, they'd have to put you away – then you'd know how I feel."

"You think I like seeing you in here?" I asked. "I don't. But after saving you so many times, it was time to save myself."

"Don't worry about me," she spat out. "I'm fully capable of saving myself. I learned a thing or two from Carl. Don't think I wasn't watching, and listening, and learning, while I was with him. Oh, and didn't you ever wonder why your other assistant left you high and dry? Why you suddenly needed to replace her?" She leaned in and whispered, "Carl took care of her, too." She stood up and pushed her chair back so hard that it tipped over and crashed to the floor. The sound echoed through the room.

The guard moved in and escorted her out, leaving me alone in the stark surroundings, aghast at all I'd just heard. What had Carl done to get rid of my first assistant? He couldn't have killed her, or her family would have contacted me when they were unable to reach her. I hadn't bothered tracking her down to ask why she'd left, because I'd had to find a replacement for her so fast. And I had, hadn't I.

Outside, Jack waited for me. "I'd ask how it went," he said, "but it's written all over your face."

"You have no idea," I said, feeling faint, and I told him what Harley had said about my former assistant.

"We'll get on that, I promise," he said, "but she was probably just trying to get you more upset."

I shook my head. "I should have known this was a fool's errand. All I ended up with are pieces to a puzzle I didn't even know existed."

"Come on," he said, "let's get something to eat before we head back."

We found a Dinosaur Bar-B-Que, not far from the police station. A regular customer in the same establishment back home, Jack ordered a House Special and a side of Drunken Spicy Shrimp, without even looking at the menu. I ordered a chopped salad and coffee. With my first forkful I realized I was hungrier than I'd thought, and my mood brightened. Between bites, he asked, "So, what else did Harley have to say?"

"She said she hoped facing Danny in court would push me over the edge, so that I'd need to be put away."

"Nice. You were in there a while, though, there must be more."

"She said she *learned* things from Carl. She watched, and learned, and listened. Those were her words. What the heck does that mean? And, of course, she blames me for her losing the money, after all the risks she took to get it." I pushed the salad around the plate with my fork. "I think those guys were really rough to deal with. And of course, she put up with all that abuse from Carl."

He shook his head. "And you still feel sorry for her, right?"

"Down deep I do, I guess," I admitted. "I mean, if I disregard all that she did, I can see her true motivation; how she thought the money would give her a better life. And she really believed she'd get away with it."

"That's why all perps get caught," he said. "They don't pay attention. They always make one stupid mistake."

"She focused on the freedom she'd have," I said, "and she was willing to share that life with me. Then I blew her in."

"And you thought about it," he said, looking at me out of the corner of his eye.

"Thought about what?"

"Going with her."

I looked down at my plate. "I know I did. At the time, it meant I wouldn't have to testify, or be afraid that Dr. Steele was going to throw a net over my head and drag me off."

"So I was the only reason you didn't take her up on it?"

"Ultimately. Once you explained what running away would mean for me, and I saw things for what they really were, and especially after you proposed, I knew I could never leave you."

"Wow," he smiled. "You must like me a lot."

"You know I do," I said.

CHAPTER 35

My office was no longer a crime scene, so I decided to drive over and take a peek at the upstairs to see what it looked like after the police had torn up the floor. The route was ingrained in my muscle memory, so even though my mind was going in a hundred different directions I soon found myself pulling into my parking space.

Yellow tape with POLICE LINE DO NOT CROSS printed on it, sagged across the front of the building and I ducked under it, unlocked the door, and went in. An eerie quiet welcomed me. A layer of dust had settled over everything and the air smelled old and musty; I opened the windows and turned on the ceiling fan. On the way up the stairs, I stopped in front of the small window; I could almost feel Carl's breath on my neck, his gun in my back.

I hurried the rest of the way up, wanting to get away from the horrible memory, but then slowed as I started down the hall toward the room where the money had been stashed; the room Harley and I had slept in while I harbored her from Carl. As I stood in the doorway, I was filled with frustration at what had gone on in this room while I was oblivious. And what made it worse was that I had contributed!

Those thugs had never had to worry about their precious money; they'd had me on their team! Carl had hidden it under the floorboards, and I'd paid good money to cover up his handiwork with carpet. *What a joke!* I wondered how often Harley had laughed about it behind my back. What a fool she must have taken me for.

At least a quarter of the floorboards had been pried up and cast aside; the room was strewn with everything from full boards to splinters of old, dry wood. From the looks of it, the demolition had been in progress for a while before I'd been able to point them in the right direction.

I tried to picture Harley pulling up the carpet, removing the floorboards, taking out the cash, replacing the wood and the carpet, and hauling the three million dollars away; a big job, no matter how you looked at it. When exactly had she pulled off the second robbery of the same damn money? In the dead of night? And where had she kept it? In those suitcases the whole time? She had to have kept them in a storage facility; she certainly didn't have them with her the day she left for Carrie's.

Feeling a chill, I rubbed my arms. What was it Harley had said back in California? She said she *had* the money. She didn't say she *took* the money. I thought I might be quibbling over words, but the question lingered. If I was confessing to the theft of something, would I say I'd taken it? Or would I say I had it? I thought I would say I'd taken it. Maybe that's what had been bugging me.

My cell rang. Jack asked, "Where are you?"

"I stopped by the office to look at the damage your brothers-in-blue inflicted on the place."

"I was going to tell you tonight," he said, "but I couldn't wait. The FBI just gave Rochester a heads-up on the money recovered in California. It wasn't all there."

"What do you mean? I saw it!"

"Only two million was accounted for. One million is missing."

"Harley was sure she had it all!"

"It's possible she hid the extra million somewhere in case she got caught," said Jack. "She may have prepared for that possibility; planned to cop a plea for immunity, and walk with the hidden money.

Then there's the possibility that either Carl or Ferdy took it from her, without Harley realizing it."

"Carl? Hell no," I said. "He would have gone into a rage if he'd found she had the money, beaten her within an inch of her life, and taken it all. Ferdy, on the other hand, might've been more inclined to share. But knowing him, he'd have confronted Harley, and in the end agreed to take half, which was better than the third he was expecting."

"I can't think of any other scenarios. Can you?"

"No," I said, "but we can talk about it later." We said goodbye and I turned off my phone.

I went back downstairs and sat at my empty desk. In all the years I'd worked here I'd only really seen the top of it once or twice, counting the day the furniture company had delivered it. I looked over at Harley's desk. For the first few years I'd filled it with interns from SUNY Oswego and SU. But about five years ago, my billing had reached a point where I could hire an actual full-time employee.

My clients had wanted more and more website work, Internet advertising, and a way to use social media to increase traffic, and for that I'd needed an honest-to-God IT pro. While the interns were wonderful, none had been ready to graduate and come to work for me full time, and it had always been a process bringing a new one up to speed at the beginning of every semester. Hiring my first assistant had eliminated all of that, offered continuity to my clients, and made them happy. But two years ago she'd left without a word, and I'd hired Harley. She'd jumped right in and handled the transition smoothly. Talk about a Trojan horse.

The first wisps of depression, like a lace curtain in a summer breeze, brushed across my mind; a familiar warning that a full-on brainstorm was on its way. I dug in my purse for the bottle of happy pills and swallowed one.

Leaning back in my chair, I closed my eyes and thought about the two Harleys; the one who had been my friend, and the one who was a thief, a liar, and worse. And then there was the question I still turned over and over in my mind; when and how had the money left this building?

Unable to come to grips with the two Harley's, and knowing the answer about the money would not be forthcoming right now, I turned my attention to the problem at hand; one pill wasn't going to cut it. Despite the last meeting I'd had with her, I put in a call to Dr. Steele. I was in trouble, and I knew it.

CHAPTER 36

Dr. Steele sat in her chair across from me, ready to write, as usual, with a pen poised over her notepad and an inquisitive look on her face. "I'm glad you called," she said. "You were unhappy when you left here the last time. I was afraid you wouldn't return."

"I wasn't unhappy, I was pissed."

"Understood," she said. "So what happened that made you reach for the phone? I was hoping you'd reconsidered my advice to take a break and work on your mental health issues," she almost whispered.

"No," I said, "although, as the trial draws closer, it seems like a way to get out of testifying."

She pointed toward my hand. "Jack gave you an engagement ring?"

"Yes."

"And marrying him will be a positive step for you?"

"I love him. More than I can ever remember loving anyone."

"The expression in your eyes says otherwise," she said. "What's the problem?"

"I worry about him. I can be a handful."

"He most likely has a sense of that already, being a police officer and all. He's most likely a good judge of character. You are not a bad person, Audrey. We've been over that. You were not responsible for your mother's death. She didn't die because you couldn't find a nurse. You were six! You deserve to be happy."

"That's the last thing Dr. Collins said to me the day I left Rochester."

"What's worried me since the day we met, is that I've had the feeling you've been holding something back; that you haven't been totally honest. And that makes it difficult for me to actually help you in a meaningful way."

"Like what?"

"Audrey, if I knew that, I wouldn't have to ask. When I read through your file from Dr. Collins, she had a concern that you might be taking the anger you feel toward yourself over your mother's death, out on other people. She felt you could possibly do physical damage to someone who made you really mad. Or ultimately, turn the anger inward and harm yourself."

I smiled. "So, you must have been worried when I was here the last time."

"Not for myself, but be honest with me. Have there been times when you wanted to harm someone else? Or took your anger out in an inappropriate way? Real, or in your head?"

I thought about being lost in the thought of smashing Carl against a wall with my vehicle. And as I looked at Dr. Steele, staring at me with that inquisitive look of hers, I remembered reveling in the thought of squeezing her throat with my bare hands until she died.

"No," I answered. "Why?"

"Because if you're given to violent thoughts, I can help you. Why keep them to yourself when we could talk through those thoughts and their triggers, and free you of them? Otherwise, Audrey, this could accelerate. And under the right circumstances it could mean a setback from which you might not be able to recover."

"No," I repeated, "I'm not having those thoughts." But I could tell that she didn't believe me.

"Would you like to bring Jack into a few sessions with you? Since you're going to marry him?"

"That's the last thing I want to do."

"So, you wanted to see me today," she said, "but you're not willing to give me anything to go on – no specific reason – you just wanted to come in?"

"I feel like I'm going to buckle under the weight of all the drama in my life. Can I increase my meds?"

"Oh, so, *that's* why you're here," she said. "I suppose I can increase your dosage a *bit*. But you have to be careful, Audrey. And for heaven's sake, do not take it upon yourself to stop cold turkey again. The zaps you experienced before will be twice as bad if you do. They could be debilitating. And listen to me. I still believe the best thing for you would be to let me admit you – just for a while – to a place where you can participate in therapy more consistently. I fear that you're headed for trouble. You can't be thinking clearly these days. I don't want you to snap and do something you'll regret."

"Like what?"

"I don't know, Audrey, I'm not inside your head. But I *can* tell you that a supervised rest would be the best thing for you and for your future with Jack."

"You can't say anything to Jack without my permission, right? I mean if he took it upon himself to call you?"

"Not without your express permission, no."

I breathed a sigh of relief. Jack's love had kept me from going over the edge so far and I hoped that it always would. But there may be a time when he too would suspect that I hadn't told him everything, just as Dr. Steele had, and try to find out for himself what was wrong with me. I didn't think he needed to hear the whole story of my mother's death, or my violent visions.

On my way back to Jack's place, I dropped off my new, stronger prescription, and diddled around the drug store while it was being filled. In this more relaxed frame of mind, a thought occurred to me. Harley's arrival and the remodeling of the office bedroom had come at the same time. In fact, other than getting her familiarized with client needs, it had been the first responsibility I had given her. I remember being thrilled at having some of the work taken off my shoulders and so impressed with how fast she'd learned the ropes, that I'd taken a much needed three days off during her first month there.

Soon I was home and pulling into my parking space, on a mission to find out who Harley had used to install the carpet. I went inside and waved at Dick, who was working the bar.

"Audrey? What the hell did you do to your hair? Did Lisa do that to you?"

"Long story."

"Okay, well, welcome home. Hang on, I'll get your key."

He was only gone a second when he reappeared and slid my key across the bar. "Want anything? A beer? Something to eat? A mirror?"

"Funny, Dick. Nothing now, thanks, maybe later." I hurried up the stairs and unlocked my door. The moment I closed it behind me, I relaxed. I lit a stick of Frankincense and then looked through boxes until I found the one I wanted; receipts from two years ago. I carried the carton to the coffee table and peeled off the tape. Although I sorted through every piece of paper, the one I was looking for wasn't there. I went through them all again, but the receipt for the carpet simply wasn't in the box.

I went back to a box of older receipts and pulled out the ones for the first year I occupied the building; way back to when I was setting up the office, had no clients, and could see the top of my desk. Thank God I hadn't thrown them away.

About halfway through, I came up with the receipt for the carpet installation on the first floor. The company's phone number was printed under its logo and I put it into my cell. After a few rings, a woman came on the line with a whole rehearsed message that finally ended with, "How may I help you?"

I introduced myself and asked if she could tell me if her company had installed the carpet in my upstairs. She asked me to wait so she could check her computer and I listened to a recording of soft rock while she did.

Soon she was back on the line. "I don't have anything listed for that address in the last five years and our records only go back that far."

"Nothing? You're sure?"

"Positive. Sorry." I thanked her and we hung up. So what carpet company had Harley used? Where had she gotten that two-for-one deal she'd bragged about when I'd returned after my three days off? I packed up the papers again and re-sealed the boxes. Now I'd have to go in search of checks from the same time period.

A knock at the door surprised me. "Who is it?" I asked.

A man's voice said, "UPS."

I opened the door to a delivery person who was standing next to two boxes I'd been expecting. He handed me an electronic device. "Sign anywhere," he said. He tucked the device back into his belt, then picked up the first box and handed it to me. I took it inside and put it next to all the other boxes I would soon have to move. Then I went back and got the second. *Soon there'll be no room in here for me,* I thought.

"Thank you," I said, as I pushed the door closed with my foot. I carried the box to where I had put the first one, found a marker, and printed KITCHEN on both, and underlined the word.

I had no sooner done that, when there was a second knock at the door. "Who is it?" I asked again.

"Flowers for Audrey Dory," a man said, and he held a bouquet up in front of the peephole. That sweet Jack, I thought, and I opened the door. "Audrey Dory?" the man asked.

"That's me," I said, grinning from ear-to-ear, as I took the basket of flowers.

"Enjoy," he said. Then he stuck an envelope under my arm. "You've been served."

CHAPTER 37

I opened the paper and read that I'd been subpoenaed to testify in Danny Stearns' trial. Just holding the thing was too much and I dropped it onto my coffee table. I'd let Jack read it to me. I'd sit next to him on his sofa and put my head on his shoulder and let him explain the details of the horrid missive. It was just like on TV – a ruse – flowers. I felt stupid on top of everything else for falling for it. I should have known it was coming. For now I would pretend it didn't exist; I was good at that.

I went into the hallway and locked the door behind me, stopped downstairs to order takeout, and headed next door to see if Lisa was still at work. My anger at her for telling Jack that I was leaving had abated. I understood why she'd done it and I wasn't about to lose my best friend over something stupid. The bell tinkled when I walked in and she looked up from her desk. Shock registered in her eyes as she stared at my hair.

"Hi," I said.

"Oh, Audrey, is that you?" She got up and came over to me. "Are you mad?" she asked, as she walked around me, checking out my do.

"I was, but I'm not any more. You did the right thing, telling Jack."

"Thank God – I was afraid you'd never speak to me again! But I thought that if I didn't say something...well, thank God you're not mad, that's all. And you're home." I gave her a hug. "Sit down and we'll take care of that hair right now; get you back to your old self."

"Pretty awful, huh?" I gave her the short version of what had happened while she stirred up the color concoction and tied a cape around my neck.

"Did Jack tell you where he was when you called him?" I asked.

"Yes, he did," she beamed. "Let's see it." I held out my hand and the ring flashed, as the diamond reflected the overhead lights. "It's gorgeous," she said. "I'm so happy for you."

"It will be a small wedding, but I'm going to need a maid of honor."

"Me? Absolutely! Just please don't make me wear something awful."

"You can wear whatever you want."

While the color was working, I sat in the vibrating chair and relaxed. Only one other person came in for a cut and then we were left alone to talk. Finally she rinsed my hair and when she put me back in the front of the mirror, I looked like myself again. "Much better," she said. "Want me to blow it out? Or are we in a curly mood?"

"Curly, I guess."

She popped a diffuser onto the blow-dryer to hurry along the process, and within a few minutes she was turning my chair around so I could see the back of my head. "It looks great," I said. "Now I'm going to pick up dinner and head to Jack's."

"Lucky girl." She gave me another hug, and when I opened my purse, she said, "Don't even think about it. This one's on me. Call it an act of community service."

CHAPTER 38

"All rise!"

The judge entered the courtroom from a door behind the bench. Jack sat beside me and held my hand. "Maybe they won't have time to call me today," I said, knowing full well that the subpoena had specified that I appear on this date.

"You're here because they *are* going to call you," he whispered. "Just get up there and tell what you remember. Then it'll be over."

I peeked around Jack to where Danny Stearns was sitting with his lawyer. He turned in his chair and stared at me, and I felt faint. I grabbed Jack's arm.

The judge asked, "Are we ready? Everyone here and accounted for?" Both sides answered in the affirmative.

The attorney for the prosecution stood. "Your Honor, I would like to call Audrey Dory."

Jack pried my hand off his arm and whispered, "You're fine, Honey, just don't look at Stearns unless you have to. Don't let him intimidate you."

I walked on wobbly legs to the stand and put my left hand on a Bible. I promised to tell the truth, the whole truth, and nothing but the truth.

The attorney smiled at me. "Please state your name."

"Audrey Dory." *So far, so good*, I thought.

"Miss Dory, were you in Rochester on the 9th of June, in 2003?"

"Yes."

"Where exactly were you?"

"I was waiting for a taxi on Franklin Street."

"And what time was that?"

"Around 10 a.m.," I said.

"Thank you. And did anything strange or unusual happen as you waited for your taxi?"

"A man ran around the corner and crashed into me."

"And did he knock you down?"

"No, he grabbed me by the shoulders, pushed me backwards into the building, and then ran on."

"Thank you. And then what happened?"

"Two police cars came around the same corner, obviously in pursuit."

Danny's attorney stood up. "Objection Your Honor. Speculation."

"The witness did not say that the patrol cars were in pursuit of the *defendant*, Your Honor," said the prosecutor, as he turned back to me. "Did the patrol cars have their lights and sirens on?"

"Yes."

"Well, then, Judge, can we agree that the patrol cars may have been in pursuit of *someone?*"

Danny's attorney stood again, "Or on their way to some emergency, Your Honor. There's no way to know where those two cars were going."

"Sustained," said the judge, and then, "Go on," to the attorney questioning me.

"What did you do then?"

"I was very upset, and I remember sitting on the sidewalk."

"Did anyone come to your aid?"

"No. I don't even remember if anyone was around."

"What happened then?"

"I saw something on the ground near me and I picked it up."

"And what was it?"

"A ski mask."

From the evidence table he picked up a plastic bag and held it out to me. "Is this the ski mask?"

"It looks like it," I said.

"And did you get a good look at the man who ran around the corner and bumped into you? The man who dropped this ski mask?"

"Objection!" shouted Danny's attorney. "The witness never said she actually saw my client drop the ski mask."

"Your Honor, the defendants DNA, and *only* the defendants DNA was found inside the ski mask. I think we can agree it was his."

"The judge agreed and the attorney continued. "Did you get a good look at the person who ran around the corner and bumped into you?"

"Yes." *Here it comes,* I thought, *the part where I have to look at him and point.*

"And is that person in the courtroom?"

Pressure built in my ears and my voice sounded very far away when I answered, "Yes."

"Will you point him out to the court?"

Shaking, I turned and pointed to Danny Stearns. My arm lingered in the air, held up by some unseen force, my finger extended toward him, while I stared into those eyes. I was paralyzed, unable to lower my arm, as before me, he appeared to be wearing the ski mask. It covered his whole head and face, with only those dark eyes glaring out at me. Then it was gone. And then it was back.

"Let the record show that Miss Dory pointed to the defendant." He turned to me, "Are you all right, Miss Dory?" The mask disappeared once again, and I was finally able to lower my arm and tear my eyes away. I looked at the attorney and nodded.

"And there's no doubt in your mind that the defendant is the man you saw running on Franklin Street that day?"

"No doubt, whatsoever. It was him."

"No further questions," I heard the attorney say.

The judge looked at Danny's attorney. "Counselor? Do you wish to cross?" I looked at Jack, who winked at me and smiled reassuringly.

Danny's attorney, who looked like a go-to guy for the Mob, strode across the room to me. "Miss Dory," he said, "you testified that you found a ski mask on the sidewalk near you?"

"Yes."

He picked up the same plastic bag from the evidence table and brought it to me. "Is this the ski mask?"

"I just said it looks like it."

"And you picked up this ski mask from the sidewalk?"

"I did."

"And what did you do with it?"

"I obviously took it with me."

"Why do you say that?"

"Because I'm the one who turned it over to the police when I heard about the robbery investigation being reopened."

"The investigation was just recently reopened, Miss Dory. Are you saying you have been in possession of the ski mask for a decade?"

"Yes."

"That's hard to believe. Why keep it? Why didn't you call the police the day you found it?"

"At the time I had no idea a bank had been robbed, and I was very upset at having been shoved into the wall of the building. I took it back to my dorm, put it in a box, and forgot about it."

"Miss Dory, what were you doing on Franklin Street that day?"

"Objection!" The prosecutor shouted. "Relevance!"

Danny's attorney spoke directly to the judge. "Goes to the reliability of the witness, Your Honor."

"I'll allow," stated the judge. "Answer the question."

"I had an appointment there." Breathe. One...two...three...

"And with whom did you have this appointment?"

Imaginary birds, pecked at the back of my neck. My face was hot. "I believe that's personal."

"We don't do personal, here, Miss Dory. Who were you meeting with?"

"My doctor."

"What kind of a doctor?"

"A psychologist." He was trying to make me out to be a nut case. I looked over at the men and women sitting in the jury box. It seemed they were all staring at me, some with looks of pity.

"And for how long had you been under the care of this psychologist?"

"Two years."

"Is this psychologist the only one you've ever seen?"

"Yes."

"Who is Dr. Karol Steele?"

I was shocked to hear her name come out of his mouth, and shaken to know that he had been digging into my life. "My psychiatrist." It had to be two hundred degrees in the courtroom. I looked at Jack. He wasn't smiling any more. Instead, he was looking at me with sympathy. *Please, no.*

"So you went from seeing a psychologist to a *psychiatrist?*"

"Dr. Collins recommended her to me. I was moving and –"

"And from what do you suffer? What is your mental affliction?"

"Objection! Calls for the witness to wave her HIPAA rights and she is not on trial, Your Honor."

I knew what that was – the Health Insurance Portability and Accountability Act, which would keep Dr. Collins or Dr. Steele from talking to Jack, or anyone else, about my diagnosis without my permission. And at the moment, it would keep me from having to explain my GAD to this ape.

"Sustained. Move along, counselor."

"Miss Dory, are you on any prescribed medication today?" Tears stung my eyes.

"Objection again, Your Honor. HIPAA."

"Sustained. Don't go there again, counselor."

But the attorney turned to the jury and smiled. "Or any *other* kind of medication?"

"Objection!"

"I'll withdraw that last question, Your Honor. But if the witness has a mental affliction, and had it when she was bumped into by some man ten years ago, an affliction she refuses to explain to the court, how are we to know she wasn't on medication at the time of the incident? How do we know her state of mind at the time? Who knows how accurate her recollection of the person could possibly be this many years later? I move that the witness's testimony be stricken from the record because it cannot be relied upon."

"I'll take it under consideration. Anything else?"

"I move that the ski mask be removed from evidence, as Miss Dory admits she has been in possession of it for the past decade, and there can be no chain of custody established."

The judge asked, "Anything else?"

"Nothing further, Your Honor."

"The judge turned to me. "You can go."

I made my way back to where Jack was waiting. "Do you want to stay and listen?" he asked.

"Are you kidding? Get me out of here." Outside, I took a deep breath of fresh air. "Oh my God," I said, "that was awful. The jury thinks I'm crazy and now they may not even be able to consider my testimony? Or the *mask?*"

"There's nothing you can do about what goes on in this trial. The facts are the facts and the law is the law and you did your best. Stearns won't get away with anything, Audrey. His DNA is in that hat. You said he was there. The jury heard that."

I leaned against him, hoping to absorb some of his strength, somehow. "Today was the hardest part," he said, wrapping his arms around me, "what you feared the most, right? And you did it. I'm proud of you. But you're the hero here. You're the reason we know who robbed the bank and how they did it. If it wasn't for you, they never would have identified Ferdy in the first place, and none of the four would be cooling their backsides in jail right now!

Think about all you've accomplished almost singlehandedly. You even located the money in California – at least the part they recovered."

"And I may still be called to testify against Ferdy."

"If you are, you'll take the stand and tell what you know. This whole saga has had so many layers. When I think of the first time I saw you at his house, how could any of us have known that it was just the beginning of so much? I don't know how you're still standing."

"I just want my life back. Or at least be able to get on with a new one."

"We can start by heading back home."

"I need to do something before I come to your house," I said. "I want to take another look for that check – the one Harley had to have written to whoever put down the carpet in that bedroom."

"Why?"

"Because I assumed she used the company I'd hired to do the downstairs; I'd left her their card. But they had no record of doing any work in the building after that first installation. I want to know who she hired."

"Because?"

"Because she wouldn't tell me when I asked her, and because I know there's more to it. It's a piece to this puzzle I don't have. And I want it."

He took my hand. "Find something on the radio and enjoy the ride." We headed back to Camillus as the sky darkened and thunder rumbled ahead.

CHAPTER 39

I sat on my sofa looking through a box of checks written around the time the work had been done in the office's second floor. Not one looked like it had been made out to a carpet company or anything close. I recognized most of the people and companies as I flipped through them, and found the check numbers to be in order and none were missing.

My head ached. I was exhausted. Gloom, like a storm cloud, settled over me, pinning me to where I sat; I couldn't even attempt to get up to take something for it. Darkness encroached on my vision, and I recognized an inner rage coming to the fore, but was helpless to do anything about it.

A vision of Harley sitting at that table in front of me in handcuffs materialized in my head. She had made such a fool of me. But I had struck back. I'd turned her in, gotten her arrested. And now I wanted more; revenge for the lowdown, back-stabbing things she had done to me. The betrayal. The deceit. I saw myself pick up the hard plastic chair I'd sat in across from her that day. I held it high in the air and crashed it down on her, again and again, until her blood was everywhere.

I cradled my head in my hands. This did not seem like revenge to me. It seemed like murderous desire. Bloodlust. I fell sideways on the sofa and sobbed. What the hell was *wrong* with me?

I woke an hour later wrung out, the impact of the vision still so strong I checked my hands for blood. I went to the bedroom and looked in the mirror; I needed a major overhaul before I could go to Jack's. I took a shower, put on a little makeup and dressed, then picked up a takeout order from downstairs and headed to Tipp Hill.

* * *

I put our food in the oven to keep warm while I gathered plates and utensils, and poured us each a beer. We carried everything to the coffee table while I told Jack that I hadn't yet found the way Harley had paid for the bedroom carpeting.

"So there's no check and no sales receipt?" he asked.

"Nothing."

Jack's phone rang. "Hang on," he said, and he got up and walked toward the kitchen. He looked back at me and mouthed, "It's Matt."

There was no question in my mind that this would be something else that would widen and deepen the tar pit that had become my life. Jack came back into the room and sat next to me. I knew by the expression on his face that I was right.

"What?" I asked.

"Ferdy's trial starts tomorrow."

My stomach tied itself into a knot. "What's he being charged with?"

"Aiding and abetting, possession of stolen property, I don't know what else. Apparently he dropped the dime on Danny and Carl to get a reduced set of charges."

"So that was it?" I asked.

"Not quite," he said. "You're on deck."

I sagged against the back of the sofa. "I'm a hamster in a wheel. I keep going and going and I get nowhere."

"You'll be fine," he said.

Jack was always so confident. Always so sure things would turn out well. How could he always be so calm? So in control? Doing my best to match his demeanor, and feeling like a total fraud, I straightened my shoulders and pasted a smile on my face. "We could go out for breakfast before we go."

"That's my girl," he said.

MARGARET BELLE

CHAPTER 40

Outside the courtroom we sat on a bench, waiting for someone to tell me it was my turn to testify.

"I'm so nervous," I said.

"You'll do fine," he tried to reassure me again. How soon would he get sick of doing that?

"I can't wait until it's over."

"When you're done" he said, "we could stay and listen to the other witnesses if you want. Maybe Harley will testify today. I would love to see her pitted against Ferdy."

The door to the courtroom opened and a uniformed officer signaled me inside. Jack followed and took a seat near the back. "Just don't look at him," he whispered.

I walked to the stand, feeling Ferdy's eyes on me. I stared straight ahead and as I had before, put my left hand on a Bible, my right hand in the air, and swore to tell the truth. I sat down and waited for the first question. Tears welled up as I spotted Sean sitting with the other spectators. He looked stricken, and here I was, about to testify against his brother, all because he'd told me that Ferdy had been a teller.

The prosecuting attorney approached and smiled at me. "Please state your name for the court."

"Audrey Dory."

"And how do you know the defendant?"

"He was a client of my agency."

"And what is the nature of your business, Miss Dory?"

"I own a small advertising agency in Syracuse."

"That's Syracuse, New York, correct?"

"Yes, sorry."

"And what did your agency do for Mr. Finnegan?"

"Full-service advertising. Radio, television, print, Internet, helped him file for patents, other things."

"And did there come a time when you went to the defendant's home because you were concerned about him?"

"Yes, I went with his receptionist. She was worried because he was uncharacteristically late to the office and he couldn't be reached by phone."

"And what did you find when you went to his home that day?"

"His car was in the garage, but he didn't answer the door. We called the police."

"And what happened when the police arrived?"

"Turned out the door was unlocked and they went in. I saw things that indicated something had happened to him."

"Like what? What made you think that?"

"Several items were scattered on the floor and a cup of coffee had been left overturned on a table."

"And had you been in the defendant's home prior to that day, so you would be able to tell things looked different from any other day?"

"No, but I knew him, and he was obsessively neat. He never would have left a mess like that."

"And tell me, Miss Dory, did you see the defendant again?"

"Yes. In California."

"And do you know why the defendant was in California?"

Obviously, he was hiding from the law, I thought. "Yes, but if I tell you it will be speculation and maybe hearsay, because he's not the one who told me why he was there."

"I see," he said with a smile. I started to get warm. My head ached. "Thank you, Miss Dory, no more questions at this time." He turned to the judge, "Your Honor, I would like to reserve the right to recall this witness at a later time."

Ferdy's attorney was a woman with a wrinkled suit and hair that looked like it hadn't seen a comb in a week. She approached me with a smirk.

"Miss Dory, my client is being accused of participating in the armed robbery of the National Bank of Rochester a decade ago. While you were the agency of record for my client, did you ever know him to act in a dishonest way?"

"No."

"Did he ever try and skip out on a bill?"

"No."

"And was it my client who contacted you and asked you to make the trip to California?"

"No."

"And when you arrived in California, did you once see my client with this money you said you saw?"

"No." I didn't like the way she'd made it sound, like maybe I hadn't really seen the money at all.

"You were in Rochester the day of the robbery, weren't you?"

"Yes."

"In fact, you were a witness in the case against Danny Stearns, who was actually convicted of that armed robbery, is that right?"

"Yes."

"Thank you, Miss Dory," she said, "No more questions."

I went back to sit with Jack. "Was I awful?"

"You were fine."

Just then Ferdy's attorney said, "Your Honor, I would like to call Simon Barr to the stand."

The prosecutor jumped to his feet. "Wait a minute Your Honor, there is no one by that name on the witness list."

Ferdy's attorney kept right on going. "We were just made aware of this witness, Your Honor. His testimony will go to show that my client was never in possession of the stolen money."

The judge thought for a moment. "I'll allow the witness."

Ferdy's attorney informed the court, "Call Simon Barr to the stand."

A lanky man, about 35, with a scraggly beard and hair that could stand a wash and cut, ambled to the witness stand. Vowing to tell the truth, he sat down, looking very uncomfortable.

"Mr. Barr, do you know the defendant?"

Without looking up, he said, "No."

"Then why are you here as a witness?"

"Because I know who took the money – not from the bank – from where it was hidden. He pointed to Ferdy, "and it wasn't him."

"And is the person who took the money in this courtroom today?"

"Nope."

"And do you know the person's name? The one who took the money?"

"Harley something. Cool name. She hired me to install carpet." I grabbed Jack's arm.

Ferdy's lawyer continued. "Your Honor, Mr. Barr is referring to Harley Bud, who testified against Danny Stearns, the convicted robber." He turned back to his fidgeting witness. "And where did you install this carpeting, Mr. Barr?"

"In one of the bedrooms in the building where she worked. And I did the stairs."

"Objection!" shouted the prosecutor, "What does installing carpet have to do with the stolen money?"

"I'm getting to that, Your Honor," said the rumpled attorney. She turned back to the witness. "And do you install carpeting for a living?"

"I did that day." A chuckle arose from the observers in the courtroom; Simon Barr smiled in response.

"How about on other days, Mr. Barr," the attorney continued, "did you ever install carpet for a living before that day?"

"When I was in high school. Summer job."

"But not since then?"

"No. Not until that day."

"And how would this Harley find someone like you?"

"I don't know how she found me. She knew a guy who knew a guy."

"And what did you charge to install the carpet?"

"I didn't have to charge. I was happy to take what she offered."

"And what was the offer?"

My heart was pounding so hard I swore I could hear it. I could hardly breathe.

"A hundred grand." A few gasps could be heard around the courtroom, including the one from me.

"You were paid one hundred thousand dollars to put down carpet?"

"Well, yeah, and to pull out some floorboards." He smiled, "There was a lot of money under that floor. She offered me a cut to pull 'em up. Then she took out the money and I replaced the boards and put the carpet back down. She told me not to say anything; I told her not to worry."

"And, Mr. Barr," she said, as she pointed to Ferdy, "was the defendant there?"

"Nope, just that Harley girl." He motioned with his hands, as though he were revving up a motorcycle. "*Vroom! Vroom!*"

"No more questions."

Before the judge had time to finish asking the prosecutor if he wanted to cross-examine Mr. Barr, he was on his feet and nose-to-nose with the guy. "Have you ever been arrested, Mr. Barr?"

"Maybe."

"Not maybe, yes or no? There's no sense in lying, because I can ask for a recess and get your record pulled before everyone files out of this room."

"Once," he answered, "for stealing a ring from a house while I was delivering a mattress."

"Any other time?"

"I took cash from a house when I was delivering furniture."

"In other words, you would take a job with a company whose employees entered homes legally to do your thieving?"

"Basically." He rubbed his beard and then ran his hand over the top of his head. "But I never did any time."

"And so what made you take this carpeting job?"

"Like I said, a hundred grand."

"Mr. Barr. Did you receive immunity to testify for this defendant?"

"I did."

"So you could say anything, is that right? And you wouldn't be in trouble?"

"That's the way it works."

"Do you have any of the money left?"

He shook his head. "I went to Vegas."

"Ah, and you lost most of it?"

"All of it."

"And why should the court believe anything a thief such as yourself, says here today?" Simon Barr shrugged and looked at the judge as if to ask, what does he want from me?

"No more questions, Your Honor."

The judge dismissed Simon Barr, who all but ran from the room. "That's all for today," he said, as he banged his gavel. "We'll reconvene tomorrow at ten."

"Want to come back?" asked Jack.

"Hell, no. I got the answer I wanted. Take me home – please!"

The ride back to Jack's house was quiet, each of us lost in our own thoughts, until Jack said, "Let's get married."

"Excuse me? I thought we already did that part." I held up my left hand and wiggled my ring finger.

"I mean soon. Tomorrow. Whatever. Let's get our license and just do it. Life is too short."

"I do have my maid of honor," I said, warming quickly to the idea.

"Lisa, right? And Matt will stand up for me."

"What about your family? I haven't even met them."

"Don't worry," he smiled, "there'll be time for that after the honeymoon."

"Worry's my middle name," I said.

"We'll find a justice of the peace and just do it."

"You know, you can be pretty romantic for a tough guy," I laughed.

"How about one week from today?" he asked. I was pleased at the excitement in his voice.

"That should give me enough time to buy a dress and shoes, and I want to at least carry a little bouquet."

"Sounds easy enough. So do you want me in uniform? Or a suit?"

"Surprise me."

"Okay, and I'll figure out a honeymoon destination, although on a cop's pay, we won't be hitting a beach in Hawaii."

"What? Cop's don't make a lot of money? I may have to reconsider marrying you under those conditions."

"Well, let me know," he said, "before I put out good money for new shoelaces."

"You know," I said, "I think I'll stay in my apartment until we get married, do you mind? I can get my things into storage, clean the place, and try to get back the down payment I put on that new apartment."

"Sure. Want to go there now?"

"Let's have dinner first and then go our separate ways."

We parked and entered Krabby Kirk's through the back door. The place was pretty full, but we were able to grab a table near the stairs to my place. "Soon the upstairs will be a billiards room," I told him. "Men will be spilling beer on my floor, telling dirty jokes, and scratching themselves in my living room. It makes me sick."

"Nothing you can do about it, Kiddo. Just remember, you'll have way more square footage when you move into my place. And I promise to never scratch myself in your presence."

I looked at him and forced a smile. While he thought that would sound good to me, it sounded anything *but* good. I'd already looked around his house to see if there was a room small enough to make my own; somewhere I could go when he wasn't home. Or when I had an anxiety attack, or when I just couldn't deal with so much space. I hadn't found one. Maybe I would leave the down payment on my new apartment alone; maybe I would need it. After all, I'd broken up with Eddie while we were engaged; what if I ended up doing the same thing to Jack?

CHAPTER 41

I spent a few days looking for a dress suitable for standing in front of a JP and went shopping with Lisa for hers. I found a sleeveless, knee-length, off-white silk dress with a bit of lace at the neck. It was fitted at the waist and then flared to a full skirt. Within an hour of the purchase I'd found shoes to go with it.

Lisa's dress was also sleeveless and knee-length. She'd picked a soft green, perfect for the time of year, and one she could wear again. We spent some time at the florist, whose shop was located on the other side of her salon, ordering her flowers and mine.

I picked a mixture of pink, white, and yellow tulips, tied with an off-white silk ribbon. Lisa's bouquet was of pale pink tulips, tied with a dark green ribbon. We giggled like school girls and I realized I was genuinely excited about marrying Jack. I ordered two small boutonnieres, just in case he and Matt showed up in suits.

Three days before the wedding, Jack called to tell me he'd found a perfect spot for the ceremony at Green Lakes State Park, about twenty minutes away, and a judge - the officiant who would meet us there at 3 p.m. on the appointed day. The location was ideal; a setting with glacial lakes, surrounded by plush, upland forest. Things were coming together.

With only three days to go, I motivated myself to get the office totally cleaned out, with the exception of the mess the police had made upstairs; the landlord could talk to them about that. I rented a storage unit and made several trips with Nelly loaded to the gills. By dinnertime, even the boxes from my apartment were stacked and locked in their new, hopefully temporary, home.

I thought about putting the main pieces to the curb, since Jack's house was fully furnished, but then hesitated, thinking about the apartment that would soon be mine. I would need them; my sofa and chair, my bed, my kitchen table, my TV; all the big stuff.

I called a moving company and made arrangements for them to move it all into storage while we were on our honeymoon. Then I called and rented a second, larger unit, with instructions to allow the moving company to gain access.

With the dress and flower shopping sprees over, I'd begun to feel a little nauseous thinking about getting married. Not so much for myself, but for Jack. He was so much like Eddie; he would love me, and care for me – he'd end up living his life for me. What if he had to eventually quit the force because I took up so much of his time? He'd no longer be able to afford the house he so clearly loved. Where would we live? Would we end up on welfare with neither of us working? I couldn't do that to him. I just couldn't.

I began to dabble in excuses as to why I couldn't marry him, but nothing that he would believe came to mind. I began to panic. Could I run away? Should I have gone with Harley in the first place? We could have taken off for parts unknown if I hadn't been working with the police.

Jack had given me a list of reasons why I shouldn't go with her – sane reasons, and at the time they sounded solid to me. But now, I thought that if I'd gone through with Harley's plan, and not been swayed by Jack and his proposal (or gotten out of my apartment before he showed up that day), I would be on the run, sure, but maybe my mind might be right. I looked at my engagement ring. It no longer seemed like a promise. It seemed like a threat. But not to me. To Jack.

My cell phone rang and it was Lisa, asking if I felt like meeting her for dinner. Wanting to rid myself of this foul mood, I agreed to meet her downstairs at the bar. By the time I got there, two frosty glasses of beer were being served.

"Man," I said, "you're quick."

"I was already here when I called you," she laughed.

"Well, I need this big time," I said, picking up my glass.

"Why?" she asked. "What happened to the great mood you were in? The mood you're still supposed be in? Come on! You're getting *married!* Look at that gorgeous ring!"

"Oh, my God, Lisa, I don't have a wedding ring for Jack! How could something like that have slipped my mind?"

"Does he have one for you?"

"I don't know – he must have. I don't even know what size he wears."

"Call him," she said. "Ask if he wants one. Some guys don't."

I nodded and pulled out my cell. I listened until the call went to voice mail. Crap. After the beep, I left a brief question: "Jack, do you want a wedding band? If so, what size?"

Lisa and I had finished dinner by the time he called back. "Of course I want wedding band. We just never talked about it, and I didn't know if you could afford one, or if you'd let me pay for both of them. It was kind of a dicey thing, so I just let it go."

"Do you know what size you wear?" I asked, not really surprised that he'd said he wanted to wear one right off the bat.

"I do. I had the jeweler size my finger when I bought your engagement ring. It's an 11."

"Do you want yellow or white gold? Or platinum?" I prayed it wasn't the latter; a wedding band in that metal would probably take every nickel I had.

"Surprise me."

"It's getting closer," I said, "any second thoughts?" Was I hoping he'd say yes?

"Not a one," he said.

CHAPTER 42

The day was warm, the sun was shining, and Lisa knocked on the door, ready to help me get dressed for my big day. I was a wreck, but had finally reconciled myself to going through with the wedding and convinced myself that I was happy about it. I loved Jack. And I was better with him than without him.

"You look beautiful!" I told her, as she breezed through the door in her maid of honor outfit. "That dress was a great choice. I like it even better today than when you picked it out!"

"Your turn," she said, and she unzipped the dress bag and pulled out mine.

"Oh," I cried, "I'd already forgotten how gorgeous it is."

"Go finish your makeup first," she said. "You don't want to drop your lipstick on it and I can see your hands shaking."

"Don't say that – it will make me more nervous than I already am!" I went into the bathroom and put on what little makeup I planned to wear, and then came back out to where she was standing, holding my dress.

"Okay, let's get you into this!" Lisa zipped and buttoned, fluffed my hair, put my shoes on the floor in front of me, and when I slipped them on, pronounced me ready. "Do you have Jack's ring?"

"Right over there with our flowers," I said, pointing to the kitchen table.

She opened the box. "Oh, Audrey, this must have cost you a fortune!"

"No kidding," I said, "but he's going to wear it for a long time, so I went for it."

A car door slammed outside and Lisa went to the window. "Audrey, come here!"

A white limousine had pulled up in front of the apartment. The driver got out and waited by the door we would use to get in. "I can't believe Jack did that!" I said. Excitement bubbled up inside me and I felt a tear slip down my cheek. We gathered our purses, locked the door behind us, and headed down to the limo that would deliver me to the spot where I would start my new life.

* * *

Following a winding roadway inside the park, the limo headed down a path that looked like it had seen more foot traffic than motorized, and I began to wonder where this perfect spot Jack had found was. We were now surrounded by forest and the sunlight dappled in and out of the trees, playing over the waxed surface of the limousine.

We rounded a corner and I caught my breath as we came upon a clearing. Two rows of white pillar candles glowed under hurricane lamps, outlining an aisle that led to an arbor made of bent and twisted twigs, with pink roses wound through. Strings of crystals dropped from the arch here and there, swaying in the soft breeze, shooting prisms of light over the entire area where Jack and I would face each other and say our vows.

"It's my wedding present to you," whispered Lisa, with tears in her eyes. "I wanted your big day to be one you'd never forget. A small wedding doesn't mean a boring wedding!"

I hugged her, wondering how someone like me had managed to snag a friend so wonderful; so unselfish and giving. "Thank you," I whispered through tears.

"Don't wreck your makeup!" she laughed, and handed me a tissue. "Just dab at your eyes. Don't rub."

"Yes, Ma'am."

Suddenly Jack and Matt were standing by the arbor with the officiant. Instead of uniforms, my groom and his best man had donned dark suits and Lisa had seen to it that they had received their boutonnieres of tiny pink tulips, which were neatly pinned to their lapels. I had never seen two more handsome men in my life.

The driver opened the door and Lisa and I stepped out of the limousine and into the light. Lisa started down the candle-lined path, looking beautiful. When she reached the arbor, she moved to the left and turned to face me. I stood at the end of the path taking it all in before I took my first step toward Jack, who would be my husband in less than half an hour. I'd never been as happy as I was at this moment.

Somewhere behind me a car door slammed, and I hoped that no one was going to start setting up a picnic or a family reunion within earshot of my wedding. I saw the happy looks on the faces of my wedding party change and then I heard a man's voice behind me.

"Audrey Dory – FBI. You're wanted for questioning in the investigation of an armed robbery in Rochester, New York."

MARGARET BELLE

CHAPTER 43

I turned to see a middle-aged man walking toward me. "FBI Agent Phillips," he said. "You'll have to come with me."

"Jack!" I shouted. Then to the man who had taken hold of my arm, "What are you doing? I'm getting married!" My vision narrowed, and tiny spots appeared wherever I looked.

"Hang on!" Jack shouted, as he and Matt ran up the aisle. "I'm Officer Jack Morey, Syracuse Police Department. Can I see some ID?"

"Sorry about this," the agent said to Jack, as he pulled his badge from his jacket pocket. "Orders."

"There's clearly been a misunderstanding," said Jack. "Audrey was a key witness in that case! There's been some gigantic mix-up here. Let us go through with our wedding and then we'll straighten it all out."

My throat tightened and my vision continued to narrow, and darken; I knew I would pass out if I didn't get some relief. I struggled against the agent. "Let go of me!" I managed to get away and started to run to Jack, but Agent Phillips caught me and snapped handcuffs around my wrists.

"She's coming with me," he called in Jack's direction, as he led me toward a dark blue sedan. "You're free to meet us at the Federal Building if you want."

"Leave me *alone!*" I screamed. "Jack! Help me! Please!"

Through a haze, I saw Lisa extinguish the last of the candles along my wedding aisle, and I heard Jack say, "I'll be right behind you." His words floated over me as I turned to see the limousine drive away. Jack followed my eyes, "Listen, Audrey, we'll work this out. I'm sorry the wedding was ruined, but we'll get it done as soon as this is over." His voice began to fade away. "We'll elope this time. Just don't..."

A storm inside my brain swirled so violently that I could no longer tell what was going on around me. Like a wild animal caught in a trap, I screamed with my mouth open so wide that my face hurt, and I struggled to free myself from the agent's grip with so much force that I thought the handcuffs would sever my hands. And that was the last thing I remembered.

* * *

I woke up in a hospital bed, squinting at bright overhead lights. Jack was sitting by my bedside, and when he saw me open my eyes, he stood and said my name. "How do you feel?" he asked.

"What happened?" I reached for him, but my wrist was shackled to the rail of the bed. "Jack!" I cried, "What's this for?" I tried my other arm and found it was shackled to the opposite rail. I looked around the small room. "Where am I?"

"You're in a place where you can get the help you need, Audrey. You lashed out at the FBI agent and resisted all of our attempts to calm you down. You fought him. And then you passed out. Those," he indicated the restraints, "were ordered because you were thrashing, even while you were unconscious."

"How long have I been here?"

"Two days. They contacted Dr. Steele and she got an emergency order to move you here from the hospital for observation."

"Dr. Steele! So that's it! She's finally had her way! She got me in here when I couldn't defend myself. How did they even know about her?" Then I realized how. "*You* told them about Dr. Steele?"

"I had no choice, Audrey, you were out of control. You need to get it together."

"Don't tell me what I need to do!"

Calmly, he asked, "Do you have any idea why the FBI wants to question you? They said you had something to do with the stolen money."

"That's ridiculous."

"Is there anything you want to tell me?"

"Like what?"

"I don't know Audrey! I'm asking you!" He rubbed his hands over his face. "Sorry. Can you tell me anything or not?"

I shook my arms and the shackles rattled against the metal railing. "I can't believe this – do they really think I'm going to try and *hurt* somebody?"

"They don't want you to hurt yourself."

Anger boiled up in me like hot lava. "Get me out of this!" I screamed. "*Now!*" And I struggled against the restraints until Jack turned and left the room. When my arms finally gave out, I threw my head back and surrendered to wracking sobs that finally expelled some of the pressure that had built up in my chest.

An hour or so passed before Dr. Steele knocked on the door and came in, even though I hadn't invited her to do so. "Hello, Audrey," she said, almost in a whisper. "How are you feeling?"

"Fuck you."

"Okay, well, we're angry. I understand that."

"So you're angry too?"

"All right," she smiled, "*you're* angry."

"You have some nerve," I hissed, "what were you doing, biding your time until I couldn't defend myself so you could squirrel me away? I know this is where you've wanted me, so are you happy?"

"Happy? No. But relieved that maybe you'll get the help you need now – if, that is, you start telling me the truth – all the things I just know you've not shared during our sessions together. How do you expect me to help you, Audrey? After all, like Dr. Collins, I've had to go by what you've told me, how you've described your symptoms. If you haven't been honest, or if you've left things out, your diagnosis may not even be valid, and in that case, your treatment would not be helpful to you. While GAD may be a part of it, you could also be suffering from a second disorder that's going unchecked. Leaving out important information when you're talking to your therapists can do you more harm than good."

"And you think kidnapping me and putting me in here – this is a psych ward, is it not? – that this will somehow make me feel closer to you? Make me want to spill my guts? Are you crazy?" And having asked that question, I laughed. "Maybe you are. Maybe it's you who needs help. Ever think of that?"

"Do you remember fighting with Agent Phillips?"

"I don't want to talk to you anymore."

"Fine," she said, "I'll go. But I'll be back tomorrow." I ignored her and refused to look in her direction until she had gone. Truth was, I did remember. I remembered my beautiful wedding being ruined by the sound of that car door slamming. And I knew why Agent Phillips had come.

It was back in California – the night Harley sat on my bed and confessed that she had the money and told me where she kept it. I'd sent her to the pharmacy, pretending I was out of my medication, which had given me time to find the suitcases and remove what I could fit into my duffle – $900,000.00. Even though the bags had been locked, I'd known the code – knew what it had to be. I'd split the remaining stacks of bills *between the three bags, rubbed down any areas I'd touched with a towel, and put the suitcases back where I'd found them. By the time Harley returned with the medicine, I'd done the deed.*

The police had been no problem. I'd told the officer about the suitcases and waited while he looked for them. I'd watched as he picked up each of the locked bags – and when he shook the largest one, I'd given him the code, along with an explanation for how I knew it. The fact that he hadn't opened all of them and counted the money was pure luck, I have to admit. But he'd had a lot to do that day – people to call, evidence to collect, a whole crime scene to direct. So I wasn't that surprised.

I'd left most of my clothes, which were the same size as Harley's, in one of the dressers to make room for the stacks of bills in my duffle, so even if the police riffled the drawers, the clothes they found would not raise any red flags.

The money had been transported to the airport, along with me, by law enforcement. I'd arrived at LAX more than two hours before the flight to Philly. As soon as the officer who'd escorted me to security was out of sight, I'd gotten out of line and hopped a bus into the city, where I'd purchased two sturdy boxes, several newspapers, and packing tape. In a public restroom stall, I'd transferred the money into the boxes, made balls out of the pages of the newspaper, and stuffed them in and around the stacks so nothing would shift. Then I'd taken the boxes, which each weighed around ten pounds, across the street to a UPS counter and mailed them to myself. I declined insurance, of course, and watched the man at the counter add the boxes to a pile on the floor. Then I'd crossed my fingers and, channeling Harley, hoped that the cosmos and someone in brown shorts would bring the money back to me.

The boxes had been delivered to my apartment, just minutes before my subpoena to testify at Danny Stearns' trial. I'd signed with a scribble and added the packages to the stacks I had readied for storage. And that's where they were at this moment - locked in a temperature controlled, fireproof, waterproof unit, with all my other stuff. Safe and sound. I had to smile; I could still separate people from their money.

CHAPTER 44

I had two surprise visitors the next day. Dr. Collins was the first. "Hello, Audrey," she said. "It's been a while."

"Ten years or so," I said, shocked to see her after all this time. "It's good to see you, even though I'm a little embarrassed to have you find me here."

"Dr. Steele called me," she said, "and I'm so happy she did. You exhibited some anger toward her and sent her away, is that right?"

"You bet I did. She had me put in here while I was unconscious. I had no say in it."

"Well, you were originally taken to a hospital," she explained. "Dr. Steele took the necessary legal steps out of concern for you, to get you moved to this facility. If it means anything, I'm of the opinion that doing so was a good thing."

"I know what she did."

"Yes," she said calmly, as she pulled the visitor's chair to my bedside. "But you're no longer restrained, so take that as a good sign; you've already shown improvement."

"They give me medication," I said. "That's as good as restraints."

"I've come to ask if you'd allow me to work with you while you're here. Dr. Steele is not going to be able to help you if you're holding onto that anger, so what do you say? We can do some hard work and get you out of here."

"And into a jail cell?"

"Well, what exactly is it you're supposed to have done?"

I explained about the robbery and the culprits involved. "They apparently think I had something to do with the money; it's ridiculous. I thought the whole thing had been solved. Danny Stearns and Carl are in jail – I don't know yet what happened to Ferdy. I heard Harley received immunity for testifying against the others, and was let go."

"Dr. Steele told me about Jack. Do you see him regularly?" she asked, changing the subject.

"He comes by most days. I expect him sometime today. I think he's bringing my friend Lisa with him."

"Well, I have to tell you, Audrey, both Dr. Steele and I feel that we haven't made the progress we'd hoped to with you, and we want you to understand that neither of us would sit in judgment, no matter what you revealed." I nodded, wondering how many of her other patients were not giving her the straight skinny. Did anyone ever tell their therapist everything? "So should I come back tomorrow?" she asked. "I can arrange for my patients to see one of the other psychologists in my practice, temporarily."

I had to get out of here somehow, and if that was what it would take, then I'd do it. "I guess."

"Wonderful. See you bright and early." She put the chair back in the corner and left with a little wave. I stared at the chair; it was like the one I'd been sitting in the day my mother died. I remembered how my grandmother and aunt had stood by her hospital bed, blocking my view of her. But I'd been able to see her hand. It was all black, and her fingernails were gone. Most of the skin had peeled away, but even so, a needle attached to a tube was stuck right into the back of it. I remember hearing someone say that it was the only spot left to put the needle in.

That morning my mother and I had been home, just the two of us, as always, because my father was already dead. I thought, as a child, that my mother didn't love me. She yelled and screamed, and accused me of doing things I had not done. "Who else could have broken this?" she would yell into my face, not remembering that she had bumped the expensive piece of crystal off the table herself. "Who else could have misplaced my cigarettes?" she'd scream, when I knew perfectly well that she had moved them herself. Nothing ever happened in the house that couldn't somehow be twisted into being my fault. A juvenile delinquent, she'd called me; a bad seed. My father would still be alive, she'd say, if he hadn't had to work so hard to provide for me.

What about you? I wanted to shout back. Didn't he provide for you too? How come he had a heart attack over just me?

I didn't understand at age six what a drunk was. Now I knew my mother was one, and that she probably never remembered what she said to me from one day to the next, and had no control over how she said it. But I was little, and helpless to do anything about my situation. Anger built up and built up and built up, until I couldn't "be there" any more.

From then on, when my mother screamed and yelled, when she struck me, when she threw my dinner plate on the floor then made me clean it up, when she pounded her fists on the walls and screamed my father's name, I would check out. My mind would shut down. And since I couldn't even hear during those check-outs, it was like watching her act in a silent movie, and often I would find her gyrations funny.

One day I laughed, out loud I guess, at her flailing fists, at her contorted face, and she'd turned on me with such hatred in her eyes that I'd run upstairs to her bedroom and hidden in her closet. She'd searched through the house for me, yelling my name louder and louder, getting madder and madder, until she'd ended up back in her room, exhausted, and collapsed on the bed.

While I waited to be sure she was really asleep, and not just pretending, listening for sounds that would lead her to me, I'd noticed some of my father's jackets hanging on a rack in the back. In the pocket of one of them was a lighter. I'd flicked it three times before a flame finally appeared, and I remember being startled that I had actually made it work; so much so that I'd dropped it. My mother's nightgowns were the first to catch fire. Then the other clothes began to smolder. Her skirts, her slacks, and the beautiful long sparkly dresses that I'd never seen her wear, all suddenly burst into flame. I'd run from the closet and tried to wake my mother, but I couldn't rouse her.

I'd stood frozen at the bedroom door, watching the flames slide across the carpet, climb up the drapes, and peel the wallpaper. When the sheets on the bed caught, I watched, mesmerized, until the hems of my mother's slacks were rimmed with fire. Her hair was next; it collapsed around her head like wet cotton candy, and I gagged at the smell. Smoke found me in the hallway and I'd pulled my shirt up over my mouth and nose as the skin on my mother's face began to darken and peel like the wallpaper.

Why doesn't she get up? I wondered. I'd tried to call to her again, but I had no voice. I turned and ran down the curved staircase, away from the screeching smoke detectors, through the foyer with the impossibly high ceilings, and outside. The driveway was long, with two jogs, and I ran as fast as I could down it and then across the yard to the house next door.

Still unable to speak, I pulled the lady who lived there outside and pointed to the house. Smoke was pouring out of the upstairs by then and the neighbor picked me up and ran back into her house and called for the fire department. An ambulance took my mother away and my grandmother arrived at the neighbor's house shortly after to collect me.

So while I was sitting in the hospital that day, looking at my mother's burned hand, I was glad that I couldn't see the rest of her. And when she died, I knew it wasn't because I couldn't find a nurse – she was dead because I had set fire to the house that morning. Anyway, I prefer the nurse story. Sometimes, in my head, I can almost make myself forget about the fire part of it altogether.

And that's why there's no picture of my mother in my gold locket. My grandmother had put one in, along with the one of my father, but I'd secretly taken it out and flushed it down the toilet. I couldn't carry a picture of my mother around with me; it would always remind me of what she looked like at the end. And I knew that with her picture inside, the chain would always feel hot around my neck. Hot with the heat of the fire. I understood that when I was six.

My father's picture I would keep forever. He was the only man in my life I had not disappointed. Had he lived, I'm sure I would have dashed his hopes and dreams for me, broken his heart in some awful way. But now I would be daddy's little girl forever, even if in reality it had only been true for a very brief time.

Later, my second surprise visitor appeared. A *real* surprise; Harley. "Hi Audrey," she said with a little smile, "can I come in?" Her many layers of love beads rattled against each other as she swooshed to my bedside in her tie-dyed maxi skirt and billowy peasant blouse.

"What's with you and all this 60s crap, anyway?" I asked. "You weren't even alive then."

"Oh, come on, Aud," she said, "don't be mad."

"No, really," I said. "You're one bead away from swapping a hippie compound for a gypsy camp."

"And you're one pill away from wearing a tinfoil hat. There. Now we're even. Come on," she said, "I came to see you, didn't I? Be nice. I brought you this," and she pulled a box of Frankincense sticks from her huge cloth tote, and put it on the table.

"I heard you were back on the street," I said. "What happened to Ferdy?"

"He was found guilty for his part in the robbery. Now he has another trial – attempted murder of Tony. I'm sure he'll be found guilty there too."

"Good. I hope he rots in jail." I noticed her face change when I said that. "I can't help that you were a couple," I said. "That's how I feel."

"Did you want me to rot in jail too?" she asked.

"I don't even think about you."

"Oh, right," she smiled. "I just wanted to tell you how sorry I am that all this happened to you; and for my part it in. I was crazy, sorry – I didn't mean – well, it was not a good decision on my part to get involved with Carl and those guys. It all just seemed to happen a little at a time, until I was stuck, you know? I wish I could make it up to you, that's all."

"You wished me a life in a place like this," I said.

"I know. I didn't mean it. We hurt each other. But I was hoping we could get passed it."

I looked at her and thought maybe there *was* something she could do to help me, but did I dare take a chance? I didn't think I had a choice. She was the only one who could possibly do what I needed.

"Harley," I said, "I'm in trouble."

"What kind of trouble?"

I motioned for her to come closer. "I have the money."

"What money?"

"You know what money."

Her eyes grew as big as saucers. "The bank's money? The part that's missing? *You* have it?"

I nodded and put a finger in front of my lips, warning her to keep her voice down. "I took it out of your suitcase when you went to the pharmacy for me that night, remember?"

"You little shit! And where is it now?"

"Can I trust you? I mean really trust you?"

"How much do you have?"

"Nine hundred thousand. And you gave a hundred grand to that asshole Simon Barr, so that's how two million ended up being left in the suitcases."

Harley broke out laughing. "Are you kidding me? I can't believe you did that! How did you get it back here?"

"I packed it in two boxes and UPS'd them to myself before I flew out of LAX. They're in a storage unit with the stuff from my apartment."

"Oh, my God." She looked at me in amazement. "What if they'd X-rayed the boxes – or opened them?"

"I sent them by ground, not air, so no X-Ray, and used my business account ID number, which indicated I was a known shipper. UPS doesn't open boxes on their trucks unless they're leaking, or smell funny, or can't be delivered because of an incorrect address. I wasn't worried."

"So what do you need me to do?"

"If the FBI finds out I have it, I'm afraid they'll put my ass in jail. Listen, when you rented the post office box in Warners, they gave you two keys, right?"

"Yes. Why?"

"I mailed the storage unit key to myself – to the same box. So go get it and take the two boxes out of storage for me. The place is on the corners of Milton and Bennett; you know where that is, right?"

"I can find it."

"The boxes are marked 'kitchen' with an underline. Drive them an hour or two in any direction – except not near Rochester – and put them in another storage unit. There's four hundred and fifty thousand in each box. We'll have to let the money sit there for a while, but we'll just keep paying the rent on the unit. I'll split it with you. Will you do it?"

Just then Jack and Lisa walked in. Jack immediately turned on Harley. "What the hell are you doing here?"

Harley took two steps backward. "I just wanted to see how Audrey was doing, that's all."

A vein in Jack's forehead swelled until I thought it would pop. "Leave right now," he ordered. "You're about the last person she needs to see. Get your ass out of here before I *help* you out."

"Okay, okay, I'm going," she said. She waved and winked at me behind Jack's back as she walked out of the room, and I hoped I wasn't going to get screwed over by her again.

"Did she upset you?" he asked. Lisa stood next to Jack and asked the same question with her eyes.

"No, I'm fine. It's so good to see you two. Jack, what's going on with the FBI? What do they think I did?"

"They have surveillance video of you leaving the airport during your layover at LAX on your return trip, and of you carrying two boxes into a UPS store. They know you sent them to yourself, and how much they weighed, and they want to ask you what was in them. Obviously, they think it was the missing money, since you were the only other person in the house with Harley and Ferdy. They think they're right and they won't give up – not if they think those boxes are out there somewhere."

"I did mail boxes to myself," I said, "but I threw them away. I unpacked them when they arrived and tossed them. All they had in them was crap I didn't want to carry on the plane, stuff I would have had to throw away when I went through security. And stuff that just weighed down my duffle bag. Shampoo, my blow dryer, shoes, just personal stuff! I was exhausted and didn't want to lug it around. What's the big deal?"

"Two boxes?" he asked. "Almost twenty pounds worth?"

I tried to look sad, and disappointed in him. "You believe me, right?"

He hesitated, but then said, "Of course I do."

Lisa said, "We *both* do," and she put her hand on Jack's arm, so easily, so familiar, that I knew in an instant it wasn't the first time. Lisa had fallen for Jack.

CHAPTER 45

I worked with Dr. Collins two days a week, and with a psychiatrist who had wormed his way into our sessions, three days a week. I finally told Dr. Collins all about the fire. She in turn tried her best to convince me that it was a terrible accident and that was all.

"You may have been suffering from a form of Post-Traumatic Stress Disorder all of these years, Audrey, and not knowing the details about the fire has kept me from delving into that with you." I almost felt sorry for her, knowing that although she considered my big revelation to be a major breakthrough, she would never get at all of the deep, dark secrets that comprised my past.

I had worked my way down to low doses of my meds by lying to Dr. Collins, and struggling with my demons on my own as best I could. Then came the day that I was to be released from the loony bin into the wild. Dr. Collins brought in an outfit she'd purchased for me to wear home, so I didn't have to put my wedding dress back on. I collected my personal effects, including my engagement ring and locket that they'd held for me in a safe. I agreed to a therapy schedule, said my goodbyes, and called for a taxi, even though I didn't know where I would have it take me. I hadn't called Jack or Lisa to tell them I'd been released – that was over now. The two of them could maybe have a normal life together, free of me; they both deserved that.

Now that I was "out," and finally free to be me, as they say, excitement rushed through me; I dabbled in hope that a bright new future was possible. I greedily filled my lungs with the afternoon's fresh air, delicious after the stinging antiseptic smell of the hospital, and reveled in the warm sunlight, a luxury after having lived under the harsh glare of fluorescents.

I gave the cabbie directions to Krabby Kirk's, thinking that maybe the plans for the billiards room had been scuttled and I could have my old place back. I didn't really believe that, but needed to at least start out on familiar turf. Maybe it wasn't too late to get into the new efficiency apartment.

I had to live as simply as I had in the past, not like I had a fortune stashed away. Harley and I would need to be careful and resist the temptation to start spending. I wondered how long it would take for her to get in touch with me, to let me know where she'd put our money. We'd decided that it was best for her to stay away from the hospital, so no one would get the idea we were becoming friends again and raise suspicions; no calls or texts that could be traced.

Soon I was in front of Krabby Kirk's, relishing the sights and sounds and aromas I knew were waiting for me, and I was looking forward to sinking my teeth into a bison burger and sipping a cold beer. I paid the fare, climbed out of the cab, and was walking up the sidewalk when I heard a car pull up behind me. I turned to see a police car, and an officer I didn't recognize got out. "Audrey Dory?"

"Yes?"

"You're under arrest for possession of stolen property and for shipping a large sum of money across state lines." He handcuffed me and proceeded to read me my rights.

I knew immediately what had happened. Harley had moved the money all right. And my guess was that she had taken one of the boxes and left the other one in the storage unit for the police to find. Goddamn her. She'd probably called in one of her anonymous tips to lead the police right to it and left the key for them. She'd been the last person I'd wanted to put any amount of trust in, but she was the only one I had left to turn to. And now she was gone who-knew-where, with $450,000.00, and I was going to jail for having the rest. I'd bet my life on it.

* * *

My court-appointed attorney, who gave me the news that no charges would be filed against me in Miller Crawford's death, managed to have the current charges against me dropped. In a nutshell (no pun intended), I didn't steal the money from the bank. There were no witnesses to my taking it from Harley and I couldn't be made to testify against myself to say that I had.

Yes, one box of bills turned up in my storage unit, but on balance, I'd worked with the police to find Harley in California, and in the process, turned up Ferdy for them. And because I am being treated for a mental disorder, and because the bank robbery was so old, and the bank got its money back (save for the $100,000.00 that Simon Barr lost in Vegas and the $450,000.00 Harley made off with), they didn't want to bother pressing charges against me. I'm glad – I heard the toilets in jail were right out in the open.

The judge, who'd made it clear he could give me jail time, said he felt that incarceration would not help the deeper problems he thought I had. He was concerned that I'd been ejected from the psych ward too soon, mostly because my involvement in criminal activity had not been known at the time of my release. He said he hoped I could be helped.

Dr. Collins informed him that I'd previously been in her care, as well as in the care of Dr. Steele, and that seemed to impress him. They'd promised that although they would be returning to their practices, I would be well taken care of in the facility. He'd spoken to me in positive terms and his eyes had sparkled with optimism. I'd tried to sparkle back, but it hadn't been easy, knowing it meant I'd be subjected to more sessions, if not with those two women, then with other shrinks who just *knew* they could set me right. They had no idea who they were dealing with.

Jack was at the hearing, of course, with Lisa. At the end, when I was given a few minutes to speak with them, I apologized to Lisa and told Jack to forget about me; that I was never going to be okay enough to be a wife and God forbid, a mother. He tried to protest, but the look on his face told me he knew I was right. I took off my engagement ring and pressed it into his hand, and they watched as I was led away to the van that would take me back to the sanitarium, which Dr. Collins was now trying to pass off as some sort of a mental health spa.

A look back confirmed what I'd thought about the two of them, as I watched Jack wrap a sobbing Lisa in his arms. I cried too, not only over lost love and lost friendship, but at the disappointment and heartbreak I'd caused two of the sweetest people I'd ever known.

As time passed, I did some thinking about why I'd packed up part of the stolen money and sent it to myself, and I managed to develop a few theories. Maybe my judgment had been permanently clouded by all the crap I'd endured in my life. Maybe I thought I deserved it for losing my business at the hands of Danny, and Carl, and Ferdy, and most of all, Harley; for being used and made a fool of by them. Maybe my thinking was skewed by my failed relationships and for the years of mental problems I've lived with because of the nightmare I call my childhood and oh, yes, the image of my mother burning in her bed, that will not let me go.

Maybe I thought I could outrun it all with the money. Taking it had certainly been an act of desperation; a decision that had to be made in a hurry, before Harley returned from the pharmacy, or Ferdy came to.

There'd been no opportunity to think through what the consequences might be, or even enough time to ask myself what taking the money would say about me personally. I'd simply taken it.

Jack had said that all perps were caught because they made one stupid mistake, but I'd made two, and they both involved Harley. I'd taken the money from her, and then trusted her to help me keep it. But who else could I have asked? I couldn't have dragged Lisa or Jack into it and asked them to move the boxes from storage – make them culpable. They wouldn't have done it anyway. Harley had been the only stinking choice I had.

What totally pissed me off, when it finally dawned on me, was that I'd completely forgotten about the reward money; $100,000.00 from Sean for finding Ferdy, and $200,000 for information leading to the capture of those responsible for the robbery. I'd done both – so in the end, if I hadn't fucked up in California, I could have had all that money and Harley would have ended up without a dime.

I received a postcard from her a few days ago. It was mailed from Dallas, Texas, which assured me she was no longer there. She'd written, *Ta-ta!* and signed it, *The New Separator*. Harley, the hippie impersonator, was the one who had set me up and brought me down. Now she was free, and I was sitting here in the booby hatch. What a world.

MARGARET BELLE

CHAPTER 46

Today is Memorial Day, here in the "spa," as well as in the outside world. I closed my eyes and pictured the parade that should be in full swing right about now in front of my old apartment. A hometown showcase of politicians, classic cars, emergency vehicles with their lights flashing, and marching bands playing patriotic music.

Kids' baseball and soccer teams would be throwing candy to the people lining the street, while men and women sold balloons from bunches that were large enough, one would think, to carry them off like extras in the movie UP. There would be scouts, Hibernians with kilts and bagpipes, and a show of horses that was always followed by at least three men carrying shovels.

I waved my arms in the air and silently cheered for the marching bands; felt the beat of the drums in my bones. I wanted so badly to march around my room, but I didn't want anyone who might be watching to think I was not in my right mind. I lowered my arms and sat quietly on my bed, smiling like a fool.

In my mind's eye I saw the spectators – children lining the street, mothers pushing strollers, and elderly citizens who could not stand for the entire length of the parade, sitting curbside in folding chairs.

Then came Drs. Collins and Steele, atop their very own float, tossing little pieces of papers filled with psychobabble to the crowd. Enlightenment shown in the people's eyes as they read their little snippets of wisdom, realizing that now their lives would be perfect.

Now what was that? A spark at the back of their float? Yes! Someone (me!)) had set fire to it, and I watched from the curb with the old ladies, as the whole thing went up like the Hindenburg. Oh, how I love a parade.

I laughed and shook my head, thinking that probably wasn't what the judge had in mind when he'd asked me to make some plans; to envision my future back in society and all that. Long-range life strategies were still difficult for me to consider, except for the one thing I knew for sure. When I *did* get out of here, I'd go looking for Harley.

I saw myself knocking on her door in some faraway exotic place. She'd open it and I'd push my way in and shove her against a wall. And that was just for starters. I'd tie her to a chair, cover her mouth with tape like I'd seen on TV, and begin to separate *her* from every one of her fingers, and maybe, if she was still conscious, every one of her toes. One-by-one. Knuckle-by-knuckle. Then I'd wave and say, "Ta-ta," and set her place on fire.

CHAPTER 47

One Year Later

A woman knocked softly on the door. "Excuse me, Miss Dory? Audrey Dory?"

I squinted at the shape in the doorway and managed to say, "Whatever it is, I didn't do it." My first thought was that she would turn out to be yet another therapist who wanted to experiment with my gray matter. I'd been treated by everything but a witch doctor. Maybe that's what this one would bring to the party; wart of toad, hair of rat, blood of swine. "What do you want?"

She was dressed to the nines in a royal blue suit, belted at the waist, hair perfect and starting to gray. Her heels clicked on the linoleum floor. "My name is Elisabeth Ely, and I've been looking for you."

"Get in line."

She pulled the visitor's chair up to the bed railing. "I was your parents' attorney; still am really, at least until this is finished." She reached into her briefcase and pulled out a large manila envelope. "I have some paperwork here for you to sign."

"I don't think I'm legally supposed to sign anything." I tapped my temple. "Nuts, you know."

She smiled. "You've been cleared by your therapists and by the court. They have deemed you mentally stable...enough...to sign these papers. And I believe Dr. Collins will be here shortly to tell you that you'll be released in less than a month."

I sat up and tried to focus. "You're kidding. So, where are these magic papers?"

"I know that you never knew your father, but you did know he was an investment banker; and he was quite a successful one. He'd started a savings account for you when you were born and it's been accruing interest since then. There's also the matter of his life insurance policies – one went to your mother, of course, and there was one for you. Then there was *her* life insurance and the insurance from the fire."

I stared at her like she was the one who should have her gray matter stirred and strained. "I was told the insurance money went into a fund for my care when I lived with my grandmother and aunt."

"Your father had also seen to both of *them*," she said. "He was a generous man who loved his entire family. And because of that, your grandmother and aunt had plenty of their own money. Neither woman had ever dipped into the fund for your care, perhaps out of appreciation."

I wanted to yell, "Objection! Calls for speculation!" but I just nodded instead.

"Don't you want to know how much money these papers will release to you?"

"Go for it," I said, trying to hear her above all the voices that were screaming inside my head.

"These papers grant you a grand total of twenty-three-million dollars."

"Why didn't I know about this before?"

"Your father's instructions were tightly written; you were not to know about, or receive, any money until the age of thirty-four, which you turned last month. I'm sorry it took me extra time to find you, and then I had to meet with your therapists and the court."

"Isn't karma great?" I asked.

She looked concerned. "Excuse me?"

"You know, *karma*," I said. "The universe, the cosmos; all that crap. It's great."

"Well, sign these and I'll leave you to it. You can come to my office upon your release; we'll meet with the financial advisor on my staff and get you all set up. You're a rich woman, Miss Dory."

"No one else knows about this, right?"

"Just your therapists and one judge – and none of them can say a word to anyone. Why, is there someone you want to surprise?"

"Oh, there sure is," I smiled.

She handed me a pen and I signed for the unimaginable amount. I'd forgotten about my birthday. I giggled to myself and thought, *when I get out of here, I'll buy myself something really nice. And then? Then I'll go find Harley.*

Acknowledgments

I would like to thank the following people for their invaluable help. In alphabetical order:

- Lisa Fiesinger, introductions
- Jill Frier, Rochester locations
- Betsy Glick, FBI
- Dick Kirk, owner of Krabby Kirk's
- John Kobliski, IT and book cover
- Mary Murphy, introductions and nursing experience
- Terry Selzer, Attorney at Law
- Connie Semel, St. Joseph's College of Nursing
- Chad Szakacs, banking procedures
- Officer Joseph Szakacs, Syracuse PD

More from Margaret Belle

- The Procedure (The Clan, Book 1)
- The Hunter's Wife (The Clan, Book 2)
- The Granddaughters

www.MargaretBelleBooks.com

Made in United States
Troutdale, OR
09/09/2023